Moon$hine Madness

Rich Finley

NovelYarns Publishing—Glendora, CA
ISBN: 979-8-9916928-0-9
Library of Congress Control Number: 2024920926
Title: *Moon$hine Madness*
Author: Rich Finley
Digital distribution | 2024
Paperback | 2024

This is a work of fiction. The characters, names, incidents, places, and dialogue are products of the author's imagination, and are not to be construed as real.

Published in the United States by New Book Authors Publishing

Dedication

To Aunt Virginia

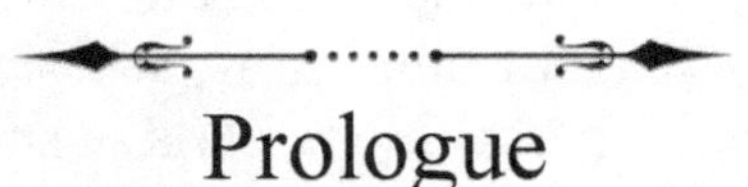

Prologue

The mood in the black SUV was tense as it pulled off the highway onto a remote dirt road, hidden in the thick underbrush, not far from North Carolina's Little Tennessee River near Buckshot Pond. The late-night air was filled with the steady lyrical cadence of frogs and crickets as the glistening moonlight seemed to dance playfully on the creek water feeding into the pond.

On any given moonlit Appalachian night, one might hear foraging nocturnal mammals, as they venture from their nests, or dens to seek berries, fruits, roots, nuts, insects, small mammals, or even reptiles as their primal food source, but the car's occupants were not interested in the natural habitat. Nor, did they care to watch the dazzling array of late-season fireflies float through the dark woods with their flickering lights. Their focus was on a barren, poorly maintained dirt road.

Behind the wheel of the SUV sat an impatient small man with tightly cropped dark hair, and a thin mustache. He was irritable, perspired and fidgeted, while staring anxiously out the window.

His easy-going, big-boned, paunchy companion was much larger, towering over six feet in height. His clean-shaven face gave him almost a boyish appearance, though, both were in their late 30s.

The men were dressed in dark clothing, rarely spoke, and smoked incessantly. Their anxiety level seemed to heighten with every cigarette they would extinguish while lighting another.

As the hours rolled by, the large man grew bored. He amused himself by blowing smoke rings of multiple sizes. After each cigarette was finished, he would triumphantly fling the butt out the SUV window. It was a game to see how far, and high, he could flick the dying embers.

At one point, the smaller man admonished him about losing focus on their assignment, but his boyish companion did not care. His interest level had begun to wane. He was tired, hungry, and bored.

Suddenly, a distant headlight appeared. It moved slowly, deliberately weaving methodology along the sharp turns. Potholes and deep ruts made from years of rain, snow, and ice had made the road treacherous and barely passable in parts where the creek water crossed. The driver was taking great care to be cautious, as he navigated each twist and turn to avoid fallen trees and debris that had been haphazardly moved to the side of the road.

"That him?" The large man asked.

"Could be," the smaller man replied.

He reached under his shirt for the hidden holster of his Glock 43. The gun felt safe and secure. Nervously, he checked his watch. The hour was later than expected.

"What time is it?" The large man asked.

"Don't matter," the small man growled. "Keep your eye on those lights."

As the headlights drew near, the small man warned the larger man to be on his "toes" and follow the "plan."

"You think he's by himself, Salvador?"

"It doesn't matter!" Salvador snapped. "Ross, do as you're told!"

"Dang," Ross said, slapping the side of his face. "Skeeters out tonight."

***

The headlights grew closer as they flickered through the trees. In the darkness, a truck could be faintly seen plodding along. It appeared to be a late 1990's pickup truck in unkept, poor maintenance condition.

Salvador turned on the SUV's ignition and checked the time on his Tissot stainless steel dress watch. He scoffed at the thought of the job being "too easy," and laughed at the stupidity of a careless driver being caught on a remote rural backroad late at night. This would be "easy money."

As the pickup made its final turn into an open clearing, the SUV bolted from its hidden location. The car skidded in front of the slow-moving truck, blocking the unpaved road.

The pickup driver was momentarily stunned. He had not expected to encounter anyone on the deserted road. There was virtually no time to react. The truck skidded to a stop in a cloud of dust as Ross emerged from the SUV.

The truck's driver watched Ross reach into his belt. In the darkness, he could not tell if Ross had a weapon. He became alarmed when he heard obscene, vulgar instructions to get out of the truck.

There was no time to lose. The road was blocked. There was no escape. Nor did the driver have any idea why he had been stopped. Instinctively, he turned the truck toward the creek. He gunned the engine. It was his only hope of escape.

Ross sprang toward the pickup truck but it was too late. The driver shifted the truck into low gear. He rammed through the creek side flora and oak tree saplings in the hopes that no fallen tree branches, logs, or rock obstructions blocked his path.

A gunshot was heard, then another. Neither bullet found its mark.

The creek's water level was low due to a lack of seasonal rainfall. Its bumpy rock bottom made for a rough, treacherous ride. The driver was tossed violently but held the steering wheel firmly as the truck splashed through the water's rugged terrain.

The driver had to find a way out of the slow-moving water. The creek's banks were walled with thick, heavy brush. There was no exit in sight. Large, moss-laden rocks were scattered along the creek's bed, causing the truck's tires to spin intermittently. Even more frightening, the driver's assailant could not be seen anywhere.

Salvador yelled for Ross to get back to the car. His hulking companion did not respond. He either did not hear his voice, or was stuck in the creek's thick brush.

By the time Ross appeared, the truck had found a sandy bank to break free from the shallow water. Only a mechanical grinding sound could be heard as it made its way onto the unpaved road.

"Shit," Salvador thought. "That prick is dead when I get my hands on him."

Salvador cursed his misfortune as the SUV backtracked along the dusty road. He was livid. He had lost the golden opportunity to wrap up a job, along with a lucrative payday.

Those thoughts raced through his mind as he wondered how to explain the botched job to his clandestine boss, the notorious Copperhead, whose renowned murderous reputation was beyond reproach.

His chain-smoking partner annoyed him further by rolling down the SUV window to light a cigarette. "Boy, those lighting bugs are sure out tonight," Ross observed. "Horny bastards, aren't they?"

The dirt road soon turned to gravel, which meant the men weren't far from the highway. The sound of the tires rolling, hurriedly over crushed gravel filled the air. Plumes of dust enveloped the car's headlights and windshield, causing Ross to cough, extinguish his cigarette, and close his window.

As the SUV eased around a wide turn, Salvador's eyes widened in startled disbelief. Even his disinterested companion's head snapped upward, stunned, as they came upon the pickup truck.

"Well, well, well," Salvador said, reaching for his Glock 43. "What do we have here?"

Both men got out of the SUV. Salvador warily fingered the trigger on his handgun, as they cautiously approached the pickup truck.

The truck had crashed into a large oak tree. The left side of the vehicle's front axle had collapsed. The hood was partially crushed and had crumpled open.

The driver's head had smashed into the windshield. He was slumped over the steering wheel, badly hurt, bleeding, and not moving. Aside from a cell phone and backpack on the passenger seat, there was nothing of apparent value in the truck's cab.

The man appeared to be young, perhaps late in his teens. A kid. It galled Salvador to think they had been chasing a "stupid" kid, which angered him more. "Get him out," he ordered.

Even without a tailgate, the truck's load they were seeking was mostly intact.

Several cases of Mad Mama moonshine had been neatly packed and sealed in unmarked boxes. Neither man knew why the boss wanted the liquor seized, but they were not paid to ask questions.

The load, backpack, and cell phone were quickly moved to the SUV, while Salvador took the young man to the creek's edge. Moments later, he returned to the car alone. Whatever guilt or regretful remorse he might have felt was exceeded by his desire for vengeance.

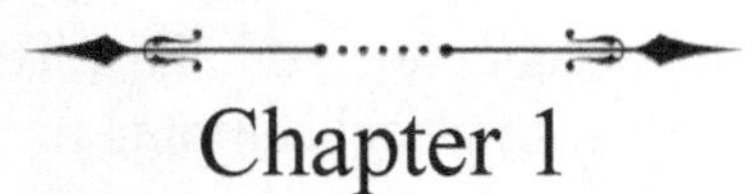

Chapter 1

When it came time for Wendall Tucker's 50th birthday, there was no question there had to be a celebration. And Wendall was the type of guy who did everything big. Real BIG. He loved life, people, and everything the world had to offer, including a pig pickin'.

Wendall owned The Red Maple Bar & Grill, not far from Bonner Falls, North Carolina. The bar and grill was a popular watering hole for local and tourist patrons alike. The Red Maple was open six days a week, serving burgers, wings, sandwiches, appetizers, beer, and drinks. It was the *go-to* place to watch televised sporting events and featured pool tables, and dart boards as well.

Weekends at The Red Maple were always special. Wendall would have local bands on Friday and Saturday nights and occasionally host open mic events for comedy and music. It was on such a night that Milt Delany learned of his friend's upcoming birthday.

Milt Delany was a stout man in his mid-50s. He had thick, calloused hands and a ruddy, leather-beaten face, the result of having worked years in the sun. He owned the Highland Ranch along the Little Tennessee River near Lake Boswell, which his son Cooper (Coop) helped manage.

The farm had been in the Delany family for generations, and part of his heritage that dated back to the early 1900s. He was proud of the farm's legacy and what he and his forefathers had accomplished. The farm had always been prosperous, even during hard economic times; though, it was not always easy.

There were substantial costs associated with maintaining the farm. Money was tight during some months. The seasonal crops were not always reliable due to inclement weather or pests. Market prices could fluctuate dramatically. Energy resources like gas, oil, or electricity were never stable, and drought could wipe out a crop.

The animals had to be fed and housed in proper shelters. There were strict state rules, regulations and ordinances that had to be followed.

Milt was fortunate to have a veterinary doctor, Doc Thomas, who could be called on short notice for any farm animal emergencies that might arise. He also had a couple farmhands, Toby and Leroy, who would often stay in Milt's fifth wheel camping trailer or shared a room in the bunkhouse above the hayloft.

Toby was especially handy when it came to mechanical repairs. The farm had a wide assortment of equipment and vehicles, including a pickup truck, tractor, livestock trailer, skip loader, and post digger. Milt was especially fond of a second-hand golf cart Leroy had restored to cruise the property, and an ATV Polaris Razor for romping in the woods.

Toby kept the machine shop's generators, air compressors, chainsaws, a log splitter, and a wood chipper in good working order. He was especially proud of an HVAC system that he and a local electrician installed to ward off those cold winter mornings and hot, sweltering summer days.

In addition to chicken and duck eggs, Milt raised pigs, rabbits, goats, cows, horses, and turkeys, leaving Leroy to monitor grain and feed storage levels. The farm also had strawberries, blueberries, blackberries, and apples, which Coop and his wife Sarah picked.

Coop and Sarah lived in the farmhouse with Milt. Sarah was an exceptionally talented homemaker. She excelled at canning fruits, vegetables, and berry preserves. She was also adept at processing raw honey. Every day, Sarah would prepare breakfast and dinner for the workers, and help with any unfinished chores.

Leroy also served as the groundkeeper and monitored the farm's green house. Aside from agriculture, the farm had a dairy barn, pig hut, hen house, duck pond, bee hives, horse stable, and corral. Leroy's job was to make sure the spaces were kept clean, properly ventilated, fully shaded, and insulated, with easy access to food.

Leroy was gregarious and lighthearted in going about his duties, whereas Toby took his responsibilities much more seriously. He tended to remain in the background, and maintain a low profile.

Milt thought Wendall's milestone birthday seemed good, as any reason to celebrate, though he also felt a tinge of sadness. His wife Ellen had died of cervical cancer at 43, and was buried on the farm's property. She never had the chance to see her 50th birthday.

Rumors circulated that Ellen had been a hell-raising city girl from Atlanta in her youth. She could hold her liquor, and shoot a gun with the best. Quick as a whip, it was said she could curse a blue streak that would peel paint off a barn. She was Milt's soulmate, and he never stopped grieving her loss.

Still, Milt sensed that the half-century mark called for more than toasting a couple beers with his occasional fishing partner. He thought Wendell deserved something better. He would throw a first-rate pig pickin' blowout.

Chapter 2

It was almost by coincidence that Milt overheard The Red Maple's part-time bartender and waitress Connie laugh at an off-handed joke about Wendell being put out to pasture. A couple of the local regulars were having fun over a beer, while making light of upcoming Wendall's golden jubilee.

That spawned several jokes, including one from someone who thought Wendell might mistake Happy Hour for nap time, while the other suggested he check *Lost and Found* for his penis.

Connie was a stocky, robust girl with short hair and a lively sense of humor. She was used to hearing younger men tell obscene jokes. On occasion, she would remind them to tone down their language, as "this 'ere's a family place, you know."

"Why, looky 'ere! I do declare, if it ain't Milt Delany hisself," Connie said. "We's 'bout to give up on you. Whereya been hidin'?"

"I was over to see Jeremy at the feed store, and thought I'd stop by."

"Well, we're glad you did!" Connie said, wiping the counter with a hand towel. "Leroy was in a while back, an' said you was fixin' to plow, or sump'n' like that."

"Yeah, it's getting to be that time of year," Milt conceded. "Hope Leroy didn't bother you much. That boy likes to talk."

"Nah, he waren't no bother," Connie smiled. "I think he'd bin over to the train station to pick sump'n up."

"He was supposed to get a baler that was shipped in, but I don't know where he got off to," Milt shrugged. "He was also supposed to swing by Tolbert's Feed Store, but Jeremy hadn't seen him."

Milt started to reach for a menu, and added, "If he came here, that explains it."

Connie paused to look at the clock. The grill was nearly empty, except for the young, crude men trading raunchy jokes about Wendall's birthday.

"Oh, my. Time's a-wastin'. I got to get to gettin'," she exclaimed. "Whatcha gonna have? The usual?"

"A Turkey Dew would be fine," Milt said. "Say, did I hear you say Wendell has a birthday coming up?"

"Oh, my! Does he ever! He's got the big 5-0!"

"That so? He around by chance, or did he get off with that fly rod?"

"Yes'm, he's out back," Connie said. "You want me to get 'em?"

"Yeah, could you please?"

Wendall burst through the grill's swinging saloon-style doors in his customary faded cutoff jeans, waterproof hiking boots and tattered AC/DC t-shirt. His casual attire gave him the appearance of a wayward gardener with his warm, friendly smile, disheveled hair, and tightly cropped salt and pepper-colored beard, rather than the proprietor of a bar and grill.

As he approached the counter, he heard Milt's booming voice. "Hey, ole boy! What's this talk about you having a birthday?"

"Yeah, it's a big one."

"You got any plans?"

"Nah, thought I'd take Darcie to the Featherstone Casino. She hasn't been out in a while."

"What? You're going to let Connie and Harold take over while you're gone? Lord have mercy!" Milt's mouth dropped in a mocking display of faux disbelief. "Besides, you can go gambling anytime."

Connie shook her head, and drifted down the counter to cash out the two men making vulgar jokes. Both customers were still laughing, as they left the grill.

"Wendell, you must be crazy," he continued. "Harold's liable to turn the oven on and blow himself up! Hell, he'll burn the place down! Yes, he will. By, God."

"Ah, he's okay. He's held down the fort before, and things were okay; except for that time I left him, and he hooked up with that gal from West Virginia." Wendall paused to shake his head. "Whew, that was a doozy."

"He did what?"

"Yeah, he hooked up with some gal who, according to him, had breasts the size of a Chinese weather balloon."

"You mean like that big balloon that they shot down by Myrtle Beach?"

"That's right, that's the one. Ummm hmmm," Wendall grinned. "Except, this was a couple balloons!"

"You've got to be kidding! As I recall, that was one of those big, fancy spy balloons. The Air Force went after it. BAM! She's gone!" Milt slammed his hand on the counter for emphasis.

"Well, yeah. Tell you what, Harold was ready to move in with her. The whole bit, till that deal got shot down." Wendall paused to gather his thoughts. "Boy, did he ever get played for a sucker!"

Wendall and Milt burst out laughing at the thought. Connie's jaw dropped, rolled her eyes, and went into the kitchen.

"Ha, that's what I'm talking about!" Milt howled, slapping his knee. "Harold might be able to cook, but it's like they say 'that boy's cornbread ain't done in the middle!'"

"Yeah, he got blinded by the light; all right," Wendall chuckled. "Big ol' headlights!"

Another wave of laughter overtook the pair, when an elderly couple walked in the diner.

"Hey, folks!" Wendall smiled. "Be right with you." He then called for Connie.

Connie came bouncing through the saloon-style doors, and gave the cackling pair the stink-eye. In a hushed voice, she said, "Y'all wanna settle down, an' grow up? We got customers."

Both nodded their heads like a couple of scolded, pubescent schoolboys. After a quiet moment of suppressed giggles, Milt changed the topic to Wendall's fast approaching birthday.

It was over a slaw burger of chili, melted cheese, and coleslaw, coupled with a lukewarm glass of Turkey Dew, that Milt suggested hosting a "over-the-hill" pig pickin' party, and offered the use of the cinder block oven pit behind his ranch's hayloft. The perfect place for a pig roast.

As the guest of honor, Wendall could invite family and friends. The afternoon event would feature food, games, dancing, and music. Guests could bring their favorite dishes and share the moment. With luck, they might persuade local pitmaster Willie Cornsilk to handle the hickory charwood honors.

It was an offer Wendall could not refuse.

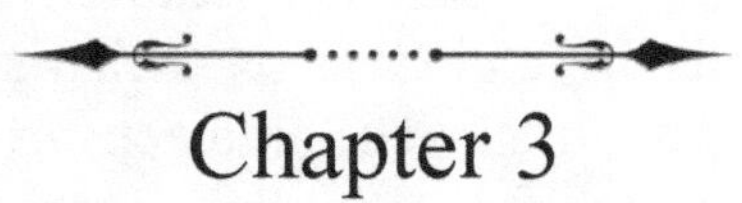

Chapter 3

The call to the county sheriff's office came early in the morning. The administrative assistant, Jo Yarborough, had scarily turned on the coffee and settled at her desk when the phone began ringing.

Detective Sonny Boy Halstead emerged from a rear office to lay a file of paperwork on Jo's desk. He had a smirk on his face, suggesting it was going to be *one of those days*, before turning to the coffee maker.

On the phone was Kaye Somerset, a mother of two boys and a daughter who lived on five wooded acres in a double-wide trailer south of town. Her husband Kyle was working as a construction superintendent on a jobsite near the Tennessee border, and had left for work hours earlier.

Earlier that morning, her young boys Kyle, Jr., and Cole had gone fishing at Buckshot Pond, which was on a farm of the same name near their house. The boys loved fishing for trout, bass, and catfish. They would wander along the pond's bank, catch frogs, and cast their lines to try their luck. By noon, they would scurry home for lunch that their mother would have ready.

The morning was slightly overcast, perfect for a short walk through the woods. The air was crisp and refreshing. The crackling sound of leaves could be heard, as they stepped over fallen trees, around downed branches, leather leaf ferns, and wooded overgrowth.

Squirrels zigged and zagged erratically across the boys' path, searching for nuts, seeds, and berries. An inquisitive finch looked on curiously as squirrels performed chaotic, acrobatic stunts, running, jumping, climbing trees, and leaping from branch to branch.

The boys traveled further along the dirt road, where the creek fed into the pond's thick, weeded bass beds. It was a favorite fishing hole, where they would rock hop with their poles. As the boys made their way around a large bend, they noticed the disabled pickup truck.

The truck appeared to have been severely damaged and abandoned.

Broken glass was strewn on the ground. Engine fluid had leaked from the truck's violent impact, several hours earlier.

Being curious, Kyle, Jr., and Cole set their fishing gear down and walked slowly toward the truck. The area appeared to be deserted. No one was around. Nor were there any cars, or trucks on the road at that early hour.

The truck door was open. The boys peered inside, and saw ripped cloth seats with shredded polyurethane padding, a cracked dashboard with exposed wiring, a hole that once held a radio, floor mats encrusted with mud, and torn speakers on the doors. The windshield was shattered with bloodstains.

Trash was scattered throughout the truck's cab, and across the seat. There were discarded fast-food wrappers, an empty Coke cup, old newspapers, candy wrappers, a biker magazine, an aluminum keychain, an empty liquor bottle, and outdated lottery tickets.

The boys were alarmed, but excited at the same time. It was Klye, Jr's., decision to rush home and tell their mother. He felt she would know the best course of action, if any should be taken, about their discovery.

But, Klye, Jr.'s mother was not in the mood for any wild, imaginative stories. She was taking care of the boys' younger sister, Tara, who was getting ready for breakfast.

As Klye, Jr., and Cole blurted news of their find, their mother, Kaye Somerset, dismissed their story as some wild yarn.

"We ain't lyin' mama," Klye, Jr. said. "We's tellin' the truth. Ain't that right, Cole?"

"Yes'm, an' that truck hit a tree, an' ev'rythin'!" Cole added. He slapped his hands together, and roared "KAPOW!"

"All right, now settle down," their mother said. "Let me get Tara fixed up, and I'll see what I can do."

The boys raced to their room. Plans for fishing were scrapped. They could not wait to tell their friends, and wondered what course of action their mother would take.

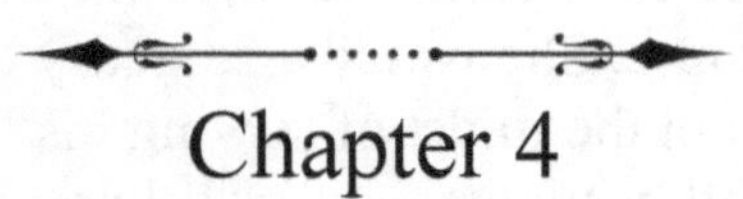

Chapter 4

When it came to co-workers, Jo Yarborough was the ultimate team player. She would arrive each morning with a ready smile, and a willingness to help with whatever task needed to be done.

Jo was 30ish, full-figured, well dressed, wore glasses, and kept her hair tied back. She was married to a security alarm technician named Ben, with their young daughter Luann and family dog Tippy.

She was always ready to greet anyone who entered the office lobby, and held a host of responsibilities, including the supervision of public records, data entry of legal documentation and secretarial assistance to the department.

Despite Kaye Somerset's skepticism about the boy's information, Jo wasn't the least hesitant to take the information when she called. In fact, Jo knew Kay through preschool activities; her daughter Luann and Tara had once been enrolled together.

"Hey, Jo," Kaye began. "This is Kaye Somerset. You know, out by Buckshot Farm. How are you doing?"

"Why, hey Kaye," Jo answered. "Been a long time since I heard from you. How's Kyle and the kids?"

"We're all fine. Just fine. Kyle's working, kids in school, and Tara's at home, but that's not why I'm calling." Kaye paused, sounding hesitant. "The boys were out fishing this morning. They say there's a truck that hit a tree out by Buckshot Pond."

"According to them, it's a bad accident," she continued. "I don't know, Jo. The boys might be telling me a whopper, but they came back all worked up. Thought you might want Max to check it out."

"Oh, my. Was anyone hurt?"

"No, they say there wasn't anyone around," Kaye said. "And that's the crazy part. Maybe the driver walked away, or got help; I don't know. But that's what they're saying."

"Okay, let me get on it," Jo said. "Max is out right now, but I'll get Bobby Wilson to run out there. He's in the area right now. You take care."

Jo gathered the details needed to file a report and made the dispatch call. Since there were no injuries on-site, the call was considered a non-emergency response. She would also notify Sheriff Max Porter.

Sheriff Porter was in the midst of serving his third term as sheriff. He was popular by all accounts, and well known to everyone in the community as the county's chief law enforcement officer, who was responsible for enforcing state laws and local ordinances for public safety, as well as maintaining security for the county jail, correctional facility, and courtrooms.

The sheriff also oversaw several divisions within the department, including routine patrols, criminal investigations, emergency response calls, warrants, and criminal arrests, as well as budgets and administrative staff.

As a leader in the community, Sheriff Porter worked closely with other law enforcement agencies, including police departments and federal agencies.

His Chief Deputy was Bobby Wilson, who was a bright, young man in his mid-30's, full of energy and anxious to take on any assignment. The deputy's role varied from being a first responder to assisting in weather-related traffic incidents, issuing court summonses, providing protection orders, and issuing eviction notices.

Deputy Wilson yearned to be in law enforcement his entire life. Even as a high school star football player who could have played for a Division I National Collegiate Athletic Association (NCAA) college team, he turned down a four year scholarship to pursue a career in law enforcement.

The call to check on a disabled vehicle was not the glamorous work Deputy Wilson had envisioned when he joined the law enforcement department, but it was part of his duties. He would make the stop as part of his morning routine.

After making the dispatcher call, Jo sat back in her chair and sighed deeply. She viewed the yellow sticky notes on her dual computer monitors, and the action item list that needed to be completed later that day.

Near her computer monitors was a picture of Luann with Tippy, which would always brighten her day. Suddenly, Detective Halstead came up behind her and set a cup of coffee on her desk.

"Having fun, yet?"

"Oh, thanks," Jo said. "I could use a cup about now."

"What's this about Bobby going out to look at some truck?"

"Ummm, there's a disabled truck over by Buckshot Pond."

"Well, I was headed out that way to look into a fraud case," the detective said. "Think I'll grab another cup of coffee, and stop on the way."

Chapter 5

A couple curious onlookers were standing near the pickup truck when Deputy Wilson arrived at Buckshot Pond. The bystanders instinctively backed away from the vehicle when Wilson's patrol car pulled into view.

As the deputy stepped from the agency's vehicle, he wondered if anyone had tampered with the evidence left on the scene. He was hopeful to find clues as to what happened to the truck.

The onlookers watched in silence as Wilson made his way toward the truck. Though they were respectful, the deputy viewed their presence as a nuisance, and concerned they might interfere with the investigation.

The deputy took a slow, deliberate walk around the truck to scrutinize the damage. His initial reaction was that whoever had driven the vehicle was lucky to be alive, if they survived.

"Anyone know who this belongs to?" he asked the bystanders, motioning toward the truck.

The men shook their heads, almost in unison.

"You guys seen this happen?"

No reaction, except blank stares.

"Any idea when this might have happened?"

Once again, no response.

"No?" The deputy did not seem surprised but nodded, shrugging his shoulders. "Okay, then."

Deputy Wilson put his hand on the door frame, and peered inside the truck. He checked for the smell alcohol. Perhaps the driver had been drinking, or high on drugs. Nothing. There was no sign indicating the driver was intoxicated, or under the influence of hallucinogenic drugs.

Moments later, Detective Halstead arrived amid a cloud of dust in his patrol car. The onlookers fell back, and turned to leave as the two law enforcement agents exchanged greetings.

"Hey Bobby, good morning," Halstead said. "What have you got?"

"Hey, Sonny Boy," Wilson answered. "Looks like a truck wrapped around a tree. I'm trying to figure out who it belongs to, and what happened to the driver."

"Hmmm, run the plate?"

"No. No plates, or registration. There's nothing in the glove compartment, under the seat, or behind it. Already checked."

"Could be stolen," Halstead surmised, rubbing his chin. "Not sure who would want to steal an older truck like this one. Am guessing it's an older Chevy Silverado. Let's get the VIN number, and run it down."

"Are there any weapons, or drugs inside the vehicle?"

"No, nothing except some trash and whatnot," Wilson shrugged. "Of course, it's hard to say whether or not these looky-loos or someone else picked her clean. They got here first."

"You might want get their names and numbers before they leave; in case you need to follow up."

"Good idea," Wilson said, running after the onlookers.

Once he returned, the two men began measuring skid mark distances, making notes, and taking photographs. Wilson drew a diagram, and noted the weather and roadway conditions. He also made a note of the vehicle's mechanical condition.

"Looks like the front left axle snapped," Wilson noted. "Hard to say if that's what put her into the tree," he paused to view the damage. "Whew, she blew right out. It could have been the road potholes, or it just wore out. I don't know."

"Yeah," Halstead agreed. "That's possible."

Halstead took a moment to look around the area. "Nice day," he noted. "I've got to get going. There's a fraud case down south I need to check on."

"Before you leave, call Harley at the garage and get the tow truck for the impound yard," he added. "Meanwhile, I have to excuse myself, and head to the creek. That coffee of Jo's, makes me want to piss like a race horse."

Deputy Wilson chuckled at the comment. He was all too familiar with Jo's coffee. As the deputy continued to write his report, he thought about checking with the office. There was still an afternoon of routine rounds to make.

It had been a long morning, and the deputy was anxious to wrap up the current call. He paused to scan the lush woods to take in the sights and sounds of their natural beauty; though, the moment lasted only for a fleeting second.

"Bobby!" Halstead yelled. "Come quick!"

Wilson's head jerked up.

"There's a body down here!"

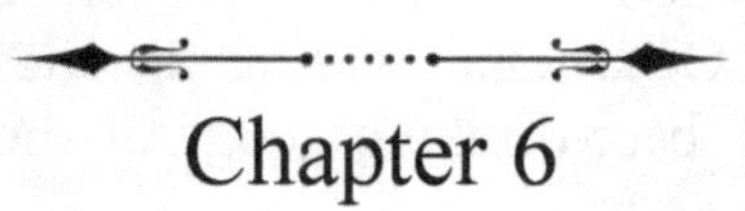

Chapter 6

The sweet tea line was longer than Skip Walker expected. He was sorry he had not gotten there sooner with his dog Fred, but he was too late. The Carolina sun had taken its toll and bore down on the pig pickin' barbecue, leaving everyone hot and thirsty.

Fred seemed oblivious to Skip's lack of enthusiasm. He shuffled his feet, sniffed the people around him, and dutifully stayed by his owner's side. Being a Labrador mixed retriever, Fred was friendly, outgoing, and playful.

As the line nudged forward, Skip patted Fred's neck and kept a firm grip on his leash. He was anxious to pick up his drinks, and get back to the celebration where his fiancée, Katie Mae Garner, was waiting.

He thought about Katie Mae sitting comfortably in her lawn chair under the shade of a birch tree with friends. She was petite, fun-loving, quick-witted, and always ready with a warm smile. Her good nature made her popular among friends and everyone she met.

Katie Mae worked as a part-time sales assistant at Two Sisters, a women's consignment shop located in town. The owners, Victoria and Veronica Jenkins were elated to have Katie Mae handle merchandise sales and consignments for the store's clothing, home goods, art, furniture, records and books. The store seemed to have something for everyone, and always had a steady flow of customers.

Skip's mind drifted as he thought about their plans later that afternoon, or if they might go out for dinner, when he suddenly heard the laughter of children in the fruit orchard behind the party's picnic tables. Squeals of delight could be heard reverberating throughout the ranch's farm area.

A bounce house with its castle-like styling had been set for the younger children. They could hardly contain their joy. The kids were busy climbing and exploring the colorful castle with its four turrets and inflatable slide, while expending every ounce of energy crashing into each other like miniature human wrecking balls and laughing hysterically.

Nearby, several older kids and adults were in a heated cornhole competition. Each toss was met with an admiring "ooh" or appreciative "aah." Occasional scoring disputes were settled by a collective group of beer-drinking judges, who tallied the points between sips of beer.

A beer keg had been taped, and was closely monitored by a group of younger men with their red disposable party cups in one hand and their other hand in a front pant pocket. Despite the good-natured, fierce cornhole competition, it was the alcohol that seemed to be the key attraction in keeping the spectators and quasi-judges riveted to the event.

Skip was still thinking about Katie Mae as a loud protest erupted over a questionable cornhole toss. Shouts of "No, that ain't right" could be heard. As the tension mounted, his attention was diverted when he heard a voice behind him say, "Hey there."

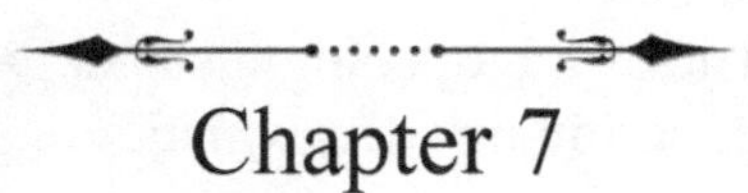

Chapter 7

Without realizing Fred's whereabouts, Skip turned around to see the dog had slipped behind him, and was intensely sniffing a stranger's leg who had a backpack slung over his shoulder.

"Oh, man. I'm sorry," Skip said apologetically. "I didn't realize he'd gotten by me." Skip gave the leash a quick tug and said, "Fred, you get back here."

"That's all right," Fred's new friend said. "You say his name's Fred?"

"Yeah, it's my Uncle Em's dog," Skip replied. "He's a good boy who likes to check things out. He doesn't mean any harm."

"He's friendly all right," the man offered.

The man set aside a backpack, reached down, and gave Fred a friendly pat. He appeared to be in his late 30s, slender and unshaven, with dark hair that tumbled from under a well-worn Carolina hat. His face was covered with pockmark scars, most likely from severe teenage acne, and limped with the aid of a cane.

Skip glanced at the backpack and saw the name Benson. He immediately asked if he was related to the Benson family, whom he knew had recently relocated from Greensboro.

"Nah, no kinfolk from there. Besides, I'm not a Benson. I'm a Bickerson. A friend found the backpack, and gave it to me. Everyone calls me Bick."

"You know, Bick, you must be a dog person or own one," Skip suggested. "Fred's been all over you."

"Yeah, I got a couple hounds back home," Bick said, fingering a silver dog whistle on a chain around his neck. "As a matter of fact, I train them."

"That so?"

"Yeah, when I get time."

"Well, I'm not sure you could teach Fred much of anything. You know what they say about teaching an old dog new tricks." Skip paused to pat Fred on the head. "On a day like this, it'd be nice if he could fetch me a cold beer."

"Tell you what," Bick said, opening his backpack. "Here," he said, handing Skip a black aluminum dog whistle on a keychain. "This is from my school."

Skip took the dog whistle and carefully examined the gift. The whistle was small, only a couple inches with a round keyring holder. "Hellhound" was imprinted in white lettering along the whistle's shaft.

"Why, thank you," Skip said as he fumbled his finger into the keyring.

"Ha, it's my pleasure," Bick laughed. "Everyone gets one with a certificate when their dog passes the class, and right now I'm about ready to pass on this line. Think I'll head over to the duck pond. I hear those boys have something *really* good to drink."

There was a loud roar at the neighboring cornhole tourney. A closely contested game had come to its conclusion, and the rowdy crowd was letting loose. Skip turned to see the commotion.

Fred twitched nervously and tugged on his leash as the line moved forward. Skip felt the tension on the leash. He instinctively moved forward as he heard Milt's son Coop make the announcement that The Gap Runners dance clogging team was about to take the stage.

Beneath the hayloft was a makeshift stage composed of recycled, reclaimed wooden boards. Partygoers sat at picnic tables, or lawn chairs that they had brought to enjoy the music and dance routines.

The Gap Runners was a local amateur clogging group of attractive young girls. They had arrived in matching colorful folk-dance blouses, skirts, petticoats, and double tap shoes.

Their show included a variety of traditional, freestyle, and precision clogging, though, that hardly mattered. It was the girls themselves that were the main attraction. A smile was all it would have taken to get the crowd's undivided attention, especially those of the inebriated party attendees by the cornhole game.

As Skip reached the front of the sweet tea line, he turned to comment about the upcoming entertainment to Bick. He was surprised to find him gone. Bick had quietly slipped away, and hobbled past the horse barn into the meadow toward the duck pond.

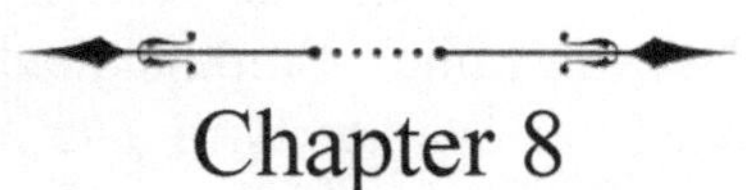

Chapter 8

At the beverage stand, Skip was greeted by Miss Faye, a slender, dark-haired lady in her late 20s, and her young daughter Emma.

The beverage stand was a simple table, covered with a red and white cotton gingham tablecloth. A crude sign had been made advertising sweet tea and several other drinks. The tea was in a five-gallon glass drink dispenser on the countertop. Additional dispensers for refills were kept ready when the tea ran out.

The stand also had cups, napkins, straws, sliced lemons, and a small inflatable children's pool that served as an ice chest behind the table. The setting was neatly arranged, with a tip jar set aside for those who were appreciative of the ladies' services.

"Hey there! Whatcha gonna have?" Miss Faye asked.

"I was going to go with the sweet tea, but what else have you got?" Skip asked.

"Oh, we got all kinds 'a' stuff. Don't we, honey?" Miss Faye said, smiling at Emma. "We got sweet tea, regular tea, cold water, lemonade, sum Cheerwine an' apple cider. You know, they make that cider here on the ranch! Ain't that right, Emma?"

"Coke, mama!" Emma blurted out.

"Why, yore right sugar. I forgot that one. We got that too. Got 'er on ice. Now, whatcha lookin' at?"

"Well, I don't know," Skip said, tugging on Fred's leash. "What do you think, Emma?"

"Sweet tea! Mama makes the best sweet tea they is!"

Skip laughed and slipped two dollars into the tip jar. "Okay, I'll drink to that. A couple sweet teas it is."

"What about your friend?" Miss Faye said, motioning toward Fred.

"Oh, Fred?" Skip asked. "He gets water only."

"Can I pet 'em? Can I pet 'em just a little?" Emma asked excitedly.

"Emma! You listen 'ere, girl. Where's your manners?" Miss Faye said firmly. "What'd I tell you about bustin' in like that?"

"Oh, sorry, mama. I didn't mean nuthin'. He's so cute!" Emma said, coming around the table. "Now, can I pet 'em?"

"Yeah, go ahead. He won't bite," Skip laughed.

"Say, you ain't that Skip Walker with *The Mountain Holler* by chance?" Miss Faye asked.

The question caught Skip by surprise. He had been watching Emma playfully pet Fred, who was relishing the attention.

"Yes, ma'am, I am. How'd you know?"

"I figured as much with that *Mountain Holler* hat yore wearin'. You reportin' this thang?"

"No, hadn't planned on it," Skip shrugged. "I was taking the day off."

"I used to get *The Mountain Holler's* eEdition on the computer, but it got too expensive. Whoo, boy," Miss Faye said, fanning the side of her face. "'Sides, internet costs through the roof these days. Ugh."

"I'm sorry to hear that."

"Yeah, well," Miss Faye sighed. "You gotta pick an' choose yer battles, I s'pose. Anyway, youn'un's was only comin' out a couple times a month, an' I couldn't see spendin' that kinda money."

There was a sudden round of applause as The Gap Runners took their places on stage. Highland's Ranch hand Toby cued *Rocky Top*, and the girls went into their choreographed dance steps to the rhythmic downbeat of the music.

"You really should do a write-up on them Gap Runners. I know some 'a' the girls, an' believe you me, them gals has bin workin' day 'an night to get into a competition."

"That so?"

"Who knows?" Miss Faye chortled. "Maybe they gonna be famous someday, an' you can say you knew 'em when they's babys! Ain't that right, Emma?"

"Yes'm, mama," Emma agreed. "I wanna be a Gap Runner!"

"Ah, honey," Miss Faye smiled. "You gonna get yore chance someday."

Miss Faye looked at the beverage line, and realized she had better move Skip along. Other customers had been waiting.

"Say, ain't this some pig pickin'?" Miss Faye asked, as Emma came around the table to pour the drinks from the glass dispenser.

"Yes, I think Wendall's going to remember this birthday," Skip agreed as he reached for the sweet teas.

"Yes'm, won't we all!" Miss Faye laughed. "Milt fixed 'em up good; real good."

Moments later, Miss Faye was heard greeting the next customer. "Hey there! Whatcha gonna have?"

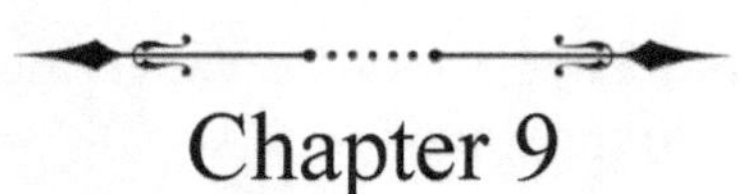

Chapter 9

"Say, look who's here?" Katie Mae smiled. "Tammy and I was starting to wonder where you got off to."

Katie Mae's voice broke off as Skip handed her a cup of sweet tea, and looked toward the stage where The Gap Runners were performing.

"Why, I do declare!" she said excitedly. "If that isn't Billie Jo and Edward over there."

Without missing a beat, she began waving. "Come on Tammy, let's go say 'Hey.' Skip, you stay here with Tom, while we go see what trouble they're into."

Tom and Skip looked at each other and shook their heads. Neither said anything. The unpredictable was always predictable whenever Katie Mae and Tammy got together.

Without delay, Fred began exploring the area under the table and chairs. Katie Mae and Tammy's fast departure did not deter him in the least. He was anxious to see what other animals might have been around. With luck, he might even find a snack that had been dropped.

"Quite a party, huh?" Skip said, tying Fred's lease to his chair.

"Yeah," Tom nodded in agreement. "I'd say so."

Skip found a small bowl that was ideal for Fred's water dish. He poured some fresh water for the thirsty dog. Then, he settled into his lawn chair.

"Those gals are stomping up a storm over there," he added. "There's no way I could make those moves."

"Me neither," Tom laughed. "I'd fall on my ass."

"Say, are you still trimming trees for Gus' place?"

"No, not right now. Gus had an accident. We had to quit for a while," Tom said, looking at his beer. "Clayborne's Tree Service is closed for the time being."

"No! Was it serious?"

"Gus got himself into a bee's nest. That darn fool fell, and got stun all over."

Tom scratched his arm. "Makes me itch thinking about it. Anyway, the doctor patched him up. He'll be all right. He's at home, right now."

"What are you doing with your down time?"

"Not much of anything," Tom paused to watch the cloggers. "Helped Lenny Watkins hang some drywall a while back. Am hoping Gus will be back on his feet soon; Tammy and I are running low on cash."

Tom sat quietly for a moment, sipping his beer. "You know, they say money doesn't grow on trees, but it sure does for me."

"Mmnn, I'm sorry to hear about Gus, you and Tammy. I hope things get better soon."

"Well, I'll let Gus know you are thinking about him," Tom said. "Besides, it could have been worse. At least it wasn't like that boy they found the other day."

"Say, what?"

"Yeah, they found some kid's pickup out by Buckshot Pond," Tom said, reaching down to pat Fred, who had stopped lapping water. "Truck was all messed up. Front end got totaled. And the boy, well, he didn't make it."

"Mmnn, mmnn, mmnn," Tom continued. "Found him in the creek. Shot in the back of the head; he was!"

"No!"

Skip's mouth dropped. He felt his stomach tighten. A sense of shock and disbelief overwhelmed him. Homicides were rare for the area. He asked if Tom knew the victim's name.

"Well, they haven't said anything yet. But, rumor has it, it was that long haul driver's son. Let me see, what's his name?"

Tom paused for a moment to take his hat off, and ran his fingers through his hair. "Oh, Benson," he recalled. "That's it. It was Les Benson's son."

Chapter 10

"Damn," Skip murmured. He tried to remember where he had last seen the Benson boy and thought it might have been at a local soccer game he reported on for *The Mountain Holler* several months ago, when Katie Mae and Tammy came bouncing back to the picnic table with black balloons.

"Hey, did you see us?" Katie Mae asked excitedly. "Tammy and I was freestyling with Billie Jo Barnes, Edward and that bunch over there." She motioned to the Gap Runners as they were leaving the stage. The group was being applauded by family and friends.

"Yeah, we were!" Tammy said enthusiastically. "That clogging will give you a workout, especially in this heat!"

She took off a French hair clip and put it in her mouth to rearrange her hair. As she finished with a tight twist and added, "Then, we ran into Milt's son Coop, and he gave us these balloons. Nice one's, huh? They're black, because everyone's in mourning on account of Wendall turning 50."

"Over the hill! Ha, it's all downhill from now on! Isn't that so, Tammy?" Katie Mae laughed, tugging at her balloon. "Pretty soon, Darci will be pushing Wendall in a wheelchair down at the senior center!"

The girls burst out laughing as Skip chirped, "Well, maybe we should have worn black."

"Looks that way," Tom grinned swirling the beer in his red plastic cup. "Not sure if it's supposed to be a party, or a memorial service."

"Katie should have gotten a sympathy card at Two Sisters," Skip joked. "Then, we could share our condolences."

"That's what Billie Jo was saying," Katie Mae said. "Say, did you know her daughter Mary Beth was one of those Gap Runners?"

Skip raised his eyebrows in surprise. "That a fact?"

"Yeah, and they're training for a tournament in Gatlinburg! It's going to be at a big fancy hotel, and everything!"

"Well, they better be on their toes," Tom quipped. With one last gulp, he finished his beer, smacked his lips and set the cup on the table.

"Tom!" Tammy raised her hand teasingly with a backhand slap, losing her balloon in the process. She made an inaudible scoff as her balloon flew away.

"All right," Katie Mae announced, tying her balloon to the picnic table. "I'm going to put my foot down before this gets out of hand, and get a dinner plate."

"You can clown all you want, but I'm hungry," she added. "Skippy, you stay with Fred, while Tammy and I get something to eat. Come on Tam."

Skip and Tom watched the girls make a beeline for the food table, which had been set with plywood planks over sawhorses. Decorative red and white checkered paper tablecovers, and tin foil pans for the appetizing side dishes were neatly arranged on the table.

"Boy, aren't they something?" Tom said. "Look at them skedaddle."

"Yes," Skip agreed as he reached in his pocket, and felt the aluminum dog whistle. "They're something all right."

Chapter 11

There was nothing special about the dog whistle. It was a simple, cheap black aluminum whistle on a keychain. Nothing distinctive or extraordinary. Perhaps a dog might respond to its ultrasonic sound, but there did not seem to be anything unique that set it apart from any other whistle of its kind.

For a moment, Skip glanced down at Fred. He thought about an anecdote his Uncle Em once told him about dog whistles being used "back in the day" on classic rock albums. There were certain records that caused his uncle to suspect a dog whistle sound was hidden in the music, probably as a joke on the musician's part, that would drive his dogs "bonkers."

Skip looked at Fred, who lifted his head. He seemed to have a sixth sense that Skip was thinking about him, and he wagged his tail.

Still, there was an uneasy feeling that haunted Skip as he scanned the party's surrounding area. Happy faces were everywhere. Laughter and excitement filled the air. Even Fred seemed to sense the overall vibe that there was a special, invigorating occasion in the air.

After pausing to take in the scene, Skip suggested Tom get a lunch plate. He would stay with Fred, while Tom joined the girls. Perhaps he was being overly obsessed with the frivolous promotional item more than he should have been, but he could not shake his curiosity. Besides, Tom could converge with the others as the pig was about to be unveiled and share in the excitement.

A crowd had gathered at the cinder block pit in anxious anticipation, as pitmaster Willie Cornsilk prepared to take the pig off the grill. Quiet and unassuming, Willie had been coaxed by Milt's emissary Leroy to handle the hickory charwood honors.

Never one to brag, Willie initially refused the invitation to be the party's pitmaster. He suggested someone else have the honor. He had spent years mastering his craft of quality and flavor, and had elevated his culinary technique to a mouthwatering artform. Willie's attitude was that he had done his share of pig roasts, and no longer cared to stand over a hot grill.

It wasn't until he accepted Leroy's offer of new Adirondack chairs for his yard that he agreed to provide his gastronomist talent for the party. Milt was thrilled. He knew that having the best pitmaster in the mountains would be a key to the party's success.

As the moment arrived to shift the pig onto the table, Willie enlisted the help of Coop and Leroy. Together, they gently hoisted the pig onto the table, where it was presented in its fully cooked splendor.

The party guests gathered to take pictures, and admire the results of Willie's hard work. The kids from the bounce house, headed by Miss Faye's Emma, had stationed themselves at the front of the crowd for a better view. Even the cornhole competitors tossed their game bags aside to share in the excitement as an intoxicating aroma filled the air.

Once the cooking was complete, Willie put on a pair of black rubber gloves, and began separating the meat from the bone. The meat was smokey, tender, and charred to perfection. It literally fell off the bone. Willie chopped some of the meat with intricate precision, leaving most for a traditional Carolina-style pork picking by the guests.

In addition to the main entrée, Coop's wife Sarah and several potluck donors had brought coleslaw, baked beans, sweet corn, green bean casseroles, cornbread, and hush puppies. The dishes were neatly laid out on picnic tables near the orchard.

A mix of prerecorded country and rock music blared through speakers that Toby had bought from Walmart for the special occasion as the crowd settled to enjoy their meal.

"Hey there!" Katie Mae said to Skip, returning with her food. "Don't sit there like a bump on a log. Go get yourself a dinner plate."

Skip nodded as he slid the dog whistle back into his pocket. Whatever feeling, or deep thoughts that were bothering him had not gone away.

He kept thinking about Bick, who had given him the dog whistle. Who was he? Where did he come from? What was he doing in the area? Was he a friend or an acquaintance of Wendall's?

And, what about Hellhound, the name imprinted on the whistle? Was it really a dog training school? If so, would it advertise in *The Mountain Holler*? And, why was Bick in a hurry to duck out of the sweet tea line?

Even stranger was the backpack. Why had a friend given him a backpack, and who was the friend? Did the friend really find the backpack? If so, where did it come from?

The more Skip thought, the more questions he raised. Nothing seemed to add up. Still, there was nothing he could do to relieve his questioning, especially in the midst of a celebration. Perhaps it was his *Mountain Holler* reporter instincts. In any event, he simply smiled and moved toward the line for a lunch plate.

"And be sure to get you some of that 'slaw," Katie Mae added. "I hear that Maggi Bellows made it, and I tell you it is to die for! You have got to get you some! Mmnn."

"Okay, keep an eye on Fred," he said. "I'll be right back."

Skip started to turn away and head toward the food line.

"You better hurry," Tammy warned. "If they put out banana pudding, they'll be a stampede. You'll get run over!"

"There's not going to be any banana pudding," Tom said. "They're fixing to cut cake for Wendall after dinner."

He called to Skip and added, "Don't pay her any mind. She's trying to cause trouble."

"Tom!" Tammy scolded. "You listen here."

Tammy was ready to give Tom a tongue-lashing when Milt walked over to the table.

"Hey! How are you guys doing?" he asked. "Are you getting enough to eat?"

"Hey Milt!" Katie Mae replied. "We're fine. Willie fixed us up good."

"Yeah," Tom chuckled. "I'll need a pushcart to carry my dinner plate. I'm loaded to the gills!"

"Now, Tommm!" Tammy in a mocking tone. "You be nice to our host, you hear? Don't go getting ugly."

"Aw, he's okay," Milt laughed. "They'll have to carry us all out of here by the time we're done."

He paused for a moment and patted Fred. "You folks be sure to stick around for the cake. There's going be music too."

"Why, thank you kindly!" Katie Mae said. "We sure will."

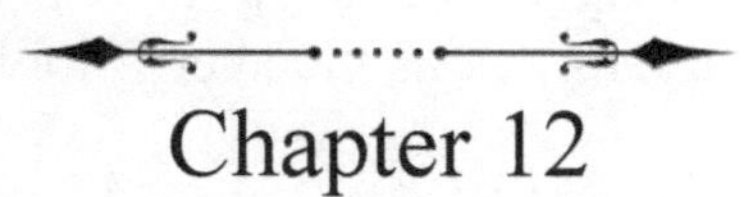

Chapter 12

When Deputy Wilson arrived at the creek, Detective Halstead was standing over a young man's lifeless body. Neither spoke as they surveyed the scene.

The body was found face down and partially dumped into the creek. Debris had started to gather around the upper torso. The body appeared to have been in the water for several hours.

"Oh, my God," Wilson said, shaking his head. "What happened?"

"Homicide," Halstead replied. "It looks like a male who's been shot in the back of the head."

Wilson starred in disbelief.

The detective took a step back and scanned the area. He did not see any signs of a struggle, resistance, or weapons.

"Lord, Jesus!" The stunned deputy mouthed. "Is there anything else?"

"He never had a chance," Halstead said woefully. "Probably dead, before he hit the water."

"Let's secure the area, and make some calls," Wilson said. "Better get rolling."

Sheriff Max Porter was called to the scene. He arrived moments before the fire department's paramedic team was on site. The county coroner's office was notified as well.

The sheriff was no stranger to violence. He was once stabbed three times in the ribs on the left side of his chest. His lung was punctured, and his heart missed by 1mm. The doctors who treated him were amazed he survived.

As the sheriff surveyed on the scene, he asked if the area was secure and the whereabouts of the Silverado pickup truck's owner.

"We're running that down," Wilson replied. "Everything else is buttoned down."

"Good," the sheriff said as he looked at the grim site. "I'm not sure, but I might have seen that truck somewhere. It looks awfully familiar."

The sheriff walked around the pickup truck. He examined the damage, shaking his head and peered inside the cab.

"You get everything out of there?"

"Yes, sir. She's been tagged and bagged."

Wilson paused for a moment as the sheriff looked at the neglected interior.

"Mostly trash, papers, and bottles. Stuff like that," he added. "We got it all."

"Good," the sheriff said, looking at the bloodstained windshield. "You and Sonny Boy comb the area. Make sure you don't miss anything."

"Will do."

"Oh, and be sure to call the garage. Have Harley impound the truck, if you haven't already. We'll need to get it to the yard for a closer look."

"Already on it!"

Before opening his patrol car door, the sheriff took one last look at the crime scene. He was anxious to return to the office, and have Jo Yarborough prepare the necessary paperwork for the criminal investigation to proceed among the various law enforcement agencies.

Once the area was properly taped off and road barricades had been set, the sheriff had Deputy Wilson formally record the identities of those individuals who had been at the scene earlier.

The deputy took note of everyone entering the scene, and gathered the evidence that was found. Notes were made of the crime scene's time, date, and weather. The deputy made a thorough sweep of the area, noting the smallest detail.

Photographs were taken to show the injuries the deceased had suffered, as well as images of the truck's accident.

"I don't get it," Wilson said to Halstead as the body was removed for the medical examiner's office.

"Neither do I," Halstead said dejectedly. "But, I'll say that fellow did not deserve what he got."

Chapter 13

Skip had barely sat down with his lunch plate when The Reedy Creek Stringbusters took the stage. The group was a well-known bluegrass band that played local events, and were often seen at The Red Maple.

The band was formed three years earlier by Jimmie "Jett" Jennings, when a group of friends gathered to play some bluegrass and gospel tunes. Soon, they were playing at weddings, festivals, and private events.

As leader of the band, Jimmie played mandolin. The band also had the traditional lineup of banjo, fiddle, standup bass, laptop, and acoustic guitar players, all capable of playing old timey bluegrass, gospel, and mountain classics.

"Whew, look at you!" Katie Mae said, examining Skip's plate. "Looks like you went whole hog with all the fixings!"

Skip smiled, tossing a piece of cornbread to Fred. Ever grateful, Fred stood wagging his tail in hopes of another tidbit from Skip's lunch plate.

"Say, that isn't Maggi Bellows 'slaw!" Katie Mae noted. "You got the wrong dinner plate!"

"No, it was gone by the time I got there."

"Well, goodness gracious," Katie Mae huffed. "You got to get a move on, once word gets out Maggi Bellows 'slaw's on the table."

"Hmmm, hmmm, hmmm," she continued. "You missed out on that one. Didn't he Tam?"

As the girls discussed Skip's coleslaw misfortune, Toby shut off the prerecorded music. Coop urged everyone to "stick around" for Wendall's birthday cake and formally introduced The Reedy Creek Stringbusters.

The band erupted with a fast-paced, toe-tapping tune bursting with energy. The dance floor became alive as people of all ages rose to their feet to join in the fun.

The sudden distraction caused Tammy to forget about Skip's coleslaw oversight and was consumed by the growing crowd around the band. "Say, is that some of those Gap Runners out there dancing?"

Katie Mae jumped up. "I believe so, come on, Tam. Let's have us some fun!"

As the girls headed to the dance floor, Katie Mae turned and said, "You guys going to join us, or be a lazy bone?"

"Naw, we're going stay here. It's too hot for that," Tom said. "Isn't that right, Skip?"

"Well, tell you what," Skip said. "You guys go on. I'll catch up later."

"Besides, I want to finish enjoying my *coleslaw*, then take Fred for a walk," he added with a wink.

Skip playfully licked his fork, while Katie Mae rolled her eyes.

"Suit yourself," Tom said, turning to the girls. "Okay, guys, let's go!"

As Katie Mae, Tammy, and Tom headed off, Wendall came by with his wife Darci. They were making their way toward the stage.

"Well, what do you know!" Skip exclaimed. "If it isn't the man of the hour, with his good-looking bride!"

Darci blushed, and Wendall laughed. "Hey Skip Walker! How are you doing?"

"Oh, fine, thank you," Skip replied. "Thought I'd come out for some fun with Katie Mae and Fred."

"We're glad you came out," Wendall said. "Isn't that right, Darci?"

"Yeah, this one's a barn burner!" Darci said.

"Connie or Harold, make it out?" Skip asked.

"No, they're watching The Red Maple," Wendall replied. "Have to keep the doors open; you know."

"I hear you," Skip laughed. "Good to have someone taking care of business."

"Tell you what," Wendall said. "We need see a couple other folks, but we'll catch up with you later."

Skip bid the celebrating couple farewell and reached in his pocket. He suddenly remembered the dog whistle and looked down at Fred.

"Come on, Fred," he said. "Let's go for a walk."

Chapter 14

Deep in the woods, near the edge of the Highland Ranch property, was a natural pond that was fed by a slow flowing creek. The pond was surrounded by oak and maple trees and covered with aquatic plants, reeds, and water lilies, making it an ideal attraction for mallard and wood ducks.

The ducks were fond of nibbling on aquatic plants, small fish, worms, eggs, algae, tadpoles, and frogs. Along the shallow part of the pond, was a dense layer of tall grass that was a favored nesting area.

Although the setting seemed like the perfect utopia for ducks and birds alike, there were hazards to consider. The ducks had to be watchful of their eggs or ducklings being taken by snakes, feral cats, raccoons, possums, skunks, and other predators, including rude, abrasive hard-drinking men.

As Skip and Fred entered the meadow, they could hear a group of younger men gathered around a picnic table near the edge of the duck pond far from the bluegrass band's hard-driving, off-beat tone. The exuberant men were talking loudly and laughing over drinks, while smoking cigarettes.

From a distance, Skip recognized Charlie Harper and Lenny Barlow. Both were in their early 20s and having a pleasurable time with their friends, while sipping drinks from red party cups, and passing around a cannabis vape pen.

Charlie was an apprentice repairman at Willis Appliance Repair, owned by old man Willis, and Lenny was the part-time shipping and receiving clerk for Marsh Auto Center on the outskirts of town.

As they walked through the meadow, Fred took a sudden interest in a moss-covered log to explore. Skip eased the dog's leash, allowing Fred to freely investigate the fallen log. As Fred examined the grounds, Skip spotted Bick amid the duck pond's group.

Bick appeared to be casually smoking and chatting amenably. He could see the shiny silver dog whistle around his neck glistening in the hot sun. The conversation centered on illegal alcohol, though Skip could only hear faint bits and pieces.

"What are you boys drinking?" Bick asked.

"Mad Mama," Charlie answered swirling his cup.

"Mad Mama?"

"Yeah, Mama. Now, that's the shit."

"You say it tastes like shit?"

"Say what?"

Some snickering was heard within the group.

"What about Helllhound?" Bick asked, tugging on his Carolina hat.

"What about it?"

"I hear it's pretty good."

"Well, 'purdy good' ain't good enough," Charlie said defiantly. "We drink the best!"

"That so?"

"'Sides, you can't get it 'round here."

"You kidding?" Bick raised his voice. "That stuff's all over the place."

"Don't matter," Charlie said, shaking his head. "That stuff sucks."

"Oh, it does?"

"Yeah, tastes like piss water. Ain't that right, Lenny?"

"Sure does," Lenny said, nodding his head. He took a drag off his cigarette, extinguished it on the picnic table and lit another. "About the only difference is the color!"

The group exploded into hysterical laughter. Bick's face fell. His intuition was to warn Lenny about not quitting his day job to become a comedian, but he did not want to sound like a smartass. Instead, he gave a weak smile.

"Just curious, what's that you boys are smoking?" Bick asked upon smelling the vape pen.

"What's it to you?" Charlie asked. "Yore not gonna rat us out ov'r a little smoke, are ya?"

"Yeah, now that there's the real deal," Lenny boasted. "That's another reason we don't drink that Hellhound piss water."

A dark, brooding scowl came across Bick's face. His demeanor took on a gloomy, ominous appearance. The group that had gathered around the picnic table stopped laughing, upon seeing Bick's uneasy gaze fixed on Lenny.

The faint sound of the bluegrass band momentarily stopped. Coop could be heard making an announcement.

"Finally, we get a break," Bick said relieved. "Beethoven would get sick to his stomach; with the stuff those guys are playing."

"Not half as sick, if he was drinking Hellhound!" an intoxicated Lenny roared. "One taste of that piss water, and he'd be hugging the commode!"

The group howled with unrestrained laughter. Bick remained silent, and glared at Lenny's crude remark. His eyes flashed an intense look of sheer, unadulterated rage.

Skip listened briefly to the laughter, then tugged on Fred's leash. "Come on, Fred," he said. "Time to turn around."

He took one last look at the group gathered at the duck pond. There seemed to be an ominous, secretive conspiration among the young men, though their jovial appearance belied any mischievous activities.

Upon hearing Coop's announcement, some of the young men left their cups on the picnic table, and headed toward the pig pickin'. They did not want to miss the birthday party festivities.

Chapter 15

The crowd around the stage had finished singing *Happy Birthday* to Wendall when Skip returned to the pig pickin' with Fred. He stood in the rear, watching the celebratory guest of honor rise from an oversized rocking chair to thank his family and friends for the party, as well as Milt's use of the farm and Willie Cornsilk's exquisite culinary skills.

Wendall cut the white sheet cake with Darci by his side. It had been prominently decorated with black balloons and an *Over the Hill* icing party theme. Pictures were taken of the memorable occasion. Paper plates and plastic forks were quickly dispersed, while Coop and Sarah began passing out dessert.

As the crowd around the cake began to thin, Jimmie "Jett" Jennings stepped to the microphone with the Reedy Creek Stringbusters and counted off the lead-in for *I Saw The Light*.

The rhythmic beat of the music electrified the crowd. Heads began to bob, and feet were moving. The excitement grew as the band seamlessly moved on with a rousing rendition of *I'll Fly Away*.

Skip could see Wendell and Milt shaking hands with party guests, laughing, and talking, while taking an occasional bite of cake. Toby stood at the far end of the stage, passing out the black balloons to the children who had been playing in the bounce house.

Willie Cornsilk sliced and diced the leftover portions of the pig. A couple guests pitched in to help with the clean-up, as Willie began filling a ready supply of plastic zip-bags for those who wanted to take home extra pickings.

"Hey silly, where have you been?" Katie Mae asked Skip with a cake plate in her hand.

"Fred and I went for a walk out by the pond."

"Say, what? You were out by those hog-eyed boys?"

"Hog-eyed?"

Tammy's mouth dropped in amazement. Tom shook his head and let out a long, guffawing laugh.

"Yes, they're hog-eyed, all right; mm-hmm," Katie Mae said. "All they do is stare at your bottom with their mouth hanging open."

"Ass," Tom corrected.

"Tom!" Tammy snapped.

"Sorry, meant boobs."

"Why, Thomas Thayer," Tammy reprimanded with her arms folded. "I'm going teach you some religion when we get home."

"Yeah, you do that."

"Ah, Tom doesn't mean any harm," Skip volunteered. "He's just telling it, like it is."

"Now you listen here, Mr. Hog Eye," Katie Mae injected, while using her fingers as quotation marks to emphasize the word "Mr. Hog Eye."

"You hush up, or else you can go back over yonder with your friends."

Both Tom and Skip laughed.

"Besides, you missed the cake," she continued. "And it was a good one."

"No, Fred and I stood by the apple trees," Skip replied. "We saw the whole thing."

"Well, if you want some cake, you better get in line."

"Yeah, and get Tam's banana pudding, while you're at it," Tom laughed.

"Tom, I'm about ready to knock you out!"

"Don't do that," Skip said. "You need a ride home."

"Right now, he can walk himself home," Tammy shot back.

The brief, good-natured exchange was disrupted when the group heard Coop announce that there were extra pig pickin' leftovers for those who wanted to take some home.

Skip thought about his Uncle Em, who had stayed home from the party. His uncle always enjoyed pitmaster Willie Cornsilk's cooking, and knew he would appreciate a luncheon plate. He quietly placed Fred's leash in Katie Mae's hand, and headed toward the food line.

The band was well into their final number, *Will the Circle Be Unbroken?* when Skip reached the food table. He overheard Milt ask Leroy to start "herding" everyone toward the exit, including the "fellas" out by the pond.

Chapter 16

The late afternoon sun's heat beat down on the pond. The ducks were no longer frolicking in the water, but had sought refuge in the shade under the densely overgrown bushes and aquatic weeds. Upon hearing The Reedy Creek's Stringbuster's final tune, the remaining partygoers at the pond's picnic bench began to leave.

Charlie was running late for work. He knew old man Willis would be angry that he had not returned to the shop on time. Being a small repair shop, the owner relied on Charlie to help move appliances within the workplace, as well as pick up and deliver customer repairs.

Earlier, he asked if he could take an extended lunch hour, and run over to the ranch for lunch. He knew about the party from a flyer he had seen at The Red Maple. His plan was to meet with Lenny, who was not working that afternoon.

"Yikes!" Charlie grimaced. "What time's it gettin' to be?"

"I don't know," Lenny said. "Who cares?"

"Half past four," Bick volunteered.

"Oh, man. Mr. Willis is gonna kill me."

"Why?" Lenny asked. "You still got plenty of time to get back."

"No, I was s'posed to be back a couple 'a' hours ago," Charlie's eyes widened as he looked down at his party cup.

"Well, in that case it wouldn't hurt none to have one for the road, and take a hit off the pen." Lenny said, slurring his words. "That stuff's hard to get."

Charlie relented, and shrugged his shoulders. He agreed to one last drink, though the cannabis vape pen had long since disappeared.

"Say, how do you get Mad Mama, anyway?" Bick asked Charlie.

"Some guy comes by, ev'ry so often," Charlie said. "Lenny knows 'em."

"Sounds like a good connection. Mind if I have a taste?"

"Nah, go ahead," Charlie said. "Lenny'll fix you up."

"Cheers," Lenny said as he poured a drink into a plastic cup and set it in front of Bick.

Bick licked his lips and took a sip. He threw back his head and coughed. "Whew, nasty," he said.

"Ah, it bites a l'il, but you get used to it," Charlie said. "Ain't that right, Lenny?"

Lenny readily agreed, though he had begun to look pale.

"Look at those ducks over there," Bick said. "Not a care in the world."

"Yeah, they's lookin' purdy happy," Charlie agreed.

"Mind if I see that jar?" Bick asked.

Lenny shrugged and passed the bottle; which was a Mason jar. Bick took a moment to study the jar, its size, shape, screw top lid and label.

"Interesting, let me get a picture," Bick said, reaching for his cell phone.

"Hey, why not take it bed, while you're at it?" Lenny suggested in a sardonic tone with his eyes half closed.

Bick lowered his eyes with an unappreciative glare at Lenny, which was followed by a smattering of laughter.

"Hey, hope you don't mind doing the honors," Lenny slurred, setting his cup in front of Bick.

"Absolutely," Bick said slowly, pouring the drink. "With pleasure."

Charlie looked at Lenny and asked if he was "okay?" Lenny had stopped smoking and looked pale. He drained his cup and jerked his head erratically. "Think I'll take a walk. I'll be right back."

"Man, I gotta get goin'," Charlie said. "Mr. Willis is gonna be madder'n than hell."

"Tell him you had car trouble," Bick suggested.

"Nah, I doubt he'd go for that," Charlie said. "'Sides, I used that one before."
Charlie and Bick stepped toward the pond's edge when they saw Leroy bouncing toward them in the ranch's ATV.

"You guys 'bout ready to head out?" Leroy called out as the Polaris Razor came to a stop.

"Yeah, we're on our way," Charlie said. "Give us a minute."

Leroy nodded and turned back toward the party to continue shutting down the festivities. He had already deflated the bounce house, taken in the cornhole games, and made sure there were no party stragglers in the remote areas of the ranch.

Bick took another sip from his drink and coughed. "Boy, this stuff will turn your insides out."

"Yeah, I'd say so," Charlie agreed. "Price is right too."

"That Mama guy ever run out of the stuff?" Bick asked.

"Oh, no," Charlie said. "We's all set."

"Well, tell you what," Bick said thoughtfully. "It'd be a damn shame if anything happened to him. Hmmm, hmmm, hmmm."

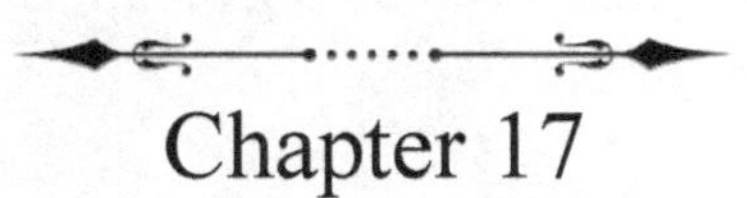

Chapter 17

Emitt Walker was not the kind of person who befriended many people. He had an abrupt demeanor, and a cold sense of humor that turned most people off. At times, he was rude, impolite, and politically incorrect. Never one to mince words, he was a straight *tell-it-like-is* talker who never strayed from an honest opinion.

Emitt, or "Uncle Em" as Skip called him, was a crusty retired project manager from Daytona Beach, Florida, who had been in the construction industry for over 38 years. He had worked from the ground level up, and did not take crap from anyone.

When Uncle Em was forced into retirement at 62 years of age, he left his profession embittered. Through the years, he had watched himself continually passed over by younger people, while his career opportunities stagnated.

Caught between disillusion, depression and boredom, Uncle Em drank heavily. Soon, his weight ballooned, blood pressure skyrocketed, and he suffered a minor stroke.

Throughout his downward spiral, his wife, Irene, offered what little comfort she could. Still, he was unable to overcome his demons. The ongoing drama was too much. She filed for divorce, leaving Emitt and his dog, Fred, virtually homeless.

Since Skip's father Thomas had long since passed away, and his mother had remarried a finance broker in Ownings Mills, Maryland, it seemed logical that he should be the one to offer him a place to live.

Skip's home was a modest three-bedroom, two-bathroom wood-framed cottage on the south of Bonner Falls. The remote location offered plenty of privacy near a wooded creek, which gave Fred freedom to explore and roam through the woods.

"Freddie!" Uncle Em exclaimed when Skip and Fred returned from the pig pickin'. "Come here, baby boy!"

Fred raced excitedly to Uncle Em's swivel rocking recliner. He propped his front paws, with his tail wagging on Uncle Em's knees.

"Ah, that's a good boy," he said before turning to Skip.

"So, where have you been?"

"We were at that Highland Ranch pig pickin' for Wendall Tucker's 50th birthday."

"How'd it go?"

"Good," Skip smiled as Fred crossed the room, and bounced off his leg. "Nice turnout, but hot."

"You should have worn a hat."

"I did."

"That stupid *Mountain Holler* thing you're wearing?" Uncle Em scoffed, shaking his head. "That's not a hat. You need something with a real brim to cover those wing-nut ears of yours."

Skip laughed, and set a bottle of water on the kitchen counter.

"What's with the water?"

"I picked it up on the way home."

"Does drinking that bottled stuff make you feel hot?"

"What?"

"You know, when I was a kid, we drank from a garden hose," Uncle Em proclaimed. "And you know what? Nobody died! We didn't have none of those fancy; what do call them? Reclaimed plastic bottles?"

"Recycled. It's to help preserve the environ…"

"Oh, yeah," Uncle Em injected, cutting him off. "That's right, we didn't have none of those cheap ass fancy schmancy recycle things with reusable pink drinking lids."

Uncle Em grimaced, shaking his head.

"Man," he added. "Back in those days, they'd have strung you up, walking around like some priss ass prima donna."

Fred bounced back over to the recliner, where Uncle Em began a frisky tug-of-war with a knotted soft rope toy.

"So, how was the food?"

"Good," Skip said. "Oh, I almost forgot. I brought a lunch plate home for you."

"Really? Well, hot damn! Hit me!"

"Yes sir, Willie Cornsilk fixed it himself."

"Mmmn," Uncle Em murmured. "No one does a pig roast like Willie Cornsilk. No siree bob."

"Funny, Katie Mae said the same thing."

"What? You still with that girl?"

"Now, don't get ugly," Skip warned. "She'd be here now if she hadn't run off with her friends after the party."

"How many times do I have to tell you about women?" Uncle Em said scoldingly. "They'll bleed you to death."

"I suppose, but that's okay," Skip conceded. "The Red Cross can figure out my blood type."

"Ha, tell that to your bank!" Uncle Em paused to review the lunch plate. "You get someone like my ex-wife Irene the Wolverine, the meanest woman you've *EVER* seen, and you'll get sucked dry! She'll run up your credit cards, like she did mine. You won't have a dime left to your name. Then, you'll change your tune!"

"Well," Skip rolled his eyes thoughtfully. "If it gets to that point, I'll close the account, and change the station."

Chapter 18

The mood in the office was quiet when Sheriff Max Porter arrived. He had been consumed with the Buckshot Pond investigation, and had not slept well. There were so many unanswered questions that led to the brutal, senseless killing that haunted him.

Upon entering the building, his senses were greeted by the aroma of Jo Yarborough's freshly brewed coffee that filtered throughout the department. The sheriff paused at the doorway to savor the moment.

The office coffee pot was the official de facto meeting place to exchange morning greetings and gossip. The lighthearted topics ranged from weekend activities, family, books, movies, weather, or sports. It was the perfect place to relax for a moment and escape from the day's demanding workload.

As the sheriff passed the coffee pot, he paused to fill a Styrofoam cup and continued onto his office. He only had a few minutes to review his notes before meeting Deputy Bobby Wilson and Detective Sonny Boy Halstead to discuss the Buckshot Pond case.

Both the deputy and detective had taken their seats with their laptop computers in the conference room. Jo had laid a dossier, complete with critical information pertinent to the case on the table.

"Hey guys, how we doing this morning?" The sheriff asked as he entered the room.

Both Wilson and Halstead nodded with an affirmative response.

"I wanted to review the procedures taken on the Buckshot Pond case and evaluate the evidence," the sheriff began. "I'd like to make sure we didn't miss anything."

Once again, Wilson and Halstead nodded and opened their dossiers that Jo had prepared.

"Bobby, you arrived on the scene first," the sheriff said. "You want to tell us what you saw?"

"Sure, I arrived at 9:07 AM and saw two white males standing next to a disabled vehicle that had crashed into a tree."

"Did they witness the accident?"

"No, they were checking it out."

"Anything else?"

"Well, I looked to see if there was anyone in the vehicle," Wilson said, glancing down at the report. "It was clean."

"The windshield was smashed and had blood," he continued. "It looked like someone hit it hard. That's about the time when Sonny Boy arrived."

"Drugs or alcohol?"

"I didn't see any," Wilson paused, looking across the room at a blank monitor mounted behind the sheriff. "The truck's interior was in bad shape; ripped seats and lots of trash, but no liquor or drugs."

"Anything else?"

"Food wrappers, old lotto tickets, a biker magazine with girlie pictures, and a keychain," Wilson stopped to gather his thoughts. "Oh, there was an old liquor bottle that'd been chipped."

"How old?"

"Pretty old," Wilson said. "It had a Mad Mama label, which I haven't seen in quite some time."

"Say," Halstead interrupted. "Isn't that the guy they shut down some time ago?"

"Maybe," the sheriff said, engrossed in thought.

"I'd be surprised if he was bootlegging," Halstead said. "He'd be a fool to start distilling again."

"Okay," the sheriff said. "What happened when Sonny Boy came on?"

"He asked if I knew who owned the truck, and I took some pictures."

"Yeah, and that's the strange part," Halstead said. "There were no plates. So, we ran the VIN number."

Halstead shuffled the papers in his dossier. He could not find the information he was after, and asked Wilson if he had it.

"Yes," Wilson said. "The truck's a Chevrolet Silverado, short bed, owned by Les Benson, with an out-of-date registration."

"Okay, I thought I'd seen that truck somewhere," the sheriff said, turning to Detective Halstead. "You talk to him?"

"Well, yes and no," Halstead said. "He's an LTL independent long-haul carrier who runs a route on Interstate 40. He's a hard guy to get ahold of. He recently had a Flagstaff delivery, and backhaul from Tucumcari, New Mexico. We're still waiting for a call back."

"Family?" Sheriff Porter asked.

"That's a tough one," Halstead began. "Jo did some research, and found his wife left him before moving from Greensboro. We don't know where she's at."

"Anything else?"

"He has a son Robert," Halstead felt his voice trail off. "We don't know much about him, or where he's at."

"Hmmm," the sheriff murmured. "You know, why don't we take a five-minute break."

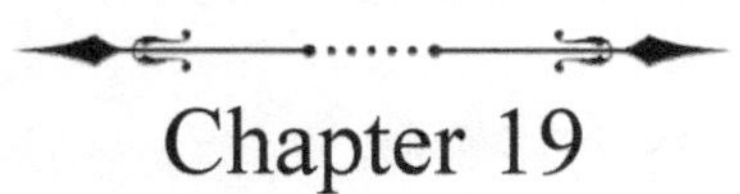

Chapter 19

The meeting break came as a welcome relief to the participants. For the sheriff, he was able to digest the information that had been forthcoming, while the others could decompress and recharge their mental batteries.

Jo set out copies of the diagrams that Wilson had drawn, and made a fresh pot of coffee for those needing an extra caffeine boost.

"Okay, where were we?" The sheriff said, bringing the session back to order. "We need to get ahold of Les Benson. Jo? Is she around?"

Jo popped her head back in the room.

"Can you, or one of the admins get Benson on the horn?"

"Will do."

As the group poured over the accident and homicide case diagrams, the sheriff wondered why the truck hit the tree. He also wondered about the kids who found the vehicle in the morning, and if they had seen anyone in the area.

"Not a soul," Halstead said. "I spoke to the boys and their mother. They stumbled on the truck while fishing. Their story was solid. Never changed."

"Okay, what was the procedure you used to canvass the area?"

Halstead silently bit his lip as Jo gathered some papers on the meeting room's storage credenza. He lowered his head in a shameful manner. "Well, uh, Jo's coffee went through me. I had to take a walk to the little boy's room."

The lighthearted comment drew considerable laughter. Jo lowered her head embarrassed, and left the room. "Well," the sheriff proclaimed. "We've all been there."

"How'd you find the body?"

"It was a white male, unresponsive. Face down in the creek. He'd been shot in the back of his head."

"At that point, what action did you take?"

"I called Bobby. He notified you, the fire department paramedics, and the county coroner's office. Bobby prepared the report with diagrams, measurements, and on-site observations. He also called Harley at the garage to impound the truck."

"Pictures?"

"They're here. We've got plenty."

The group took a moment to examine the photos. There was a moment of respectful silence when the sheriff finally said, "Boy, my heart goes out to this guy and his family."

"Any signs of a struggle?"

"None."

"Any footprints or damaged branches?"

"Not really," Halstead said, shaking his head. "There were some drag marks."

"Drag marks? Do you think he was shot in the truck?"

"Hard to say," Halstead acknowledged. "It looks like someone hit the windshield. It doesn't appear that he was shot him in the vehicle."

"Nothing in the truck that might indicate otherwise?"

"Not that I could see."

"Well, the coroner's report should confirm that," the sheriff said. "Someone must know something. I cannot believe a young man gets murdered in cold blood, and someone gets away with it."

The meeting concluded with further investigation planned. It was the sheriff's hope that the evidence, witness leads, and coroner's report might be helpful in solving the case.

As the group was leaving the room, Jo stepped through the door. She had an ashen, worrisome look of concern on her face.

"Sheriff, Highland Ranch just called," she said. "They found a body."

Chapter 20

The scene at the Highland Ranch was chaotic. Leroy had gone to the duck pond, as part of his morning chores. During the duck's migratory season, he would regularly check the wood duck nesting stands and mallard nests near the wetlands surrounding the pond.

As Leroy searched in the shallow water through the thick underbrush, he came across a mallard's nest of nearly a dozen greenish-colored eggs. He was cautious not to disturb the nest, and make sure it was safe from predators.

Leroy quietly backed away. He knew there were other nests in the area, and continued to prod along the pond's edge in his insulated synthetic rubber hip waders while checking on the wood duck stands.

It was near the pond's most remote area that he saw a body partially hidden in the bushes. The body lay motionless, curled in a fetal position.

At first, Leroy thought it might be a trespassing fisherman who had fallen asleep. It was not uncommon for kids to enter the ranch illegally, and try their luck fishing. In those cases, Leroy would round up the offenders, and escort them off the property.

Leroy called to the man but got no response. As he continued to tread through the water's thick blanket of aquatic plants and reeds, he sensed the individual was not moving. Alarmed, he raced back to the Delany farmhouse, where Sarah was clearing the breakfast table.

When Deputy Wilson arrived, Leroy took him to the man's location. It was apparent that the individual was deceased.

Wilson immediately secured the area, and took a preliminary statement from Leroy. Close examination did not reveal any signs of foul play.

"Whattaya think?" Leroy asked.

"I don't know," Wilson replied. "If I had to hesitate a guess, I'd say drugs, but we'll have to get a toxicology report from the coroner."

"Well, folks 'round 'ere ain't into stuff like that fenny-all."

"Fentanyl," Wilson corrected.

"Whatever, but that's big city stuff," Leroy said. "That don't happen 'ere."

It was then, Sheriff Porter could be seen turning the corner past the horse corral, with Coop in the front seat of his cruiser.

"Hey, Bobby!" the sheriff said, stepping from the patrol car. "We've got to quit meeting like this."

"Yeah, I know."

"What do we have here?"

"Over here, Max," Wilson said. "He's under a tarp."

The sheriff followed Wilson into the thick underbrush. "Careful," Coop warned. "Leroy spotted a timber rattlesnake a couple days ago."

"Sho' did," Leroy said emphatically. "A big'un too."

"Thanks for the heads up," the sheriff said. "The last thing I need is to get my ass bit by a damned snake."

The group stood back for a moment to carefully scan the area.

"Drug overdose?" the sheriff asked.

"That's what I'm thinking, but I can't tell for sure."

"Any evidence?"

"We found his wallet," Wilson said. "His name's Leonard Barlow. He lives northwest from here."

"Okay, anything else?"

"Possibly," Wilson shrugged. "I believe he's 24 years old. There were a couple party cups from that pig pickin' they had the other day."

"Yeah, heard they put on the dog."

Wilson thought for a moment. "Chain smoker. Had six dollars and some change in his pocket. Couple keys and a plastic keychain."

"He also had a diamond stud in his ear," Wilson said.

"Jeeze," the sheriff scoffed. "I never did get that style."

"Me neither."

"You talk to any of the Delany's?"

"No, Milt and his mechanical guy, Toby went to look at farm equipment out of town. Sarah's in the house; she's upset," Wilson paused to look at Leroy. "Oh, and Leroy's been running all over this morning."

There was a sudden commotion in the horse corral. A horse could be heard kicking, snorting, and pawing the ground. Alarmed, Cooper and Leroy excused themselves, and hurried to the corral.

"You get anything out of Leroy?" the sheriff asked.

"Not much," Wilson began. "He talked about the party, and said some guy was hanging with Charlie Harper."

"Isn't he that the kid at Willis Appliance Repair?"

"That's right," Wilson confirmed.

"They worked on my dryer," the sheriff said ruefully. "Still, doesn't work right."

Both men studied the body for a moment, then turned their attention to the pond. The ducks in the pond were gliding over the water, with their heads bobbing sporadically. On occasion, they would dive downward for a minnow or to nibble on an aquatic plant, and surface victoriously to shake the water off their heads.

"Well, tell you what," the sheriff began. "We need to call the paramedics and county coroner's office."

Wilson nodded vigorously in agreement as he prepared to diagram the scene.

"Also, let's have Sonny Boy get ahold of Charlie Harper," the sheriff said. "It'd be nice to know, if he knows anything. Plus, let's get with Barlow's next-of-kin."

Wilson made a couple notes on his clipboard. He knew the drill, as the sheriff turned toward his cruiser.

As Wilson looked down on Barlow's covered body, the glint of a shiny object caught his eye. Curious, he pulled on his disposable gloves. He reached down to find what Barlow might have processed in his final moments.

Chapter 21

In the early pre-dawn hours, the black SUV made its way along a single-lane road deep in the wooded mountains above Bonner Falls. The men in the vehicle were tired and spoke little.

As the car neared its destination, its driver, Salvador, was tense, apprehensive, and irritable. His focus was finding a virtually hidden, obscure driveway that was heavily fortified by a steel gate.

"Is this the place?" Ross asked as the car pulled to a stop.

"Looks like it."

"The gate's locked."

"Of course it is," Salvador said, opening the driver's door. Using the headlights to view the gate, he toggled the numeric code on the lock and slid the gate open.

Salvador's instructions to Ross were to "close her up," and lock the gate after the car had passed through.

Ross dutifully got out of the car and walked to the gate. "Damn," he said, swatting the side of his face. "Skeeters are eating me alive!"

"Hurry up," Salvador urged. "We don't have time for that."

Once inside the car, the two men rolled along a long, heavily wooded semi-gravel driveway that led to a fenced compound. Dogs could be heard barking.

"Oh, lord!" Ross exclaimed. "If this place doesn't look like Fort Knox!"

"Hush," Salvador said. "They want us around back."

"Who's 'they'?"

"None of your business," Salvador snapped. "Just listen to me and do as you're told."

The car slowly drove around the side of the property. The road was well illuminated from the moonlight, and Salvador had no difficulty finding the rear gate.

Once again, the Salvador pulled up to the gate and got out of the car. There was a doorbell on the side of the gate. Without hesitation, Salvador pressed three times, which was the designated signal. Moments later, the electronic gate slid open.

A building emerged behind the gated fence. It appeared to be a large storage complex. The faint sound of an unrecognizable Johann Strauss waltz could be heard, as Salvador pulled the car forward. He parked in front of a metal roll-up door, and watched the electronic gate closed behind him.

Suddenly, a slender man wearing a well-worn Carolina hat, with a pockmarked face and silver dog whistle around his neck appeared holding the two vicious dogs on a tight leash. The dogs were raging rottweilers. Both monsters primed to attack.

As the man limped with a cane toward the car, the dogs strained forward on their leash. Their terrifying, gruesome fangs on full display.

"You got everything?" the man asked.

"Yes, we're good to go," Salvador replied.

"Any issues?"

"No, everything went as planned."

The dogs continued to snarl and growl. "STOP!" the slender man yelled as he forcefully pulled back on their leash. At the command of "quiet," the dogs backed off.

"That's better," he added. "Now, where were we?"

"You asked about the 'plan.'"

"Oh, yes," the slender man said. "Did you take care of our young friend?"

"We tried, but there was an accident."

"Hmmm, too bad."

"Anyone see anything?"

"No, all quiet," Salvador replied. "The place was clean when we left."

"Did you remember to drop off the souvenir?"

"Yes, we did exactly as you asked," Salvador confirmed.

"Good," the man said as the dogs moved uneasily. "Our resident corn mash expert, and master distiller Cornelius will help you unload. He'll also take care of you when you're done."

"Great," Salvador nodded.

The man limped through the side door of the storage unit with the dogs. The metal door to the large storage complex began to rise. An elderly, stooped man with short gray hair and a pleasant, warm smile emerged. He introduced himself as 'Corny' who oversaw the facility and kept the Hellhound distillery 'juices' flowing.

"Whatcha got?"

"Some boxes in the back," Salvador said, opening the SUV's rear compartment.

"Hmmm," Corny said. "Lemme get a dolly."

The men quickly unloaded the boxes from the SUV into the storage unit. The backpack and cellphone found in the Silverado were also given to Corny.

As promised, Corny pulled an envelope from his pocket and handed both men a wrapped package. "Nice doin' business with y'all."

Chapter 22

Ross Parker was an unemployed garage door installer who lived in an aging single-wide mobile home with his girlfriend Candi O'Neil near the Tennessee border.

He was a heavy smoker and avid deer hunting enthusiast who had worked for the Sweet James Garage Door Company until he failed a drug test, which he blamed on Candi's immoral influence.

Candi lived a fast and loose nomadic lifestyle, and was frequently seen hanging around bars when bikers rolled through town. She loved to drink and smoke, but most of all, take drugs.

She had moved in with Ross on a temporary basis. The arrangement was initially fine, until Ross realized her addictions were detrimental to his frugal lifestyle. It was then that things began to deteriorate.

The couple frequently bickered over money, while Ross scrambled to make ends meet. During the tourist season, Candi cleaned hotel or Airbnb rooms, but those jobs were few and far between.

Upon falling on hard times, Ross took whatever opportunities came his way. It was through word-of-mouth that he heard Salvador DiMarco needed help with some pickup and delivery jobs. It was a position he accepted, on the condition that he was never to discuss the nature of the business.

The work was easy, and the hours flexible. Ross would be given a specific address, or location to meet a customer and either pickup or deliver boxes. He never questioned the contents of the boxes, or the nature of the business, though working with Salvador could be trying.

Salvador was impatient, critical, and moody by nature. He worked fast and expected 100% loyalty from his subordinates. He rarely, if ever, spoke of the company or its enigmatic owner.

He would trust Ross to complete a given task on his own, unless the job was critical. At that point, Salvador would personally take the lead with Ross on a given assignment.

Despite being kept in the dark, Ross didn't mind. He needed the money. His laid-back, passive attitude made him the perfect foil for

Salvador's emotional outbursts, and infrequent demonstrative demands.

When Ross got home after the meeting with Corny in the morning, he opened the envelope and was dismayed to find $300. He thought the job was going to pay $500.

In addition to the envelope, there was a jar of Hellhound, a high-proof distilled spirit. The gift disappointed Ross but delighted Candi. Ross preferred beer, while Candi would drink anything.

Nevertheless, Ross unscrewed the jar's lid and recoiled at the acidic, ethanol smell that burned his nostrils. He jerked his head back and replaced the lid. The alcohol, he could do without. The money was another matter.

"Whew, boy," Candi said. "We're going have a good time with that!"

"No, we're not," Ross firmly replied.

"What?" Candi said, looking amazed. "You've got be crazy. People pay good money for that stuff."

"Well, in that case, they can have it," Ross said. "I'm not drinking that shit, and I'm going get ahold of Salvador for the rest of my money."

"You do that," Candi said, rubbing her eyes. "Besides, it's too early, and I'm going back to bed. There's no point in jabbering with a dang fool."

As Candi headed to the bedroom in the rear of the mobile home, she turned and warned "You best keep your promise that we were supposed to go out today."

"Say what?"

"That's right, you said you were going to score a big job, and we'd have some fun."

"That all you can think about?"

"Darn right, honey," Candi snapped. "Now, don't go getting ugly. Remember, you got to be sweet to get some sugah."

Ross shook his head. In fact, he was still shaking his head later that afternoon when they walked through The Red Maple doors.

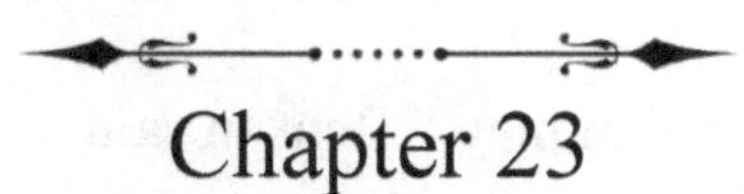

Chapter 23

It took several calls until Jo Yarborough was able to reach Les Benson. He had finished delivering a backhaul load in Memphis, which helped him avoid a deadhead trip home.

Ever since his divorce, Benson had an aversion to law enforcement. His opposition stemmed from an incident while living in Greensboro. He had an argument with his wife. A misunderstood scuffle got him arrested for domestic spousal abuse. It was an experience he never forgot.

Upon returning home, he agreed to meet with Detective Halstead at the sheriff's station to discuss the whereabouts of his son. He had been unable to reach him since leaving for Flagstaff.

Benson was in disbelief when he was notified that his son's truck had been in an accident. He immediately asked if he was "okay," which was why he had agreed to come into the sheriff's office to review the photos and answer questions.

At first, he was relieved to learn his son was not in the wreckage, but saddened to learn he had disappeared. No one knew his whereabouts.

Benson's son, Robert who went by his nickname "Bo" was a 19-year-old renegade. He was unemployed, kept irregular hours, and rarely saw his long-haul truck-driving father.

When Benson finally met with Detective Halstead, he was horrified to learn that Bo was dead. Though the detective spared Benson from seeing the gruesome pictures, Benson was shown enough evidence to confirm his worst nightmare.

The detective offered grief counseling to Benson, which he flatly refused. Instead, Benson sobbed lightly and vowed to kill the "son-of-a-bitch" who murdered his son.

Once calmer heads prevailed, the detective tried to learn more about Bo, his associates, and activities.

"Can you tell me about his personal life?" Halstead asked.

"What's to know?" Benson said defiantly. "He had his; I had mine and his mother..."

"Go on."

"Well, God only knows where the hell she run off to."

"Did he have any money?"

"Yeah, he always had money," Benson said.

"Did he have a job?"

"No."

"No job?" Halstead paused for a moment to gather his thoughts. "Any idea where it came from?"

"No, not really," Benson responded. "I was on the road most of the time."

"Was he into drugs, or anything like that?"

"Not to my knowledge."

"Did he have any friends, or a girlfriend?"

"To be honest, I don't know," Benson said, rubbing his eyes. "I never kept tabs on what he was doing."

Benson was becoming restless and irritable with the questioning. He had a myriad of things on his mind. A nosey detective was the least of his concern.

Detective Halstead sensed Benson's discontent with the conversation, but still had many unanswered questions.

"Okay, shifting gears," the Halstead said. "Err, no pun intended; let's talk about the truck."

Although the comment was meant as a lighthearted segue, the mood was not captured. Benson stared blankly at the ceiling's fluorescent lights without listening.

"Were you aware that the truck's registration was out of date, and had no license plate?"

"Yes, I meant to take care of the registration, but we had plates."

"Okay," Halstead paused as his eyes rolled in thought. "Any idea why Bo would be at Buckshot Pond late at night?"

"No."

"I'd like to show you a list of things that were found in the truck," Halstead said, sliding an evidence sheet across the table.

"I don't know what all Bo had," Benson said, glancing at the sheet.

"That's funny; there wasn't a backpack or cell phone with him?"

"What?"

"Yeah, he never went anywhere without that stuff."

"Hang on, let me make a note," Halstead said, jotting the comments on a notepad.

Benson checked his watch. He was growing impatient.

"There was also a jar of Mad Mama," Halstead continued. "Did he drink that stuff?"

"Beats me."

"Okay, last question," Halstead rushed ahead. "Any idea why he had a dog whistle?"

"Ha, you guys are so stupid," Benson sneered. "We got cats."

Chapter 24

It was a typical luncheon crowd when Candi and Ross walked into The Red Maple. There was a boisterous sense of unity among the noontime crowd, creating a vivacious sense of togetherness within the diner. The crowd's energetic, infectious fraternal enthusiasm overtook everyone sharing in the excitement, except for Ross.

Ross was ready to leave the moment he walked through the door. He felt trapped. Being among crowds was not his idea of fun. Furthermore, he wanted the rest of the money that Salvador owed him. He had even brought the jar of Hellhound, in case someone might want to buy it.

Candi, on the other hand, was ecstatic to be among the cluster of people. She found the excitement intoxicating, and was enthralled by the rollicking camaraderie.

As some patrons stood with their drink, others table hopped to visit friends or chatted on their cell phone, Ross and Candi slid into a side booth near a window. Ross found the outdoor view a welcome distraction.

"Hey, look who's 'ere!" Connie said, tossing a towel onto the table. "If'n it ain't Candi O'Neil herself!"

"Hey, Connie," Candi said. "Boy, your busy today!"

"Yeah, they got me hoppin'," Connie smiled as she finished cleaning the table. "Who's this with y'all?"

"This here's Ross."

"Hey," Ross said.

"He doesn't get out much," Candi said. "Except for smokes and beer."

"Ha, wish I could say the same," Connie laughed. "Whatcha gonna have?"

"I'd like sex on the beach!"

"Wouldn't we all?"

Instantly, several heads turned to see who the ladies were having the bawdy discussion.

"What about you, hon?" Connie asked Ross.

"Beer," Ross said. "An IPA would be fine."

"You got it!" Connie said, turning away.

After Connie left, Ross glared at Candi. "You don't have to tell the world that I smoke and drink beer," Ross admonished. "Besides, Salvador told me to keep quiet."

"Well, Salvador can kiss my…" Candi's voice tailed off as Connie returned to the table with the drinks and a bowl of Chex Mix.

"Lemme know if you folks'd be needin' anythin' else," Connie said. "Harold's on the grill today. The special is a smashburger with slaw. Cheers!"

Ross started to take a pull on his longneck beer when a man heading to the restroom stopped at his table. "Hey, it's the Sweet James garage guy!"

Ross smirked.

"You're the guy who changed the springs on my garage door!"

Ross nodded, though, had no idea if he had ever worked for this person. Instead, he sniggered and tipped his beer, as the man continued onto the restroom.

"*Sweet James garage guy*," Candi said in a mockingly sarcastic singsong voice.

"I'd still be working there if it wasn't for you."

"That so?"

"Yes, how was I to know they'd be drug testing?"

"Ross, you're full of yourself," Candi said taking a sip from her drink. "Besides, ever since we got here you've been looking at that gal with the big tits by the bar!"

"That so?"

"Yeah, you've been eating that shit up."

"Well, I got news for you," Ross said, taking another pull from his beer. "They aren't so big."

"Ohhh, so now I know you've *REALLY* been checking her out."

The slightly inebriated man who had passed the table earlier, slowly made his way back from the restroom. He gave Ross a thumbs up as he passed and exclaimed, "Sweet James!"

Ross nodded with a weak smile as the man moved on.

Connie returned to the table to check on the couple's drinks. She asked if they would like another round. Candi began to answer when Ross said, "No, thanks."

"We'll take the check."

"Pfff," Candi huffed. "Some fun."

"Say," Connie said, looking down. "Whatcha got there?"

"Huh?" Ross glanced down, not realizing the jar of Hellhound was on the booth seat. "That there's some Hellhound."

"Hellhound?"

"Yeah," Ross said. "Let me know if you want to buy a jar for the backroom. Tastes better than Turkey Dew."

"Ha, don't tell Harold," Connie laughed. "He says that stuff ain't fit for a hog!"

Chapter 25

Skip was running late when he got home. Earlier, he had called his Uncle Em with plans to stop by a sandwich shop for their dinner. By the time he walked through the door, his uncle was more than annoyed; he was furious.

"Where the hell have you been?" Uncle Em barked.

"I got caught in a meeting with Mr. Andrews," Skip said, placing Uncle Em's sandwich bag on the counter.

"What? Isn't he the publisher of that rag you work for?"

"Uncle Em, it's not a rag. *The Mountain Holler* is a popular publication that's well respected in the community," Skip said. "You know that."

"Hump, still a rag," Uncle Em said as Fred walked across the room to sniff Skip's shoes. "What'd that fat ass want, anyway?"

Skip paused to reflect on his meeting with *The Mountain Holler* publisher Colin Andrews. The publisher was a heavy-set, no-nonsense man who had spent years in the newspaper industry.

Andrews was a fire breathing heavy smoker who went through a pack of unfiltered cigarettes a day, and kept an open can of Coca-Cola at hand, which he called his "go juice."

In relocating to the Appalachian Mountains from Newark, New Jersey, Andrews intended to retire to a tranquil, docile lifestyle. Instead, he found himself bored and short on cash.

As a result, Andrews sought to subsidize his monthly income with a bimonthly newspaper geared toward community events that was supported by local advertising. Almost immediately, the publication, dubbed *The Mountain Holler*, was a success.

Andrews was constantly nagging Skip to generate more advertising revenue while placating the current advertisers. It was a fine line, but Skip made it a priority to work with the publication's sponsors and report local news.

"The usual," Skip said. "Get more ads."

"Money," Uncle Em huffed as he opened the sandwich bag. "It's always about money. That's all people care about."

"Well, that's kind of the way it works," Skip replied, being philosophical.

"I'll tell you what, there's other things in life than money," Uncle Em said, taking a bite from his sandwich. "Big guys, screw little guys! It's always been that way! I learned that doing construction. CEO's make millions, and the little guys get nothing. NOTHING!"

Uncle Em paused to swallow his food. "They treat people like shit, and expect everyone to kiss their ass! Like that fancy pants finance guy your mama run off with to Ownings Mills. Well, you won't catch me bootlicking. No siree bob. And another thing."

"You're retired," Skip reminded his uncle. "You don't work anymore."

Uncle Em tossed a small piece of bread to Fred. The dog eagerly gulped down the treat.

"Well, if I was working, they wouldn't have a thing on me," Uncle Em asserted. "I'm not some damned fool that doesn't know any better!"

"No one said you were," Skip said, attempting to assuage his uncle's ego.

"Hmmm," Uncle Em muttered, having had his tirade momentarily placated.

Fred paced the floor looking for another treat, but there was none to be found. As a result, he sought solace lying near Uncle Em's living room recliner.

"Oh, I forgot to tell you that Katie gal called," Uncle Em said, finishing his sandwich.

"Did she leave a message?"

"Yeah, she wants you to call her," Uncle Em said. "She said something about that pig pickin' thing you were at."

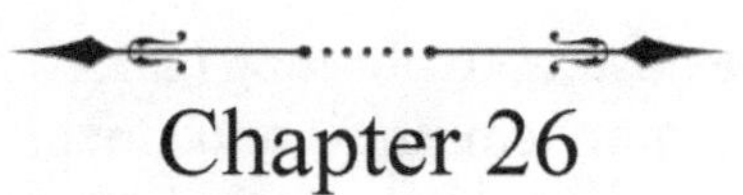

Chapter 26

Katie Mae lived in a small wood-framed cabin deep in the woods north of Bonner Falls. The cabin was fully furnished with a cozy fireplace, living room, kitchen dinette, and large bay windows. A rustic wraparound porch with two rocking chairs added the perfect touch for a place to relax with a glass of wine, and enjoy the evening sunset.

A boyfriend Katie Mae met, while attending a liberal arts program in community college, had coaxed her to drop out of school and relocate to the area. Unfortunately, the move was a mistake. The relationship was short lived. The boyfriend was not ready to make a long-term commitment and moved on.

The move left Katie Mae stranded. With no means of support, she had to forge ahead, and find a job. One day, while shopping in town, she saw a bulletin board posting that advertised customer service help needed at the Two Sisters consignment shop.

The moment Katie Mae met the shop's owners, Victoria and Veronica Jenkins, they clicked. She was hired immediately. Her effervescent, vivacious personality made her a joyful hit with the customers and owners alike. And, it was during an unscheduled advertising sales call that Katie Mae's dynamic nature caught Skip Walker's eye.

It was late when Skip returned Katie Mae's call. His Uncle Em had been on the warpath, and was not ready to relax until he turned in for the night.

"Hey, sorry I'm late," Skip said apologetically. "Uncle Em gave me holy hell about being late tonight."

"Uh-huh, I got that," Katie Mae agreed. "He was madder than a wet hen when I called."

"Yeah, he gets that way sometimes," Skip said. "Especially when we're running late for supper."

"Where did you get off to, anyway?"

"I had a meeting with Mr. Andrews about advertising."

"Again?" Katie Mae moaned. "That smelly old guy?"

"Smelly?"

"Yeah, that guy's a poster boy for lung cancer," Katie Mae asserted. "He smokes worse than my chimney, and smells like it too."

For emphasis, Katie Mae added, "Ugh, he's nasty."

"I don't know," Skip said. "I listened to what he had to say, then and left."

"Well, then you did good," Katie Mae said. "Miss Victoria just about threw him out of Two Sisters the last time he came begging for ad money."

Even with the most ingratiating manners, the owners of Two Sisters did not look kindly on Mr. Andrews presence in their shop. Neither were fond of northerners, and would never endear themselves to a Yankee from New Jersey.

"Any chance the Sugah Express might be around tonight?" Skip asked, trying to lighten the conversation.

"Oh, honey," Katie Mae laughed. "You missed that train hours ago. Besides, that wasn't why I called."

There was a sudden change in Katie Mae's voice. The tone was serious and solemn.

"You remember those hog-eyed boys at the pig pickin'?"

"Hog-eyed boys?"

"Yeah, the hog-eyed boys who were staring at women's bottoms?"

"You mean those guys at the pond?"

"Yes, that whole bunch of perverts."

"Well, okay," Skip said, perplexed. "What about them?"

"I overheard someone tell Miss Veronia that they found one of them dead!"

"You're kidding?"

"No, I'm not," Katie Mae confirmed. "Someone at Highland Ranch found one of them, and called the sheriff."

"Wow, I hadn't heard that!" Skip said stumbling over his words.

"I knew they were up to no good."

"I wonder what happened?"

"Who knows," Katie Mae replied. "They're still trying to figure it out."

"How so?"

"Well, I heard them tell Miss Veronica that the sheriff knows who it is, but can't find the next of kin."

"Really?"

"Yeah," Katie Mae paused. "He's going to have a fine time with that mess."

"What do you mean?"

"Once word gets out, those hog-eyed boys will head for the hills and leave Sheriff Max high and dry," Katie Mae said. "Hmmm, they'll hide in the weeds like dogs, and take their fleas with them!"

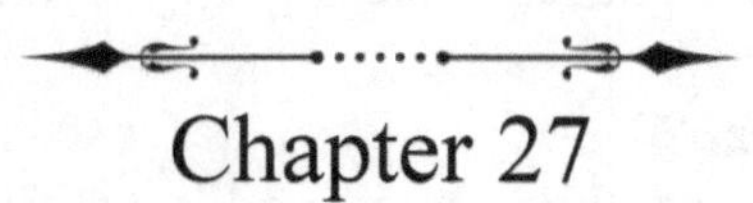

Chapter 27

Detective Sonny Boy Halstead was perplexed by what he had learned about Leonard Barlow. None of the information on file seemed to fit the facts surrounding the case.

The detective's initial suspicion was that Barlow was a potential drug user, though he had not received the official toxicology report. It would be weeks before the forensic analytical testing results from the medical examiner would be available.

It was Halstead's thought that Barlow might have taken an overdose, or gotten ahold of bad drugs ranging from fentanyl, heroin, hydrocodone, methadone, morphine, oxycodone, cocaine, methamphetamine, alprazolam, or diazepam. The possibilities were endless.

Furthermore, if there were illegal drugs being sold within the community, he wanted to know if they were manufactured locally, or being shipped into the area. An even bigger question was who was the individual, or organization behind the illicit operation.

The detective was even more baffled when he went to Barlow's residence. He was stunned to find a dilapidated single-wide mobile home that could easily have been mistaken for a run-down, condemned building.

The mobile home's roof sagged, creating streaks of rust from warped rain gutters, while the outside shattered skirting panels had fallen, creating a haven for raccoons, skunks, rats, snakes and possums.

The yard was in equally dismal condition. It had a broken washing machine, car parts, a motorcycle frame, a rusted gas barbecue, remnants of a patio swing, and an abandoned Ford Pinto with a decomposing vinyl top hidden by overgrown weeds. The occupants could easily have been mistaken for hoarders, though being in a remote, heavily wooded area, the eyesore went unseen.

Music could be heard within the home, which the detective took as a good sign. He was hoping Barlow's family or roommates could answer some questions about his lifestyle, and locate his next of kin, as he politely knocked on the torn screen door.

After getting no initial response, the detective knocked again on the screen door. A young lady appeared to peek through a curtain, but did not answer. Once again, the detective resumed knocking on the screen door.

A clean-shaven young man with facial sores, greasy hair and a protruding Adams apple tentatively opened the door a few inches, behind the tattered screen. Two scantily dressed young ladies with unkept hair could be seen standing behind the man, peering over his shoulder.

"Hey, I'm Detective Halstead with the County Sheriff's Department, and I'm looking for Leonard Barlow's residence."

"He don't live here."

"What?"

"I don't know who that is," the young man said.

"There must be a mistake," the detective explained. "I was given this address."

"They ain't no one here by that name."

The detective turned to point at the mailbox, near the bottom of the driveway. "That's his name on the mailbox, isn't it?"

"I s'pose so."

"If he's not here, do you know where he lives?"

"No," the young man said firmly. "I don't know who that is."

"So, did you just move here?"

"Look, I told you ev'rythin' I know; okay?" the young man said, growing impatient.

The detective sensed the conversation was fast becoming futile, but kept his composure. Instead, he tried a different tact.

"Say, is that the frame for an Apollo DB-X18 bike?" Halstead asked, motioning toward the motorcycle frame. "I'm a bike guy myself."

"Could be," the young man replied. "I dunno."

Halstead could see any further conversation was pointless. If the young man knew anything, he wasn't talking. Instead, the detective offered his business card.

"Look, I am trying to reach anyone who knows Leonard Barlow, or related to him. I didn't mean to bother you," Halstead said. "I'd appreciate it if you'd let me know if you hear anything."

The mobile home door closed, as the detective turned away. His card fell unseen on the doorstep, behind the screen. It would soon be part of the yard's unsightly collection.

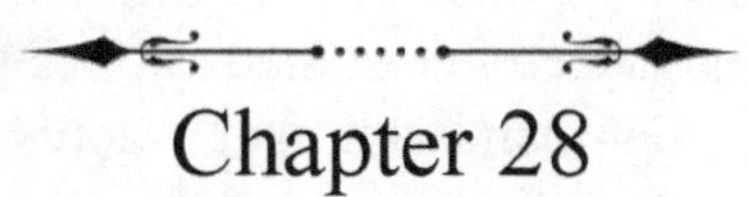

Chapter 28

It was early evening when the black SUV eased to a stop under the dazzling lights of the Mandalay Bay Resort and Casino's entrance in Las Vegas. A hotel valet opened the driver's door. Salvador stepped out of the vehicle, looked around, pausing to soak up the sights, smells, and excitement within the area.

The trip to Las Vegas had been given to him as a gift, with the opportunity to lay low after the Buckshot Pond assignment. It also provided a chance to relax, and get away from the bothersome messages Ross had been leaving for more money.

The car's trunk was opened, and a hotel porter took the suitcase to the hotel's registration desk. Inside the lobby, the Salvador paused to admire the beauty and splendor of the hotel's immense fish aquarium.

As Salvador checked in, he presented his reservation confirmation, and was greeted at the front desk by an attractive young lady in glasses with short dark hair, dressed in the hotel's uniform and a name badge that read "Jana."

"Ah, Mr. Robert Ryan," she said upon finding his assumed name logged into the computer. "We have you for a three-night stay."

"That's right," Salvador said. "It should be prepaid."

"Yes, you're all set, Mr. Ryan," the young lady smiled. "Could I see some ID?"

Salvador nodded, and happily complied with a current out-of-state driver's license registered to Robert Ryan.

"Would you like one or two keys for the room?"

"One is fine, thanks."

"Oh, you have a package," the young lady said, reaching for the card key. "You can pick it up at the Business Center."

Again, Salvador thanked the young lady and checked into his room.

Salvador's room was a clean, spacious suite with a breathtaking, panoramic view of the Las Vegas strip. The hotel had other amenities, such as an enormous pool complex, entertainment facilities, restaurants, shops, a massive casino, and even a shark reef aquarium attraction. But it was the plush bed with its fluffy pillows that he hoped to use the most.

After picking up his package at the Business Center, Salvador took a seat in the hotel lounge and ordered a margarita. A quick peek into the envelope revealed $5,000 cash, which brought a smile to his face; another gift from Corny. It was time to unwind with money to burn.

His first order of business, after checking his Tissot stainless steel dress watch was to reserve a cab and head to Fremont Street. He had often heard about the famed street in downtown Las Vegas, and wanted to experience the spectacular canopy screen light show that covered the pedestrian mall.

As Salvador walked among the throngs of people with their eyes glued to the ceiling screen, he haphazardly bumped into a woman with her cell phone in one hand, and a drink in the other.

At first, the woman reared back defensively, as the drink splashed on her shirt. She was certain Salvador's mishap had been intentional, and was deeply offended. He immediately threw up his hands apologetically, and explained that he meant no harm.

"Hey, watch where you're going," she said. "Look what you've done!"

"I-I'm so sorry," Salvador stammered. "I didn't mean it."

"You trying to kill me, or something?"

"No, not hardly," Salvador laughed weakly. "If anything, I'd want to save you."

"Hmmm, that so?" she said. "Well, I can live with that."

Once the ice had been broken, Salvador could see the woman was short, rather plain, with unkept shoulder-length hair, brown eyes, and possessed a wicked smile. She had a playful wit, which he found attractive and challenging.

"My name is Rob," he said. "Thought I'd check out the show."

"Oh, I'm Cricket," she said, putting away her phone. "You from around here?"

"No, I'm from Ohio."

"Really, a Buckeye?" she said. "You're a long way from home."

The light show was nearly finished when Salvador asked if Cricket would join him for dinner. Despite having a wet shirt, she readily accepted and returned to his hotel.

For the next few days, Salvador entertained Cricket at upscale hotels on the Las Vegas strip. They viewed the spectacular Bellagio water show, had drinks in the Rio's Voodoo Lounge, gambled, went to a couple shows, rode a gondola at the Venetian Resort, and marveled the city's breathtaking nighttime panorama from the top of the Stratosphere Tower.

On the final morning of Salvador's trip, he woke alone. At some point during the night, his romantic partner left a smiling face emoji in lipstick on the bathroom mirror with x's through the eyes, and slipped away. Cricket was gone, as were his Tissot watch and money.

Chapter 29

Detective Halstead was unsettled after the debacle at Leonard Barlow's former residence. There were so many unanswered questions, which made him even more determined to uncover whatever truth Barlow might have had hidden in his past.

To learn more about Barlow, the detective paid a visit to the Marsh Auto Center on the outskirts of town. He thought his former employer might shed light on whatever activities might have led to Barlow's demise.

It was apparent when the detective arrived at the used car lot that the manager, Ed Meyers did not care to discuss Barlow. His work habits had been less than stellar, nor was he a reliable employee.

"The guy wasn't worth a shit," Meyers said, as he spat on the ground. "Never got here on time, and couldn't get anything right."

As the detective pressed for more information, Meyers became contemptuous. "I can't tell you how many times I warned that kid to get his act together, but he didn't listen."

"Any idea where he came from?"

"Who knows?" Meyers said. "With Lenny, you never got a straight story."

"What was his job?"

"You mean what he was supposed to do, or didn't do?" Meyers sharply replied. "We *still* haven't straightened out the mess he left in shipping and receiving."

"Oh, man," he added. "You wouldn't believe it. We got parts coming out of our ass that we don't need, and stuff that's older than Methuselah."

Meyers paused to spit on the ground. "Our controller, Billy Ray's about to have a heart attack."

Both Meyers and the detective took a moment to look at the handful of cars under strings of colorful streamers swaying in the gentle breeze. Each car had a neon green year, price listed on the upper left corner of its windshield, and were spotlessly clean.

"I'm sorry he's gone," he added. "I don't know, maybe Charlie, that kid he hung out with, would know more."

The detective thanked Meyers for his time. His next stop was Willis Appliance Repair Shop, where Charlie Harper worked. Harper's name had already appeared on his radar from Deputy Wilson's notes, and he had a prepared interview ready.

It was Wilson's good fortune that the Highland Ranch groundskeeper Leroy recognized Harper at the duck pond when he was closing the pig pickin' for Wendall Tucker. Without the lead, the case could have gone cold.

With a ding of the doorbell, the owner old man Willis appeared from a room behind the counter. Elderly, bespeckled with a white wispy beard, dressed in a plaid shirt and overalls, the reticent owner was familiar with the detective and his family.

"Hey, Sonny Boy," Willis said matter-of-factly. "What can we do fer you?"

"Hey, Mr. Willis," the detective began. "I'd like to have a few words with Charlie Harper, if he's around."

"Sure, he's out back loadin' the truck," Mr. Willis said, motioning toward the back door. "I believe he's got a delivery; he's fixin' to make."

"I thank you kindly," the detective said respectfully. "And please give my regards to Mrs. Willis."

"I'll do that," Willis said. "Next time I'm at the cemetery."

Chapter 30

When Detective Halstead introduced himself as a member of the sheriff's department, Charlie Harper thought he was in trouble. He was standing on the liftgate of a flatbed Ford truck, and preparing to tie down a washer and dryer with bright yellow cargo rachet straps.

"You know, I never could thread those things," the detective said.

"It's easy, once you get 'em started," Charlie said. "Lemme show you."

The detective edged closer for a better look.

"You open the release lever an' feed the strap through the bottom of the rachet, an' loop 'er through with the teeth up," Charlie demonstrated. "Grab the loose end an' tighten till she's taunt; connect to the truck's side wall bolt and crank."

"Huh, I'll be dogged," the detective grinned. "Looks like you've had experience."

"Yeah, I've done a few," Charlie said slowly. Mr. Willis taught me.

Charlie seemed to relax once the truck was loaded and secure. He tied off the appliance hand dolly near the rear of the truck bed and raised the truck's hydraulic lift gate.

"So, Mr. Willis teaches you how to fix this stuff?" Halstead asked, motioning to the appliances Charlie had loaded.

"Does he ever!" Charlie exclaimed. "He's teachin' me how to fix major appliances, an' what tools to use."

"That so?"

"Yeah, an' I'm learnin' the basics of electricity, how to read appliance diagrams, gas fixtures, an' pumps too!"

"Sounds like the whole ball of wax."

"Yes sir, an' someday I might have my own place!" Charlie's eyes widened at the thought of owning his own business.

The detective sensed Charlie was getting comfortable. He decided to steer the topic to the purpose of his visit.

"Seeing that you keep so busy, does Mr. Willis ever give you time off?"

"Oh, sure," Charlie said. "Except, he don't like you bein' late."

"That ever happen?"

"Well, yeah," Charlie admitted sheepishly. "I got back late from a pig pickin' the oth'r day. My bad."

"That the one for Wendall Tucker?" The detective asked innocently.

"Yeah, that's the one."

"What happened?"

"Well, I was with some friends," Charlie began. "We had a couple drinks, an' lost track 'a' time."

"Were you with Leonard Barlow?"

"You mean Lenny?" Charlie asked. "Yeah, I was."

"Was he drinking?"

"Yeah, he was the one who brought the stuff."

"What'd he bring?"

"He got hold 'a' some Mad Mama."

"Any idea where he got it?" the detective asked, leaning forward.

"Lenny knew some guy who'd come around," Charlie acknowledged. "I think he's out by Lake Boswell, or someplace like that."

"Was Lenny taking any drugs that day?"

"No, we were drinkin'," Charlie said quickly, not wanting to mention the cannabis vamp pen that had been passed around.

"Did you leave him alone at any time?"

"Not that I can think of, though…" Charlie paused. "Yeah, we did leave 'em to look at the ducks."

"Was anyone with him?"

"An older guy wearin' a Tar Heels hat. I didn't know 'em," Charlie said. "As I recall, he got bent outta shape, 'cuz we was pullin' his leg."

"Oh, about what?"

"We made fun 'a' some liquor he was talkin' about," Charlie folded his arms thinking. "Lenny said sump'n he didn't cotton to."

Charlie paused to tighten a cargo strap.

"How many guys were there?"

"I dunno," Charlie said. "Five or six."

"Did you know the other guys?"

"No, they jus' come ov'r for a drink, an' get some shade."

"Was Lenny alone with the guy?"

"Maybe, I can't recall," Charlie said thoughtfully. "I know the guy was ready to punch his lights out."

"What was Lenny's condition?"

"Lenny said he had a headache," Charlie began. "He looked pale, an' dizzy."

"Then, what happened?"

"He went for a walk," Charlie said. "It was late, an' the party purt near ov'r. I had to get back to Mr. Willis. 'Sides, I thought Lenny went home."

At that moment, the detective and Charlie could hear Mr. Willis calling from the shop.

"You fellas 'bout done?"

"Yes sir, I'll there right quick," Charlie said.

"You realize Leonard Barlow never made it home?"

"Yes, I heard the news, an' it about killed me."

Detective Halstead wanted to say something to lighten the mood, but offered condolences about Charlie's friend and said, "Okay, if you think of anything else, please take my card and call me."

Chapter 31

The cursing Skip heard had become progressively louder. The tsunami of volatile obscenities seemed to literally shake the foundation of the house.

At first, Skip could not identify the location until he peered onto the back porch. There, before an unlit propane gas grill, was his Uncle Em. He was screaming in vain as he tried to light the burners with a butane fire starter.

"What's all the hollering about?" Skip asked.

"I can't get this damn thing lit!" Uncle Em bellowed. "I'm about to throw this piece of crap out."

Skip walked onto the porch. His uncle had planned to grill his specialty of beer can chicken, okra and roast potatoes, but his frustration had overwhelmed him.

"You got the valve open?"

"What the hell?" Uncle Em screamed. "You think I was born yesterday?"

"Okay, hang on," Skip said coolly. "Don't go getting riled."

He reached down and lifted the propane tank.

"Empty," Skip said. "You got an empty tank."

"WHAT? That was new last week."

Uncle Em exploded with another wave of vulgar expletives, which Skip ignored. He calmly walked over to the yard's utility shed, and brought out another propane tank.

"Somehow, the valve might have been left open," Skip said dismissively as he swapped tanks. "No big deal. I was talking to Jeremy at Tolbert's Feed Store awhile back, and bought an extra one."

With the disaster averted and the beer can chicken roasting over a low flame, Skip sat on the porch to enjoy a beer with his uncle and an observant Fred.

Being no stranger to Uncle Em's rants, Fred kept a safe distance until the bombastic rhetoric had ended. Fred waited for the dust to settled, and take his spot near Uncle Em's feet.

"Anything new that *Mountain Holler* rag?" Uncle Em asked.

"Not really," Skip said. "Mr. Andrews wants more ads."

"That fat ass," Uncle Em huffed. "He's never going to have enough money."

"We already talked about that," Skip acknowledged.

"You watch," Uncle Em said, setting his beer aside and petting Fred's head. "That fat ass will die of lung cancer before he's able to spend it."

Skip brushed off the comment. He looked at the grill. A curl of dark smoke began to rise.

"Your chicken's on fire."

"Oh, shit," Uncle Em carped, making his way to the grill. "Can't have that."

Skip watched Uncle Em move the chicken to a lower flame, while Fred stood stretching his legs.

"There's a barbecue fundraiser at The Red Maple coming up, that Mr. Andrews wants me to cover."

"Fundraiser?" Uncle Em growled. "What the hell for?"

"There's a clogging dance group of kids called The Gap Runners," Skip began. "They're collecting money so they can go to Gatlinburg for a big competition."

"Meh, panhandlers," Uncle Em groused. "So, what's The Red Maple got to do with it?"

"They're doing the fundraiser at their place."

"Well, I still don't get it," Uncle Em said, checking the chicken. "What's in it for fat ass?"

"The Red Maple is a good advertiser," Skip said. "It's a way for Mr. Andrews to promote them and the kid's fundraiser, as well."

"Ah, ha!" Uncle Em exclaimed. "So, it is all about the money!"

"Oh, good lord," Skip said.

"It's for a good cause," he added. "The Reedy Creek Stringbusters are going to play, and there's talk that Willie Cornsilk might work the grill."

"Why, hells bells!" Uncle Em exclaimed. "You know it's serious, if you get Willie over there."

"Too bad he wasn't here right now," Skip said.

"Why's that?"

"Your chicken's burning."

Chapter 32

The distribution of Mad Mama had come to a virtual standstill with the passing of Bo Benson. The owner of the still, Jack Fuller, preferred to keep a low profile and was not the kind of person to create waves.

The loss of Benson weighed heavily on Fuller's mind, but everyone involved in the illicit business knew the risks. He also knew that at any moment, his operation could be shut down by the county sheriff, or an unscrupulous competitor.

The custom distillery, Fuller maintained, was a small but profitable business based in the rural Lake Boswell backcountry. It was comprised of a stainless-steel alcohol distiller with copper tubing, a built-in thermometer, and a water pump that kept a steady production schedule. It was ideal for producing several gallons of Mad Mama at a time.

Despite being a small operation, Fuller maintained the utmost secrecy and relied on Larry "Latch" Hall as his master distiller, who took deliberate, cautious steps in the distilling process.

The process of making moonshine was complicated. Even the slightest mistake could lead to blindness or have fatal consequences. Latch was careful when making the mash and allowing the proper time for it to ferment.

Benson had been a reliable carrier, or "mule," as Fuller called him, to get the product onto the street, but he needed to reactivate his pipeline source. In doing so, he hired Ricky Ehler, a shameless self-promoter who was older and wiser than Benson and ready to take on the task, though he liked to talk.

Ehler maximized his "good ol' boy" skills to promote sales and charm the ladies. He was warm, friendly, and outgoing. His affable nature easily won over Fuller's customers, which helped spike sales, but also brought on unwanted attention with his trademark backward ballcap and Ray-Ban sunglasses.

Once Ehler became acquainted with Benson's former route and burner phone, he would make his deliveries with the panache of a carnival barker. Whereas Benson would discreetly handle customer transactions, Ehler's arrival was always met with bravado and braggadocio.

It was not uncommon to see Ehler stop into The Red Maple, ogling Connie, while boasting to anyone within earshot that Mad Mama was the "elixir of the gods."

Upon hearing that Ehler was boastfully extolling Mad Mama's virtues, Jack decided to put an end to his exuberant enthusiasm, and called him into his office.

"Listen Ricky," Fuller began. "I hear you have been talking about Mad Mama."

"Ah, Jack!" Ricky began in a virtual breathless voice while removing his sunglasses. "If'n that ain't the hottest thang on the market, I don't know what is. I'll bet Whole Goods'd buy it by the truckload! By God, they ain't no way they'd be able to keep it on the shelf! People'd be comin' from Hiawassee to git a jar!"

Fuller started to interrupt, but couldn't get a word in edgewise.

"Imagine, Hiawassee! You ev'r bin there?"

Fuller shook his head.

"That there's some 'a' the finest bass fishin' in Chatuge Lake. Hmmm. As a kid, I used to camp down that way, an' also spent alotta time in the Chattahoochee-Oconee National Forest."

"Listen," Fuller said. "You're not a kid anymore, and you DO NOT talk about Mad Mama to anyone; got it?"

Ehlers looked perplexed, and nodded his head.

"What we do is confidential," Fuller said firmly. "Our customers treat us good, and we treat them with the utmost respect."

As Ehlers opened his mouth, Fuller put up his hand.

"You load and deliver," Fuller continued. "You do not ask questions, and most of all keep your mouth shut!"

Ehlers was still bewildered, as Fuller added, "We've got some nice orders coming our way, and cannot afford any slip ups."

"Besides, you need to be extra careful after what happened to Bo, because that score hasn't been settled." Fuller warned pounding the desk. "Mark my words, you keep barking up the wrong tree, and you'll get hung by the balls."

Chapter 33

When Salvador DiMarco left Las Vegas, he faced a long, laborious ride home. To worsen matters, he was nearly broke. Cricket had stolen nearly everything he had, including his Tissot stainless steel dress watch. Fortunately, he had some cash hidden in the sole of a shoe, but it would not last.

Throughout the ride from Las Vegas into Albuquerque, Salvador cursed himself for being so careless and thoughtless for trusting Cricket. Despite having a good time, he was furious that he had been scammed. He was further enraged by the taunting lipstick emoji she had left on the bathroom mirror.

Outside Albuquerque, he pulled off I-40 and found a secluded rest stop to park for the night. He had to sleep in the car, because he had no money for a hotel. Aside from a light jacket, he had neither a pillow or a blanket. Instead, he curled up on the backseat until dawn.

The next morning, while heading through Amarillo, Salvador realized he would be unable to travel much further without additional funds. He was tired and hungry. Ross had been calling for money, which was also a bothersome annoyance.

At a Love's Travel Shop, Salvador decided to take a chance and call Corny for help. Perhaps after explaining his dilemma, he could lend him enough cash to get home.

Corny was busy clearing warehouse space for a vendor delivery of maintenance supplies when Salvador called. He was initially surprised, then burst out laughing at Salvador's predicament.

"Ha, it sounds like you stuck yore pecker in the wrong place, *Mr. Ryan*," Corny laughed. "Hang tight, I'll check with the boss an' call you back."

Salvador wandered through Love's souvenir store, waiting for the call. The shop was well stocked with hats, t-shirts, and miscellaneous gifts. He laughed to himself as everything in Texas, even the souvenirs, seemed big, excessive, and oversized.

He checked his pockets at the snack bar and found enough change for a hot dog, which was a welcome relief. He had not eaten since the night before and was starving.

When the call came, Corny said the boss was transferring a few hundred dollars to Salvador's bank account. The money would cover the rest of his trip.

"You caught 'em in a good mood," Corny said. "The Copperhead has a job comin' up for y'all."

"Is it anything like the last one?"

"Well, I don't know," Corny said thoughtfully. "I know he was mighty glad you called, but wonders 'bout yore choice in women. Next time, fish in yore own pond."

"Great," Salvador said, relieved. "I can always use the work, and any help on the ladies would be appreciated."

The clanging sound of a pallet jack could be heard on the phone. Salvador could faintly hear Corny yell "put 'er ov'r 'ere," over the deafening roar of a pallet jack dropping its load.

"He said you an' that oth'r fella'll be workin' outta town," Corny added.

"Okay, that's good to know," Salvador said. "I'll have my bags ready to pack."

Once the money came through, Salvador got into the SUV and headed east on I-40. It was late at night when he got into Memphis. There was another message from Ross asking about money.

Despite being tired, Salvador knew he would need Ross' help on the next job. He sent a text message promising to put $200 in his mailbox on his way home. He also told him to be prepared for their next assignment, which would take them out of town.

In Memphis, Salvador was able to find an inexpensive hotel room, enjoy dinner, and stop at a strip club for a nightcap.

As he took a seat at the bar, a masculine-looking lady, heavily made up with bright red lips, short cropped hair, and an intricately embellished sun and half-moon tattoo above her left breast, sat next to him.

The lady was animated, ordered a drink, and tried to initiate a conversation, but Salvador could not get past her bright red lips. Cricket's crudely drawn smiley face on the bathroom mirror still had him seeing red.

Chapter 34

It was early in the evening when Ross found two crisp $100 bills in his mailbox. He was relieved to receive the money, and happy to have a nagging Candi off his back. Her criticism about getting a job had mentally worn him down.

In addition to the money, there was a note from Salvador. The message was vague but alluded to an upcoming job out-of-state. He wanted Ross to call regarding the details.

As expected, Candi went ballistic. She wanted him to cut ties with Salvador, and return to work for the Sweet James Garage Door Company. Unfortunately, the owner James Cunningham was a devoutly religious Christian who viewed drug usage as dangerous and highly immoral. It was unlikely that the company would ever rehire Ross, though Candi refused to give up hope.

Cunningham was fond of Ross, but not willing to jeopardize his company's reputation with an unreliable employee. He had replaced him with a young intern who was excited to learn about the garage door installation and repair business.

Despite Candi's lack of enthusiasm, Ross called Salvador. He was willing to take another job if the money was right. Besides, he knew deep down that the Sweet James Garage Door Company was not going to rehire him.

The job Salvador described seemed easy. It was a two-day run to meet a truck dealer in Tennessee. The only stipulation was that Ross could not tell anyone about the meeting. It was to be kept a secret.

At first, Ross balked. Something did not seem right. Salvador was being overly polite on the phone, which was a dramatic departure from his normal rude, harsh personality.

It wasn't until Salvador offered $1,200 that Ross became attentive. Ross, never a fast thinker, cautiously said he would have to think it over.

Salvador was not taking any chances. He wanted a commitment and warned Ross that he had been working covertly, for Copperhead, an elusive felonious regional criminal figure with a callous reputation for brutal violence. By turning down the request, he could be facing a death sentence.

It was an alarming threat, which Ross did not take lightly. When Salvador raised the offer to $2,000, Ross' head was spinning. It was a big pay day. He had never made that kind of money, while working with Salvador and could not resist.

Salvador's advice was to "lay low" and stay "under the radar." He warned Ross about not being seen in public, or saying a word to anyone. One false move would jeopardize the job, and there would be severe consequences. Their discussion was to be kept in total secrecy.

"You're not going to take another job with that loser, are you?" Candi asked.

"I don't know," Ross said dismissively. "Does it matter?"

"That guy's a creep. You need to get away from him," Candi urged.

"I would, if I could."

"What? You must be batshit crazy!"

"That might be, but I need the money."

"Call Mr. Cunningham," Candi said. "Tell him you're sorry, and want another chance. He'll understand."

"Nah, that's not going to happen," Ross said. "That job's long gone."

"Want me to call him for you?"

"Hush," Ross said scoldingly. "No one's calling anyone."

"Oh, that so?" Candi shot back. "You keep hanging with Mr. Big Boots, and the only call you'll be making is for me to bail your sorry ass out of jail; and that's not going to happen! Not on $200!"

Ross laughed at the absurdity of the situation. Candi was notorious for dramatizing the simplest discussion.

"Look," Ross said assuredly. "One more job, and that's it. Okay?"

"Why can't you quit now?" Candi asked. "What's the difference?"

"This job's going to be a money maker," Ross explained. "I'm just going for the ride; easy peasy."

"Easy peasy," Candi groused. "I don't know what you and Mr. Big Boots are smoking, but it can't be legal!"

Chapter 35

A thick layer of hickory smoke rose from The Red Maple parking lot as the crowd gathered for The Gap Runners barbecue fundraiser. The intoxicating aroma was a seductive tease for those supporters who could not wait to sink their teeth into the thick, juicy lunch plate entrees being served.

Wendall Tucker offered to stage the event when he heard the clogging troop did not have enough money to enter the national clogging competition in Gatlinburg, Tennessee. He and his wife Darci, immediately called The Gap Runners to offer their help.

Flyers promoting the event were distributed throughout the town, and Mr. Andrews promised to provide front-page coverage in the next issue of *The Mountain Holler*.

The Reedy Creek Stringbusters were tuning their instruments as Skip and Katie Mae pulled into The Red Maple's parking lot. An area outside the diner had been cordoned off for the event where pitmaster Willie Cornsilk, wearing a colorful Red Maple apron, was manning the barbecue smoker.

Cornsilk was deeply engrossed in preparing a variety of mouthwatering delicacies with his *secret* rub, including brisket, ribs and pulled pork. Side dishes included coleslaw, macaroni and cheese with cornbread.

A beverage stand manned by volunteer Miss Faye and her daughter Emma were nearby, as well as a cookie stand with cookies baked by members of The Gap Runners.

Several familiar faces were on hand, seated at tables borrowed from Milt Delany's Highland Ranch. The mood was lively and festive as The Stringbusters opened with *Blue Moon of Kentucky*.

"Hey, there's Tammy and Tom!" Katie Mae squealed as she tugged on Skip's arm. "Let's see what's going on!"

After exchanging initial greetings, Skip and Tom went to the beverage stand.

"Hey there!" Miss Faye said, cheerfully. "What's *Mountain Holler* gonna have?"

Skip smiled at the recognition, while Tom asked for a double Jack Daniels on the rocks.

"Ha, you gonna hafta go inside for that one," Miss Faye laughed, motioning to The Red Maple. "Connie'll help you out."

Miss Faye turned her attention to Skip, who was smiling at Emma. He ordered a couple bottles of water, and dropped ten dollars into the donation jar.

"An' The Gap Runners thank you kindly," Miss Faye said.

Standing by her mother's side, Emma blurted out, "I'm gonna be a Gap Runner someday, huh, mama?"

Both Miss Faye and Skip exchanged smiles. "You sho' are honey," Miss Faye said. "You gonna be there, right in front."

By the time Skip returned with the water, Tom had disappeared into the bar, while the girls had gotten their luncheon plates. They were joined by the Two Sisters owners, Veronica and Victoria Jenkins, who had wandered over to The Gap Runners table.

Billie Jo and her husband Edward were holding court with anyone who would listen about how excited they were that The Gap Runners were going to compete on the national level. They were ecstatic that the community was offering their support.

"What are you going to do when you bring home that big ol' trophy?" Katie Mae asked.

"I don't know," Billie Jo said. "What do you think, Ed?"

"Oh, man," Edward laughed, waving his right hand. "We're going to have us a ball! I'll tell you what! We'll be running wide open!"

Skip excused himself to mingle with the crowd, and take pictures. Mr. Andrews was very specific about getting candid shots of The Gap Runners and The Red Maple owners together.

As Skip surveyed the crowd, he noticed Jo Yarborough from the sheriff's station had brought her husband Ben and daughter Luann. He also spotted Milt Delany chatting with Wendall Tucker and his wife Darci, while Connie and Harold served customers inside the diner.

The ever-chatty Leroy from Highland Ranch had Jeremy from the feed store cornered as deputy Bobby Wilson looked on. Kaye Sommerset could be seen with her kids listening to the Stringbusters, while they enjoyed their Coke and cookies.

Ross and Candi made a brief appearance with a jar of Hellhound neatly tucked in a bag, but left empty handed after having a lunch plate. Candi was, as always, was in a celebratory mood, but Ross would have none of it.

Tammy became alarmed when she hadn't seen Tom, since he'd gone into The Red Maple for a drink. Skip came to the rescue, tracking him down near the bar where he thought he saw Bick standing among the crowd.

"Oh, good lord!" Katie Mae exclaimed upon seeing Tom. "Hmmm, hmmm, hmmm."

"Tom!" Tammy bellowed. "You're three-sheets to the wind!"

Tom dropped his head with a skirmish grin, then mumbled something about a jar of Hellhound that was being passed around.

Skip's eyebrows raised on hearing Tom mention Hellhound. He inadvertently reached in his pocket, and felt the dog whistle keychain.

"Well, Thomas," Tammy huffed. "That hellhound of yours better shape up, or It's going to the pound when we get home."

Chapter 36

It was with great anticipation that Sheriff Max Porter received the toxicology report on Leonard Barlow. For weeks, the office had speculated on his cause of death, but the report would erase all doubts.

Once again, the sheriff could smell Jo Yarborough's fresh coffee as he entered the office building. After making his usual stop to fill a Styrofoam cup, he headed to his office to prepare for a follow-up meeting on the case.

Both Deputy Bobby Wilson and Detective Sonny Boy Halstead took their usual seats in the meeting room. They had come prepared with their notes, and were anxious to hear the report's results.

"Hey guys," the sheriff said warmly as he entered the room.

Both Wilson and Halstead appeared somber, and nodded their heads.

"Well, we got the report," the sheriff began. "It doesn't look good."

The sheriff reviewed the blood, urine, and tissue specimen collection process by the pathologist and the testing procedure afterward.

He took time to review the medical examiner's toxicology drug testing summary analysis results.

The deputy and detective listened intently, as they were assured there was no chance of specimen contamination during the field investigation.

"The lab went through Barlow's urine and blood," the sheriff continued. "They looked for opiates, amphetamines, cocaine, heroin, meth, marijuana, alcohol, barbiturates, all that stuff."

The sheriff paused to sip his coffee. Upon setting the cup down, he rubbed his brow and shook his head, muttering "pills" before continuing.

"It looks like the lab is calling it 'polysubstance usage,' which means he mixed fentanyl with alcohol. BAC .040, with a little THC."

"Jeeze!" Wilson exclaimed. "That blood alcohol concentration would kill anyone."

"Wait, there's more."

Detective Halstead asked if the report mentioned any signs of long-term substance use abuse, such as (SUD).

"No, there was no indication that he was a heavy drug user," the sheriff said. "But based on your interview at Marsh Auto about his erratic behavior, it's hard to tell what this guy had going on."

The sheriff scanned the papers laid on the table and finished his coffee. With a sigh, he turned to Detective Halstead and asked, "Sonny Boy, what'd you hear about Barlow's condition at the ranch?"

The detective related that Barlow had become lightheaded and dizzy. He seemed tired, incoherent and was breathing heavily.

"Any word if his eyes were dilated?" the sheriff asked.

"I spoke with Charlie Harper, who was with Barlow," the detective confirmed. "He didn't say anything about Barlow's eyes; except he wasn't right."

"How so?"

"Well, he had slurred speech and was stumbling," the detective replied. "Everyone there felt Barlow had too much to drink and left the table to take a piss."

"Anything else?"

The detective thought for a moment. "You know, Bobby found a lid from something they might have been drinking."

"Mad Mama," Deputy Wilson injected. "Sonny Boy was told Barlow picked it up for the party."

The sheriff turned to the detective, and asked, "Where'd he get it?"

"Good question," Halstead replied, draining the last sip of coffee, which had long since gone cold. "He said Barlow got it from some guy out by Lake Boswell."

"Hmmm," the sheriff pondered. "Any idea who?"

"That's the million-dollar question," Halstead countered.

"That's out by Buckshot Pond," the sheriff thought out loud.

"Yeah, it is," Wilson agreed. "But I don't see the connection."

"It's a hunch," the sheriff said, rubbing his forehead. "But, if I'm not mistaken, that Benson kid lived out that way and had an empty jar of Mad Mama in his truck."

The sheriff added his concerns about fentanyl and illegal alcohol usage escalating within the county. "In terms of drugs, you're looking at something 50 times stronger than heroin. You combine that with alcohol…" He slowly shook his head.

As the sheriff finished his thoughts, he looked up to find Jo Yarborough placing a note on the table next to him. There was an urgent call waiting for him on hold.

Chapter 37

The ride to Tennessee took a couple hours, but Ross did not mind. He was absorbed in thinking about the money he would earn on the trip. Nor, did he care about the slow-moving traffic or construction delays. He was content to let Salvador handle the steering wheel, and view the pleasant scenery.

As the SUV headed north, Salvador raged whenever the car would fall behind a slow-moving RV or farm equipment. He would curse when a road construction maintenance crew would stop traffic to repair areas of damaged asphalt, or concrete that had been worn by cracks, erosion, or general wear.

"What time we getting there?" Ross asked.

The question broke Salvador's concentration. Being unable to check the time reminded him about the Tissot stainless steel dress watch that Cricket had stolen. The memory was still a sore spot.

"Oh, for chrissakes!" Salvador exploded. "We're an hour away."

"Okay," Ross slumped under the seatbelt. "Just asking."

"Hold your water till we get there," Salvador said irritably. "You'll follow me once we get the truck."

Ross gazed out the window, and lit a cigarette. Between the long ride and Salvador's ill temper, he was clearly bored.

"Looks like a good place to hunt deer," he observed.

"Oh, my God!" Salvador barked. "You're not going to start in on that damned deer blind of yours, are you? If so, I don't want to hear it."

"No, but it looks like a good place for one," Ross said, taking a drag from his cigarette. "Should have brought the Browning with me."

"I swear, Ross," Salvador snarled. "One of days some deer's going to come along when you're asleep in that blind, and shove that damn rifle up your ass!"

Ross took a long drag from his cigarette, inhaled deeply, and flicked it out the window with a laugh.

The pair were headed to a remote location near Badger Creek, on the Tennessee border near Virginia. They planned to meet a commercial vehicle broker who was selling a Ford E-350 16' white panel box truck with a tuck-under liftgate.

The box truck they were buying was loaded. It was fully equipped with an automatic transmission, 7.3L V8 gas engine, power windows and locks, cruise control, AM/FM stereo, tilt steering wheel and AC/Heat. The truck had a vinyl interior, dual rear wheels, a drop step, and nearly 60,000 miles on the odometer, which seemed like a steal at $28,700.

The meeting place agreed upon was behind an abandoned flooring company off the main highway. The building had long since been closed with padlocked doors and boarded windows. A For Sale sign had been tapped to the front window by a local realtor.

As Salvador edged the SUV around the building, he saw a casually dressed man, with an attractive young lady standing in front of the truck. A Nissan Altima had been parked alongside the truck, as well.

"Hey, Sal?" The man shot forward. "I'm Billy 'Turbo Joe' Lewis, the car man, an' this gorgeous gal with me is Gracie Leigh."

Gracie dipped her head with a shy, warm welcoming smile.

Sal nodded, opening the SUV car door. Ross followed close behind.

"Any trouble finding the place?" Lewis asked.

"No, none at all," Sal replied, looking at the box truck. "So, this is it?"

"Yes sir, isn't she a beaut?" Lewis said in an admiring tone. "This 'ere's a Ford E-350 16-foot box truck with dual wheels, a liftgate, an' side door. GVWR of 12,500. New tires, an' runs great! Wanna take 'er for a spin?"

"I believe so," Salvador said, opening the cab door. "Ross, jump in."

After a 15-minute test drive, Salvador had made up his mind. He would buy the truck and deliver it, as instructed by his boss, Copperhead.

"What was that price, again?" Salvador asked in a nonchalant, unenthused sounding voice.

"She's at 28.7, a real bargain!"

"Mmmn," Salvador said, rolling his eyes. "That's a bit out of my reach."

"I might be able to swing a thousand lower."

"Look, I know a guy offering the same deal at 25 over at Black Mountain," Salvador said. "I like what you've got, but I can't work with the numbers."

"Okay, if you got cash, I can roll at 26," Jett said. "Mind you, this is only 'cuz I like you."

"Fair enough," Salvador said on a handshake.

Once the deal was made, money was exchanged, and the truck's pink slip signed was over, Billy and Gracie Leigh bid Salvador and Ross farewell.

"Ah, hold on," Salvador said. "Not so fast."

Billy and Gracie Leigh turned to see Salvador's Glock 43 pointed at them.

Chapter 38

The Leonard Barlow toxicology report meeting had left Sheriff Porter emotionally and mentally drained. There were so many questions still to be answered as he rushed to his office.

The sheriff hastily took a seat at his desk as Jo Yarborough placed a fresh Styrofoam cup of coffee before him. With a nod of thanks, he picked up the phone's receiver.

The caller was Les Benson, who had been drinking heavily. Through a bombastic flurry of slurred vulgar epithets threatening to kill his son's murderer, the sheriff assured Benson that the county also wanted justice, and to gather any additional information that might shed light on the case.

During the drunken haze of violent, aggressive threats, the sheriff learned that Benson had found a notebook in his son's room. It appeared to have cryptic notes about Bo's activities prior to his demise at Buckshot Pond.

Although Benson was not enthused about seeking help from a law enforcement agency, his outrage over Bo's loss was enough to forgo any past biased legal discrepancies he had experienced during his divorce.

His anger was further provoked every time Benson looked in the front yard and saw the damaged Silverado truck that the impound yard had returned. As a result, he conceded to the sheriff's suggestion that Detective Halstead review the newly discovered material.

By the time the detective arrived at Benson's residence, he had passed out on the living room sofa. The sound of Tammy Wynette's music could be heard from inside the house, as the detective made several attempts to bang on the front door's torn screen.

When Benson finally stumbled to open the door in a drunken stupor, his rage had dissipated into tears. In his sorrowful state, he recounted emotional memories of his son and the last time they were together, as a short-haired gray cat wandered into the living room from the kitchen.

"Let me show you his room," Benson said, wiping his tears.

As the detective moved along the hall, he was surprised at the lack of family mementos one might expect to see hanging on the walls. There were no pictures of past relatives, family or cherished events. Instead, the walls were bare, with peeling paint in need of repair.

Bo's room was small, laid out simply with a bed, computer desk, dresser, small bookcase, and several wall posters. Unkept clothes were scattered across the floor, and a guitar with missing strings sat in the corner.

"Nice guitar," the detective commented, trying to brighten the conversation. "I tried taking lessons once, but couldn't get the hang of it."

"He'd mess with it every so often," Benson said. "The guitarist for the Stringbusters used to come over and show him some licks."

On the wall were several posters, including the Atlanta Braves, musical groups, and a Carolina Panthers card collection. There was nothing notable that seemed out of the ordinary to the detective.

Quietly, Benson reached down next to the bed's bureau to retrieve a well-worn, frayed red Scholastic notebook.

"Here," Benson said, handing the notebook to Halstead. "I'm not sure if there's anything of interest here, but I thought you might like to have a look."

Halstead opened the notebook to find several scrawled notations with times, locations, partial addresses, and phone numbers. There were also vague notes alluding to people and places to avoid.

"Mind if I take this?" Halstead asked. "I'd like to check into it."

"No, go right ahead," Benson said. "I hope you guys find the son-of-a-bitch that killed my boy. When you do, I want a piece of him."

Halstead gave Benson a solemn, empathetic understanding nod. His anger was beyond questionable doubt, and he did not want to aggravate the grieving father further.

As Benson led Halstead to the door, he complained of an excruciating headache.

"By the way," Halstead asked. "Just out of curiosity, what's that you were drinking?"

"I don't know," Benson said, rubbing his head. "Some Mama shit I found under Bo's bed."

Chapter 39

It was early morning when Skip slipped through the rear door on the patio deck near the propane grill. He did not want to wake his Uncle Em or disturb Fred.

Almost on cue, Fred came bounding out of the bedroom. He could not wait to greet Skip and head outside into the yard.

Skip paused to watch Fred as he cavorted about the yard. Ever since he was a pup, Fred was a fun-loving, high-spirited playful dog. Even the simplest activity, such as chasing a ball or Frisbee, would provide Fred ample entertainment of immense pleasure and joy.

Having satisfied his morning constitutional, Fred returned to the house triumphantly, wagging his tail. Skip bent over to give him a gentle pat on the head as Uncle Em emerged in a bathrobe from his bedroom.

"Well, look what the dog dragged in?" Uncle Em grumbled, heading to the coffee maker.

"Okay, I'll confess," Skip chuckled. "You guys caught me."

"Hmmm, at least someone did," Uncle Em growled. "Where'd you get off to anyway?"

"I was out with Katie Mae and some friends at The Red Maple last night," Skip said. "They had that fundraiser for The Gap Runners, and I stayed at Katie Mae's."

Uncle Em let out an inarticulate, disdainful groan as the final drops of coffee finished brewing.

"I figured you were covering the fundraiser for that *Mountain Holler's* fat ass," Uncle Em said, reaching in the cupboard for his stained Daytona 500 souvenir coffee mug that had seen better days.

Skip brushed off the comment and picked up Fred's sock toy. The dog immediately grabbed the toy, and a playful tug-of-war ensued.

"Did fat ass show up?" Uncle Em asked, pouring his coffee.

"No, I didn't see him."

"I don't suppose so," Uncle Em groused. "Probably too busy counting his cigarette money."

As the tug of war progressed, Uncle Em became increasingly annoyed.

"You know, back in my day, you had to earn your money."

"Well, I have a job," Skip said. "That's kind of the same thing; isn't it?"

"What?" Uncle Em shouted as his coffee splashed on the counter, and his bathrobe loosened. "I can remember when a dime was worth a dime!"

"Ha, still is," Skip laughed. "Last time I checked, you could even spend it!"

"Okay, smart ass," Uncle Em fired back. "You go throwing away your money on that gal of yours, and you'll wind up like me!"

The tug-of-war had ended. Fred victoriously grabbed the sock puppet and went to his sofa bed in the living room. There, he took pleasure in chewing on the toy until his interest waned.

"That's fine by me," Skip smiled. "You get a pension, 401K distribution, and Social Security check every month. There is nothing wrong with that."

"That may be so, but you can never have enough!"

Skip burst out laughing. "Okay, I get it."

"Get what?"

"So, you're saying it's good to stash all the cash you can, like Mr. Andrews?"

Uncle Em shook his head. He poured another cup of coffee, and went into the living room.

"Yeah, well, I earned it," Uncle Em carped. "It still galls me that a fellow can work 38 years for a place, then get replaced by someone half his age."

Skip thought for a moment and suggested that new technology was among the factors in career advancement. He added that well trained employees who possessed the newest technology were apt to help the company's business progress.

"Oh, good God almighty!" Uncle Em exclaimed. "Progress my ass! You're telling me experience doesn't count for nothing? What's wrong with young people. You guys think you know it all. Well, let me tell you, you don't know shit!"

Skip tried to inject a comment, but Uncle Em was on a roll.

"I'll tell you what," he growled. "In my day, you worked your ass off! You earned what you got, and the money was good too! People stayed with their company, and no there was no jumping around to change jobs; like today. And once you got married, you stayed married; except in my case."

Uncle Em took a deep breath, then let out a sigh. "If you don't get it right, you'll wind up with someone like Irene the Wolverine, who'll eat you alive, or worse like that couple they found in Badger Creek."

Chapter 40

The news that two bodies had been found slain execution style, face down in the woods near Badger Creek, spread through the region like wildfire. TV crews, radio stations, and newspaper reporters descended on the site. The murders were foremost on everyone's mind; including, Sheriff Porter.

The sheriff was puzzled by the similarities to the Buckshot Pond case. A single bullet hole through the back of the skull, with an exit wound through the forehead, was a chilling reminder that a killer was on the loose.

As his agency compared notes with the Badger Creek authorities, the sheriff made a formal request to network with other regional agencies to gather further information on the case. He also monitored public plea requests for additional information being made through local television, radio, and social media.

The sheriff could not help, but wonder if the killings were a copycat, or an ironic coincidence. Either way, the brutal slayings were cause for concern, and the public was in a panicking nosedive.

Further investigation revealed Billy "Turbo Joe" Lewis was a popular sales rep for a car dealership, and Gracie Leigh Rhodes was a lady whom he had recently started dating. Neither had any organized crime ties, or known criminal records.

A thorough investigation was made of the area including the Nissan Altima, which turned up clean. There were no signs of a struggle or any sort of resistance. The victims had met the killer willingly.

The mood inside the sheriff's station was somber as the normal daily law enforcement activities proceeded. The sheriff wrestled with the tragic news, and felt it was critical to maintain the department's physical presence within the community. He wanted to assure residents that their safety and well-being were of the utmost concern.

Sheriff Porter had a longstanding commitment to working with the community to develop good relations with citizens and business owners alike. It was his goal to develop mutual trust. Above all, he greatly valued the public's feedback and was always open to hearing their input at local council meetings and city meetings.

The murders that occurred at Badger Creek put residents throughout the region on edge, and the sheriff sought to quell any general hysteria. Still, everyone was on high alert. People throughout the community looked to the sheriff for protective support and answers, which brought a wave of concerned calls.

"Looks like they're giving Jo a run for her money on the phones," Detective Halstead said, popping his head into the sheriff's office.

"Yeah," Sheriff Porter agreed. "I can't blame them, though."

"What do you make of the Buffalo Creek news?"

"I don't know," the sheriff said. "Seems strange. No money, or personal belongings were taken from either victim."

"You'd think that'd be the motive," the detective offered.

"I'd agree, but something isn't right."

"What about a hit?"

"Could be."

The sheriff took a moment to reflect on the matter. His chair squeaked as he leaned back with folded hands in thought, touching his lips as though in prayer.

"You know," he said slowly, "you wouldn't think something like that could happen in a place like Badger Creek, but then again, maybe that's why it happened there."

The detective stepped further into the office and leaned on a file cabinet. He could see the sheriff was deep in thought.

"What about a business deal gone bad, drugs, or domestic issue?" he suggested.

"Possible," the sheriff agreed. "At this point, we don't know enough. We'll have to see what turns up."

In addition to the concerned calls Jo Yarborough was receiving, members of the press began leaving messages. They were seeking a comment and sought whatever information the sheriff might have, which resulted in a brief press release.

In the sheriff's press release, he reassured local citizens that everything possible was being done to protect the community and offered his department's full assistance to Badger Creek's law enforcement agencies seeking the arrest and conviction of those responsible. The sheriff's statement brought a barrage of additional phone calls, including one from *The Mountain Holler's* Skip Walker.

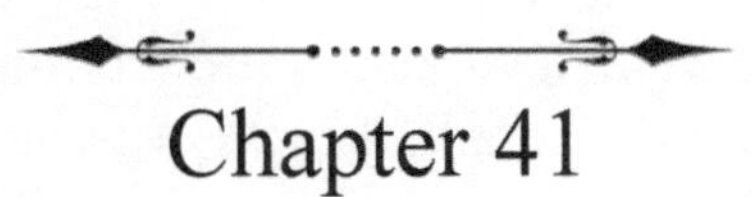

Chapter 41

Whether Ricky Ehlers took Jack Fuller's advice seriously about being vigilant during his Mad Mama deliveries was anyone's guess. His devil-may-care attitude seemed to make him an easy predatory, haphazard target; not that he cared. He approached each task with the same nonchalant, carefree attitude and great gusto.

As business picked up, Fuller began changing Ehler's burner phone on a regular basis. He worried that the deliveries were being tracked, and was cautious about taking greater security measures. Delivery routes and schedules were constantly changed as well.

To capitalize on Mad Mama's increased demand, Fuller changed his route-planning strategy. He began to focus on efficient *milk run* deliveries within targeted geographic areas. Rather than have Ehlers zigzagging across the countryside, he concentrated on a single area at a time.

None of this mattered to Ehlers. Once he got into his Ford Escape, he would crank up his music to an ear-splitting level, tug on his backward ballcap with the ever-present Ray-Ban sunglasses, and head to the next destination.

"Where we headed, boss?" Ehlers asked at a quiet, undisclosed meeting place near Highland Ranch.

"You are headed south to the Firestone Reservoir with several stops along the way," Fuller said, handing him delivery notes with addresses and instructions. "You'll need to keep moving, and won't have time to stop at The Red Maple."

Fuller warned Ehlers about unwanted distractions. He reminded him that his job was to drop off the delivery, collect the money and return. He was not to socialize or fraternize with any of the customers. Above all, as a safety precaution he was to be wary of anyone who might follow him.

At the first stop, Ehlers was scheduled to meet a customer named Mark, who had ordered a case of Mad Mama. The meeting was to be held in a field at the end of a dead-end road.

The following stop was with a college student named Brian. The meeting was to take place in the parking lot, behind a small convenience store near the local community college dorm.

As a favor on Fuller's behalf, Ehlers was also asked to visit an elderly man named Roy, who was a handicapped shut-in. He had been a faithful, loyal customer for many years and drank Mad Mama on a regular basis.

Roy lived on a limited income in a small, one-bedroom house near the Firestone Reservoir's cemetery. Fuller wanted Ehler to give him two jars of Mad Mama. He thought the liquor would brighten his day.

Ehler's final destination was a secluded estate in Wedgefield Heights, on the banks of the Firestone Reservoir. The owner was a wealthy patron named Tom. He was to meet with the property caretaker Bubby, who would provide delivery instructions upon his arrival, deliver four cases of Mad Mama and return home.

"As always, you can call if you need anything," Fuller said. "Any questions?"

"No, not really," Ehlers said. "I haven't been down that way in a long time. Used to go fishin' at Firestone with my daddy when I's a kid."

Fullers opened his mouth to speak, but Ehlers kept rolling.

"Hmmm, lemme tell you, them's some good times!" Ehlers said excitedly. "In fact, they's a bait shop by the marina I used get my red wiggler worms, an' we'd..."

"Ricky!" Fuller shouted. "Listen, I don't care about worms."

Ehlers sat back, bolt upright, like he had been electrocuted. His eyes widened, and mouth snapped shut.

"I know you like to fish, but that's not why you're here," Fuller said. "I'm going to tell you one more time, you're not a kid anymore."

Ehlers sat motionless. He watched as Fuller shook his head, visibly shaken.

"I don't know how, but I'm going to have to knock some sense into you about being a mule," Fuller added. "You do not repeat anything you see, hear or do; and most of all, keep your mouth shut!"

Ehlers nodded. He was aware of Fuller's insistence on keeping his assignments confidential.

"You might see some things that you haven't seen before on this run," he added. "If you do, look the other way, because if you don't, your ass will wind up in a sling, or worse."

Chapter 42

It was late morning when Ross arrived home to find Candi angrily pacing the floor. She was no mood for excuses. Candi wanted to know where he had been the night before, though Ross was not much for conversation.

Ross was exhausted from the late night he had spent with Salvador. At Copperhead's instructions, they had taken the box truck to Gilbert's Body and Paint Shop outside of town, where the pair spent the night.

Salvador did not want to risk being caught on the road late at night. Chances are they would be sitting ducks alone on the highway if they were spotted by a patrol car.

By waiting until dawn, the box truck could be taken to the garage and hidden. Gilbert's Body and Paint Shop had an acclaimed reputation for its vinyl wrap work as well as illicit VIN cloning.

Since it would take days for the garage to complete its work, Salvador and Ross could take a leisurely ride home in the SUV. They were able to easily blend in among the mid-morning traffic, and would pick up the truck at a later date.

Candi was enraged that Ross had taken a job with Salvador, but relaxed when he opened an envelope stuffed with $2,000. She whooped for joy and began to dance around the living room, until she was overcome by a wave of suspicion.

Once her joyful emotions had subsided, Candi wanted to know where Ross had been and why he was out overnight. She also wanted to know what he had done to earn the money.

Ross was vague. He was tired, and wanted to go to bed. Candi's questions would have to wait, which did not sit well with her.

"Where were you last night?" Candi asked.

"With Salvador," Ross said. "You know that."

"What were you doing?"

"We ran an errand for his boss," Ross said nonchalantly. "Easy money."

"Easy money?" Candi exclaimed. "If that's so, why is everything such a secret?"

Ross pulled off his shirt and turned toward the bedroom. He was too tired to get into an extensive discussion, but Candi persisted.

"There's no secret," Ross said. "Salvador says I can't talk about it."

Ross' reluctance to talk fueled Candi's suspicions to unbearable levels. She followed Ross into the bedroom, and stood at the doorway as he pulled off his pants.

"Oh, is that so?" she asked. "Why would anyone want to listen to that copper headed snake in the grass?"

"Ha, not me," Ross chuckled. "I hate snakes."

"Well, then get yourself a rake, and get rid of it!" Candi roared. "You keep hanging with that one, and it'll bite your ass!"

Ross eased into bed. He pulled the sheet up to his neck and rolled on his side, while Candi kept pounding about his relationship with Salvador. He made a feeble attempt to remind her that they would no longer be working together in the future, but Candi was relentless.

"You guys weren't out by Badger Creek last night, were you by chance?" Candi asked.

"What's Badger Creek got to do with it?"

"They found two people shot," Candi said. "It's all over the news."

Ross' senses were suddenly jolted awake. It was as though he had stumbled into an ice-cold shower. Although he maintained his ignorance in his fatigued, drowsy, slumbering state, Ross was shocked upon hearing the news.

"They're dead as a doornail," Candi continued. "Sheriff's got people looking all over the place for the shooter."

"Really?" Ross said with a startled, alarmed look on his face. "Any idea who did it?"

"No, but they're going string them up when they find them."

"I'll bet they will," Ross hesitantly agreed.

Candi turned to leave the room. She had exhausted all attempts to get any information from Ross, and was frustrated with his lack of response.

"Well, I hope for your sake you and that batshit friend of yours didn't have anything to do with it," she said. "Otherwise, you're both going to hell in a handbasket."

Chapter 43

It had been a long time since Milt Delany had stopped at The Red Maple. Usually, he would send Leroy or his son Coop into town to run errands, but he wanted to take a well-deserved break from the ranch.

The daily routine on Highland Ranch was industrious, if not challenging. There were constant concerns about the weather, animal feed and grain supply, equipment, and general maintenance repairs that needed attention on an ongoing basis.

Hard work never bothered Milt. In fact, he relished keeping busy and thrived on being active. Making a run to Tolbert's Feed Store was almost like taking time off. Still, it was on such a trip that he decided to check in on Wendall at The Red Maple.

"Say, look who's 'ere!" Connie said, greeting Milt as he walked into The Red Maple.

"Hey, lady," Milt said. "The ol' man around?"

"He sho' is," Connie laughed. "Lemme get 'em."

Wendall came bounding through the grill's saloon swinging doors wearing his customary AC/DC t-shirt, cutoff jeans, and hiking boots. He had been working with Harold in preparation for the evening's happy hour.

"Well, look who they let out of the house!" Wendall laughed. "What's the matter, you hiding from the revenuers?"

"No, they know where to find me," Milt said good-naturedly. "Besides, I drank everything before I left."

Both Milt and Wendall shared a laugh as Connie walked over to the table, tossed a damp towel down, and asked what he'd like to order.

"You ain't gettin' off that easy, Mister," she said, wiping the table. "We gotta make a livin', you know."

"Alright, you got me," Milt said, throwing up his hands. "I'll take a Turkey Dew."

After Connie left, Milt shifted into a quiet, subtle mood. Wendall could tell he was concerned about something that was bothering him.

"You know, I was talking to Jeremy at Tolbert's about what happened in Badger Creek," Milt began. "Man, he's about ready to keep his .32-20 loaded under the counter."

"Hmmm," Wendall said. "I'm not surprised. Harold was saying the same thing."

"It's hard to say what went down," Milt said. "Coop, at the ranch, thinks it was a domestic dispute."

"Say, what?"

"In fact, he thinks it was some sort of love triangle."

Connie arrived with Milt's Turkey Dew, and a glass of water for Wendall.

"Well, whoever did it must have had a hard on," Wendall said, shaking his head. "Because, the guy and gal were both shot in the back of the head. At point blank range, he wasn't going to miss."

Milt swirled his glass and took a sip. He glanced out the window and saw a couple girls walking home from school. The girls made him think about The Gap Runners, which reminded him about the fundraiser.

"Say, how'd those Gap Runners make out at that deal you and Darci put on?"

"Oh, man, we did good!" Wendall said, smiling. "We got those gals covered!"

"Mmmm, when were they headed to Gatlinburg?" Milt asked. "It'd be nice if they win."

"Don't know," Wendall said. "Should be sometime soon."

Connie wandered over to the table to check on Milt's drink. Seeing the two in deep conversation, she turned to other customers in the diner, while Milt thought back to the Badger Creek murders.

"You know, the weird thing about that shooting?" Milt paused to choose his words wisely. "Is that the Benson kid got shot the same way."

"Yeah, I thought about that," Wendall said. "That don't seem right."

The girls across the street had stopped to talk. Both Wendall and Milt watched them burst into giggling laughter as a boy rode past on a mountain bike.

"I sure hope that sheriff in Badger Creek can figure out who's behind that mess," Wendall said wistfully.

"That makes two of us," Milt agreed, finishing his drink. "It'd be nice."

The girls across the street had stopped giggling and turned away. Both Milt and Wendall smiled at the fun they were having.

Milt looked at his watch and rose from the table saying, "Well, you better get back to Harold before he burns the place down. If that happens, you'll wind up killing him!"

Wendall chuckled at the comment, as Milt added, "Lord knows, the sheriff's already up to his ass in alligators."

Chapter 44

After the Badger Creek murders, *The Mountain Holler* publisher Mr. Andrews became acutely aware that there were national headlines being made over the recent spate of unsolved, ghastly murders. And headlines to Mr. Andrews meant one thing: money.

To capitalize on the ongoing investigations, Mr. Andrews encouraged Skip to write a biweekly column recapping the latest developments. He prodded Skip to create tantalizing headlines that were designed to hook the reader into craving further information with a follow-up story.

Mr. Andrews knew that an increase in *The Mountain Holler's* readership would not only sell more papers, but increase advertising. It would also, hopefully, raise the publication's profile in the community.

Skip pondered the stylistic approach. He never considered himself a hardened news reporter, but rather a photojournalist along the lines of Superman's sidekick Jimmy Olsen.

With Mr. Andrews' eyes on *The Mountain Holler's* bottom line, Skip was thrust into an uncomfortable investigative reporter's role of creating a tabloid approach, which he considered immoral and unethical. Skip preferred dealing with community news and announcements.

As Skip wrestled with his journalistic options, he broached the subject to Uncle Em, while taking Fred on a morning walk.

"Where you guys off to?" Skip asked as Uncle Em took down Fred's leash hanging by the porch door.

"Time for the morning constitutional," Uncle Em replied, opening the door, followed by Fred. "Come on, Fred."

Fred bolted forward. Within a flash, he was seen scouting throughout the backyard, and creek nearby.

"Yours, or Fred's?" Skip joked, despite Uncle Em's rueful glare.

"A little early to be a smart ass," Uncle Em said as he watched Fred dash around.

Skip grinned sheepishly and followed Uncle Em down the steps.

"Aren't you working today?" Uncle Em asked as he leaned on the porch rail.

"Yes, I need to come up with a new storyline."

"Storyline?" Uncle Em said, with an incredulous look. "What's fat ass got you doing now?"

"He wants a story on that Badger Creek deal."

"Good God almighty!" Uncle Em exclaimed. "That story will be old news by the time your rag gets printed. Besides, are you writing stories or news?"

Uncle Em went on to point out that *The Mountain Holler* was published only twice a month. The news would be outdated by the time it hit the street.

"Yes, I know," Skip admitted. "I told Mr. Andrews…"

"Mr. Andrews my ass," Uncle Em fumed. "That fat ass doesn't even know what day it is, except when he goes to the bank."

Skip gave a faint smile, and shook his head as Uncle Em launched into profanity-laced tirade about the *The Mountain Holler's* coverage of the recent murders.

"You know what?" he began "They'll never figure that deal out."

Uncle Em moved into the yard to call Fred. The dog had moved out of sight by the creek.

"I'll tell you right now, they can look till the cows come home and they won't find a thing," Uncle Em stated. "Whoever did it is long gone; probably some crazy bastard laying on the beach by now."

"You think?"

"Yeah," Uncle Em said slowly while looking for Fred. "I'd imagine that fellow is chasing women, and getting ready for Bike Week in Daytona."

"Well, I'd better move along," Skip said. "I need to come up with something for the paper and head over to Katie Mae's for supper."

"What?" Uncle Em bellowed. "There you go, throwing your money away. Lord, have mercy. What'd I tell you about women; especially, after the crap I went through with the Wolverine?"

Uncle Em spat on the ground, and shook his head. "I'll tell you right now, I've been places you don't ever want to go. You'll get eaten alive!"

With a quick clap, Uncle Em summoned Fred and clipped the leash to his collar.

"And I can't say that your father didn't warn me about the

Wolverine," Uncle Em continued. "Hmmm, hmmm, hmmm. He saw the whole thing coming."

A distant, misty look appeared in Uncle Em's eyes, as he muttered, "What in the hell was I thinking?"

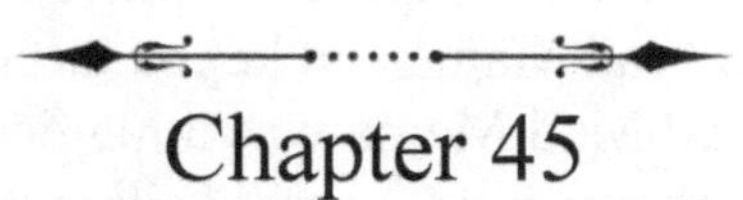

Chapter 45

Ricky Ehlers was ahead of his Mad Mama delivery schedule. His first stop had called to reschedule for the following day. The plan was to meet at the same place, around dusk.

The ever-exuberant Ehlers promptly agreed to the meeting without notifying, or consulting Jack Fuller. He felt that the warnings he had received about unwanted distractions were overblown, melodramatic exaggerations. There was no need, if any, to worry. Everyone loved Mad Mama, or so he thought.

With extra time on his hands, Ehlers decided to stop at The Red Maple for a beer. He always enjoyed chatting with Connie, and could not resist an opportunity to indulge himself.

Being busy, Connie scarcely had time to spend with Ehlers. While he was absorbed in trying to engage her in a conversation about a "big" job he was working on, she could not be bothered. There were other customers who needed service.

Undeterred, Ehlers left a sizable tip and promised to return after finishing his "big" job. Connie nodded her appreciation, tossed her damp rag on the counter, and made ready for the next customer.

Once in his Ford Escape, Ehlers slipped on his Ray-Ban sunglasses, cranked up the radio's music to ear-spitting levels, and headed to his first stop. He was to meet a college student named Brian behind a convenience store.

The meeting was a quick exchange that barely took five minutes. Brian had contacted Jack Fuller on behalf of several friends who were Mad Mama enthusiasts. A case of Mad Mama would be an instant party favorite.

Near the Firestone Reservoir, Ehlers pulled into the driveway of a small cottage at the edge of town, near the local cemetery. There, on the front porch, was a thin, elderly man seated in a wheelchair. At Fuller's instructions, Ehlers placed two jars of Mad Mama on a table next to him.

Rather than leave immediately, the man introduced himself as "Roy" and invited Ehlers to "set a spell."

Together, they shared a sip of Mad Mama as Roy regaled Ehlers on his past hellraising, youthful escapades. Being a longtime customer of Fuller's, Roy favored Mad Mama and kept a jar handy for "medicinal purposes." He believed Mad Mama was a magical, therapeutic elixir capable of curing his rheumatoid arthritis ailments.

The ever-grateful Roy repeatedly thanked Ehlers, and told him to thank Fuller. Ehlers was overwhelmed by the heartwarming joy and gratification that such a simple gift could bring as he drove away.

The final stop was a country estate in Wedgefield Heights. The property was in a gated, secluded community on the banks of the Firestone Reservoir, which Ehlers knew well. He passed the campground and bait shop that he used to frequent with his father as he wound around the lake.

The estate was a magnificent house that had been built decades ago by a retail furniture entrepreneur. The house was built to enjoy a truly extravagant lifestyle, featuring a dramatic entry with turret ceiling and clerestory windows that led into a large open area gathering room with inlaid marble floors, covered by fine embroidered carpets.

The luxurious living spaces included a formal living room with a double-sided stone fireplace crystal chandelier leading onto a foyer that eased onto a private indoor swimming pool and spa area with inlaid seahorse mosaics.

The yard was perfectly landscaped with honeysuckles, twig dogwoods, Carolina Allspice and Miss Kim Lilacs. An additional touch of elegance was added near the lake's multi-slip dock with a group of manicured hydrangeas, Pearl Glams, Aphrodite Sweetshrubs, and Miss Mollies butterfly bushes.

Ehlers was in awe of the estate as he was buzzed through the driveway's imposing security gate, and spied a pair of regal stone lion statue sculptures prominently placed near the estate's front door.

The property caretaker Bubby greeted Ehlers as he pulled his Ford Escape around the long-curved driveway to the main entrance, and was told to drive to the rear of the property.

As Ehlers opened his car door, he could see there was much activity in preparation for a party. Bubby instructed him to deliver the cases to the resident bartender Ace, who was setting up a bar near the indoor pool.

"What's this shit?" Ace asked as Ehlers began to unload his delivery.

"This here's Mad Mama!" Ehlers declared. "You got four cases, and believe you me, it don't get any better than this."

"That so?" Ace said. "Hellhound would probably disagree."

"Well, now," Ehlers said boldly. "They ain't here are they?"

"No, but it'd be a shame for you if they were," Ace said. He motioned for Ehlers to put the cases inside the swimming pool area.

As Ehlers moved the cases into the pool area, he emerged with his sunglasses off and eyes bulging.

"Hey, there's a couple naked girls in there!" he said. "They's layin' by the pool! Naked as jay birds!"

"Yeah, what about it?"

"Nuthin', you got some nice scenery around here."

"You done, yet?" Ace asked, reaching for his cell phone.

"Almost, I believe I forgot my sunglasses in thar."

"No, I don't believe so," Ace said, pointing to the pair on his hat. "Where you headed next, anyway?"

"Oh, man," Ehlers shrugged. "I gotta see some guy down south tomorrow. Some ol' farmhouse at on a dirt road that cuts through the woods at dusk. Damn. No girls, nuthin' like this place."

"Hmmm," Ace said dismissively. "Sucks to be you."

Chapter 46

It was early in the evening when Salvador got a text message to call Corny. He had spent the day touring Pigeon Forge's historic district, and just settled into bed with an attractive brunette at a quaint bed and breakfast.

Corny's message was terse, and to the point. Copperhead had received a call that Mad Mama was on the streets again. He was dismayed to learn that he had lost a major account, and wanted to eliminate any future intrusions into his territory.

An agreement was quickly struck. Although he wasn't able to provide complete details, Corny provided enough information about Mad Mama's next move for Salvador to move ahead the following day.

Time was of the essence. Salvador had to move fast. He would need help if he was going to catch Mad Mama. And once again, he would need Ross' help.

Having sworn to Candi that he would no longer work with Salvador; Ross was less than enthused about Salvador's call. At first, he flatly refused to work together. Fortunately, Candi was not home, which gave Ross a chance to hear Salvador's offer.

The job was simple. Ross would ride with Salvador the following afternoon. Toward evening, he would move a couple cars to an undisclosed location and return home. Chances were, he would even be home for a late dinner and earn $500.

Ross pondered the offer. Candi was already burning through the $2,000 he had earned from the Badger Creek job, but he did not want to risk being involved in any illicit activity. Still, Ross was hard-pressed to turn down the offer.

"Nah, Candi doesn't want me going out any more," Ross said. "She wants me to get back on at Sweet James."

"What?" Salvador shot back. "That place fired you! You know why? She set you up!"

"What do you mean?"

"There's no way you would have failed a drug test, if she hadn't given you the drugs in the first place."

"Well, I hadn't thought of that," Ross said.

"Listen, run the math," Salvador said. "She's out running around, having a good time on your dime!"

Salvador paused. He knew Ross was wavering, but time was short. He had to press his point and needed a commitment.

"Ross, you don't get it!" Salvador exclaimed. "She's spending your money! That's your cash she's throwing away! And what's she doing? Cleaning Airbnb rooms? Come on, man."

Ross thought for a moment and meekly acknowledged Salvador's comments.

"Look, this job's easy," Salvador pressed. "Move a couple cars, and bam! You're done. In and out. Home free. It's money on the table!"

"It sounds okay," Ross offered. "I don't know, I have to think about it."

Salvador could no longer wait for Ross' decision. He had to have an answer.

"Okay, how about $1,000?" Salvador asked. "That's a lot money to move a couple cars."

Ross agreed, but still demurred. The thought of facing Candi's wrath was a prospect he did not care to endure.

"Alright," Salvador said. "How about $1,000 and an all-expenses-paid weekend for you and Candi at Myrtle Beach?"

The offer perked Ross' interest. "Seriously?"

"Yeah, everything paid," Salvador confirmed. "You guys can stay wherever you want, ride the SkyWheel, hit the Funplex and do the whole deal."

"Hmmm, Myrtle Beach," Ross murmured. "That does sound good."

"Good?" Salvador laughed. "You're getting a deal!"

"Okay," Ross said. "I'll do it, but I don't want any trouble."

"No, now come on," Salvador said. "You know me. There isn't going to be any trouble; besides, you have my word."

Before getting off the phone, Salvador quickly gave Ross the meeting details. They were to meet for a late lunch without Candi's knowledge, then head to the job. Once the cars were moved, he would race home for dinner.

Salvador was extremely pleased as he eased back into bed with his brunette friend. Unlike his previous experience with Cricket in Las Vegas, he was looking forward to an adventurous evening of romance as well as a big payday the following night.

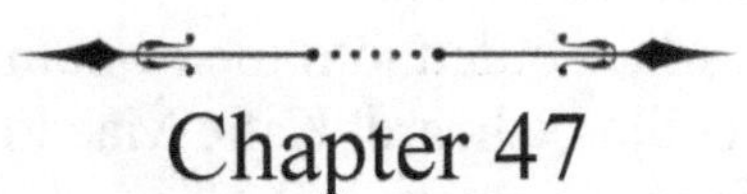

Chapter 47

Skip was running late when he left Uncle Em and headed to Katie Mae's for dinner. He hastily stashed his current news story notes into his coat pocket and headed out the door.

He barely had time to give the upcoming *Mountain Holler* article any thought as he pulled up to Katie Mae's cabin. Despite being preoccupied, the article would have to wait, though he quickly realized his fiancée did not share the same mutual interest.

"You're late," Katie Mae said. "You realize what time it is?"

"Yes, I'm sorry," Skip said. "I got tied up with Uncle Em, and work."

"Hump, I would have thought you'd have been here an hour ago," Katie Mae. "You've got to stop that yapping."

Skip hung his head sheepishly. He knew better than to antagonize Katie Mae further, and moved fast to lighten the subject.

"Say, how about we go out for some sushi?" Skip suggested. "I hear there's a new place in town."

"Sushi!" Katie Mae exclaimed. "No, I'm not eating bait!"

"Sushi's not bait," Skip explained. "I thought we'd try something different."

"They cook it?"

"Kind of, it's rice and raw fish…" Skip struggled to find the right words, but shrugged his shoulders.

"Kind of?" Katie Mae shot back. "Oh, good heavens. That's not right. Tammy told me she ate it once, and threw up!"

"You ought to try it, if you've never had it."

Katie Mae reared her head upward with a revolted look. She made no effort to hide her repulsed feelings about Skip's dinner plans. Her normally adventurous spirit was devoid of exploring any new cuisine.

"Let's go to Mrs. Mary's," Katie Mae said flatly. "I hear they got a crab quiche to die for!"

Skip duly nodded his head. Being late and suggesting an undesirable dinner had already given him two strikes on the night. Instead, they'd opt for Mrs. Mary's Azalea House, a well-known restaurant that favored a lace decorated boutique style restaurant located in the heart of Bonner Falls.

As Skip and Katie Mae settled into their booth at Mrs. Mary's, the beep of a cell phone could be heard. Katie Mae looked in her purse. It was a text message from Tammy.

Over a glass of Chardonnay, Skip watched Katie Mae exchange messages with her friend. Although he viewed the interruption as an intrusion, he did not mind, as the distraction was enough to brighten Katie Mae's mood.

"Oh, now isn't that precious!" Katie Mae squealed. "Tom bought a kayak for Tammy! Isn't that something? They're going to take it to Lake Boswell."

"Hmmm," Skip nodded between sips of Chardonnay. "Sounds like fun."

"Boy, she's high as a kite!" Katie Mae blushed.

In her excitement, Katie Mae had barely looked at the menu. She was still absorbed by Tammy's text messages as she ordered the crab quiche and stuffed potato, while Skip took a less adventurous route of a bacon cheese smashburger with a side order of sweet potato fries.

Throughout the meal, Tammy's phone beeped. Like a circus ringleader at a three-ringed choreographed show, she skillfully answered her text messages, chatted with Skip, between hurried bites of dinner.

By the time Katie Mae was served the restaurant's signature strawberry shortcake dessert and Skip's butter pecan pie, he was ready to bolt home. At every phone message "ooh" and "aah," he gave a weak smile or raised his eyebrows, feigning interest as Katie Mae fawned over a cute animal picture, or a joke Tammy sent.

Skip woke Uncle Em who had fallen asleep in his easy chair with the television on, when he arrived home. Fred rose from his living room mattress, sauntered to the door greeting Skip, then returned to his bed.

"How'd it go?" Uncle Em asked.

"Meh," Skip shrugged. "I wish they had never invented cell phones."

"You and me, both," Uncle Em said. "Sounds like a rough night."

"Yes, seems it went that way."

Uncle Em reached down to pat Fred. He then turned to Skip and shook his head.

"Well, live and learn about cell phones," he said slowly. "Next time when they go off, you go off!"

Chapter 48

Detective Halstead had combed through the worn red notebook Les Benson had given him many times for a clue that might lead him to resolving the Buckshot Pond murder case. He examined every nuance, scribble, and squiggle in the notebook.

Much of the notebook was illegible. Bo Benson was not known for neat handwriting. Still, there were numbers, jotted notes, and sketches that the detective took time to carefully analyze. The notebook could be a potential treasure trove if properly deciphered.

In addition to studying the notebook, the detective reviewed Benson's personal information, including Motor Vehicle Department information, academic school records, past photographs, and anything else he could find.

In reviewing the notebook, the detective noticed several references to "J." There was another seemingly lighthearted note about a "mule roundup." The most interesting was a circle with a line through it. Inside the circle, was the printed word "Dog," and another with an "HH."

As Deputy Wilson passed the detective's office one morning, he noticed his frustration while pouring over the notebook at his desk. He was deep in thought, trying to untangle the seemingly unbreakable code.

"Hey, there," the deputy said. "Any luck?"

"Not really; nothing makes sense."

"Mind if I have a look?" The deputy asked, edging toward the desk.

"No, go right ahead," the detective replied, sliding the notebook across the table.

The deputy turned the notebook for a better view. His head nodded briefly as he scanned the book.

"Mule roundup?" The deputy said aloud. "What do you make of that?"

"Don't know," the detective said, shaking his head. "No mules around here, unless Milt Delany's got a couple at Highland Ranch."

There was a brief pause as the deputy and detective starred at the notation.

"Mules are used as pack animals," the deputy volunteered. "Maybe Benson got into some backcountry stuff?"

"Could be, but his pa didn't say anything about him backpacking."

The deputy continued to flip the pages until he found the crossed-out "HH."

"What about this?" He pointed to the crude, crossed-out lettering. "A girlfriend?"

"Could be," Halstead said. "Benson's pa wasn't up on his personal life after his divorce."

A few more pages were flipped. More smudges, odd disjointed maps, ripped pages, crossed-out letters, numbers, and times that made little sense.

"There are a few J's here with a smudged-out name," the deputy noted. "Must be someone, because he's even got one marked with a star to call J."

The detective leaned over the desk and nodded thoughtfully. "J seems to stand out, which might be a name, but that's not what gets me."

The detective flipped several pages until he came to the crossed-out word "Dog" in old-style, capitalized English letters.

"Check this out," he said, lightly tapping his finger on the page.

The deputy looked baffled. The crossed-out, scrawled word seemed no different than anything else he had seen.

"Okay," the deputy offered. "I don't get it."

"You wouldn't, and neither would I," the detective said. "Benson didn't have any dogs."

"Okay, now you really got me," the deputy said, bewildered.

"If they didn't have any dogs, then why was there a dog whistle in the truck?"

As the deputy pondered the thought, the detective held up his hand. "Wait," he said. "There's more."

He reached into his desk drawer and put a Bushnell trail camera on the table.

"I went to Buckshot Pond awhile back and noticed a trail cam strapped to a tree down the road," he said. "Jo tracked down the owner, who was a hunter. He said I could check the SD card to see what was on it."

The deputy starred at the trail cam. His eyes widened and jaw dropped in disbelief as the detective turned on his computer monitor and inserted the SD card.

Chapter 49

At the urging of his friend Andy Dodge, Mark Sanders was encouraged to buy a jar of Mad Mama. He had never tasted moonshine. The prospect of something new appealed to him as adventurous and exciting.

Unbeknownst to his wife Staci and young daughter Kylee, Sanders planned to buy a half-case through a clandestine contact. He thought it would be fun to share the secretive, mysterious drink with his friends at an informal gathering.

Sanders lived in a small, two-bedroom prefabricated house with a carport southeast of town. He worked as a seasonal paint subcontractor and drove a weather-beaten GMC Sierra pickup truck. His average day was spent prepping surfaces, mixing paints, and operating various pneumatic guns.

Jobs were often few and far apart, and keeping up with the bills could be a challenge. As a diversion from the daily boredom, it was not uncommon for Sanders to enjoy a beer with friends, or fish at a local creek.

It was early evening when Staci became concerned that her husband, had not returned home from an errand. She began calling friends, but no one could determine his whereabouts.

By morning, Staci began to panic. She had exhausted her list of contacts and called the sheriff's office. A short time later, her worst fears were realized. Outside Bonner Falls, her husband's truck was found abandoned.

Jack Fuller was experiencing similar emotions to Staci's. He had not heard from Ricky Ehlers since he left the Wedgefield Heights estate. Nor, did he have confirmation that Ehlers had made his delivery's first stop.

Frustrated, Fuller headed to the rear of his property, where he found Latch cleaning the still in a well-concealed tool shed.

"Giving her a bath?" Fuller asked as he opened the shed's door.

"Yeah, getting her ready for the next batch," Latch said. "Am almost done running the vinegar wash."

"Whew, hot," Fuller said, wiping his forehead. "It feels like a sauna."

"You might want to step out," Latch suggested. "She's going to start steaming."

Fuller stepped back and watched Latch dump water into the still. He worked slowly and meticulously with the intensity of a mad scientist to ensure the copper retained its clean, natural lustrous sheen appearance.

A propane tank was lit to bring the water to a boil. Moments later, steam began to come out of the outflow spout as the condensed water began to run off.

Once the process was complete, Latch stepped back to prepare for a sacrificial run that would finalize the distillation process.

"How are we fixed on orders?" he asked. "Got anything coming through?"

There was a folding chair outside the shed, which Fuller brought inside and set opposite Latch's workstation. He sat leaning the chair back on two legs with his back against the wall.

"Yes, we have orders," he said. "As a matter of fact, we're full up."

"Hmmm," Latch said, spot-cleaning the still's copper. "We're good to go, when you are."

"Ahh, that's why I'm here," Fuller said. "You heard from Ricky?"

"No, not a word," Latch said as he took care to polish the still's copper tubing.

Latch stepped back for a moment. He appeared satisfied with the still's shiny appearance and added, "That damned mule would talk your ear off if you let him."

"Well, he missed his first stop yesterday," Fuller said. "And I haven't heard from him since."

"Ha, God only knows where that mule's kicking around," Latch sneered. "That guy doesn't even breathe when he talks."

"That's what I'm afraid of," Fuller said gently, bringing his chair forward. "I have a bad feeling that Ricky got himself into trouble talking too much."

Latch could sense a higher level of concern in Fuller's voice. He tossed his rag down, folded his arms and leaned against the counter.

"I want to shut her down until I know what's happening," Fuller said.

Fuller shuffled uncomfortably in his seat and looked outside the door, seemingly lost in thought. "You know, when Bo went down, I got a text message. It read, 'Grrr!' Am guessing someone got his phone as a prank."

"This time, someone got Ricky's phone and sent another message," he said, looking toward Latch pensively. "It read, 'UR mule's been put to pasture!'"

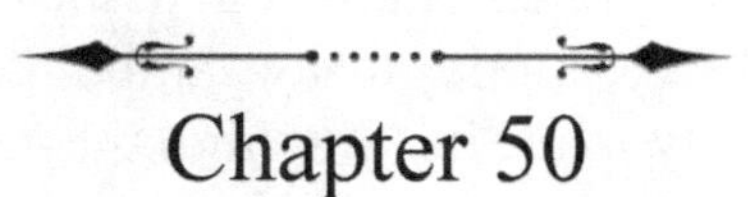

Chapter 50

Having never been to Myrtle Beach, both Ross and Candi eagerly accepted Salvador's offer of an all-expense paid weekend getaway. Despite Candi's skepticism of Salvador's generosity, she kept her suspicions to herself. The allure of visiting the world-famous Myrtle Beach Grand Strand was an opportunity she was not going to pass up.

The ride to Myrtle Beach took Ross and Candi through Columbia and the heart of South Carolina. Not being used to traveling, Candi found the long ride boring and tedious, with the heavy traffic heading into Myrtle Beach unbearable.

Her outlook changed, once the couple found themselves comfortably settled into a luxurious, Polynesian-style oceanfront resort hotel, which Salvador had arranged. Together, Ross and Candi looked forward to a weekend of lavish entertainment, dining, and shopping.

The first thing Ross and Candi did after checking into their hotel was head to the *Broadway at the Beach* shopping and entertainment complex. They were anxious to experience the ongoing hub of energetic activity.

On the boardwalk, they strolled along the crowded promenade, getting lost among the shops, restaurants, bars, carnival attractions, arcade activities, and entertainment. The evening was capped with a ride on the gigantic SkyWheel with its stunning, mesmerizing views.

At times, Candi found the activity at Myrtle Beach electrifying. Although she was captivated by the craziness of the exhilarating party atmosphere, Ross was uncomfortable being around such large crowds of people.

Amid the excitement, Candi and Ross took time to lounge at the hotel's pool and soak up the sun at the beach, which offered a variety of activities including paddleboards, jet skis, and paragliders. All of which; Candi found fascinating.

Being flush with cash, Candi pressed Ross for a visit to the nearby riverboat casino. She wanted to try her luck on the slot machines, while Ross enjoyed the live entertainment in the bar. He did not share Candi's enthusiasm to toss money away gambling, but watched mildly amused as she hurriedly made her way into the casino.

Candi attacked the slot machines with a vengeance. Every nerve in her body was focused on the LCD screen before her. She wanted to win at all costs. She'd whoop and squeal with joyous delight at every winning spin and moan angrily at each loss.

As the evening wore on, it became apparent that Candi's luck was not going to hold. Had it not been for Salvador's generosity, the couple would have been hard-pressed to pay their hotel bill. As a result, their trip home was a long, arduous journey.

At home, the couple collapsed in front of the television to decompress after an adventurous weekend of non-stop activities. The money they had taken to Myrtle Beach was gone. They had spent recklessly on whimsical things without bothering to consider the future consequences.

Without any thoughts or regrets, Candi immersed herself in a haze of drugs, while Ross stared blankly at the television. He privately cursed his carelessness at having spent his savings and wondered how he would recover when a news bulletin caught his attention.

The local authorities were searching for a young man named Mark Sanders, who was missing. They were requesting that anyone with information contact the sheriff's department.

Ross thought it was ironic that Sanders drove a GMC Sierra pickup truck, which was one of the vehicles Salvador asked him to move on their recent job. After giving the matter a brief thought, he discounted the possibility of the two being related due to the different locations.

With Candi passed out, Ross decided to call Salvador to see if he had any jobs lined up in the near future. Perhaps there was an upcoming opportunity where he might need an extra hand.

Since it was never easy reaching Salvador on the phone, Ross was hoping to get lucky and reach Salvador with Candi asleep. She would give him a scathing tongue-lashing if she knew he was making the call, but it was a chance he'd have to take.

The discovery of Mark Sanders abandoned truck hidden in the woods drew an onslaught of curious onlookers. Everyone was concerned about Sanders' well-being and offered whatever help was needed.

Among the crowd of spectators was a young teenage couple, Wes Harder and Eli Mills, who turned out to view the commotion. They arrived to find a chaotic group of people descending on Sanders vacated GMC Sierra pickup truck, while few people paid scant attention to the Ford Escape that was parked nearby.

The couple had recently met at a local convenience store, where Wes worked, and started dating. Eli had stopped by the store after attending a holistic nursing class at the nearby community college.

Eli found Wes engaging and a good-natured conversationalist. She was immediately struck by his charm. Wes was attracted by Eli's wholesome, virtuous personality and captivated by her sincerity.

Since neither had any desire to be drawn into the massive confusion surrounding Sanders abandoned vehicle, Wes suggested they take a ride to enjoy some privacy and enjoy the quiet afternoon together.

Wes headed to a vacant tobacco farm north of town, located at the end of a winding, dirt road. As he parked near the farm's dilapidated barn, Eli asked where they were.

"Don't worry," he said. "This place has been deserted for years."

"Are you sure?" Eli asked tentatively. "Looks spooky."

"Ha, it's the old Carter farm," Wes laughed. "He's been dead for years."

The couple got out of the car and walked toward the field. It was overgrown with weeds, brush, and kudzu. The lush kudzu vines were dense, and literally blocked the sunlight in the thick, tree lined foliage from reaching the woodland floor. The invasive vine had overtaken the edge of the woods, field, and even the roadside leading into the farm.

"Looks like he could have used a couple goats," Eli quipped. "Bet they'd have a field day eating this stuff."

"I hear Carter had the place in good shape when he was alive," Wes said, taking a few steps into the field. "Place went to hell after he passed."

Wes bent down to tear off a piece of kudzu. He examined it briefly, turned it over, and flung it in the air.

"Hard to believe this stuff grows about a foot a day," Wes said as the vine fell to the ground. "Used to drive my daddy nuts if it'd get in our yard. Am sure Carter felt the same."

"What'd he die of, anyway?" Eli asked curiously.

"Well, you see that house over yonder," Wes said, pointing across the field. "That was his place. There's no one there now."

Wes slid his arm around Eli and drew her close to his side. "Place is haunted," he joked mimicking a poor imitation of Boris Karloff's voice.

"What!" Eli exclaimed. "Wes Harder, I declare! You brought me to a haunted house?"

An amazed look appeared on Eli's face as she shook her head in disbelief. Her mouth fell open, and eyes widened in exasperation.

"No need to be scared," Wes said. "There's nothing to worry about."

Eli pushed her arm away from Wes. The thought of paranormal activity gave her an uncomfortable, creepy feeling.

"Want to have a look?" Wes asked. "There's nothing there that'll hurt you."

"No," Eli balked. "I want to go home. This isn't right."

Wes took Eli's hand. He gently coaxed her toward the desolate farmhouse.

"Tell you what," he said. "Let's have a peek in the window."

In the spirit of adventure, Eli reluctantly agreed. She was still dubious about being on a remote property with a sketchy past, but willing to give Wes the benefit of the doubt.

As the couple traipsed their way through the tangled kudzu vines, Wes began to reveal more of the farmhouse's past.

"The story goes, Carter had a dog that used to give him fits," Wes said. "One day, the dog got out and he went to get him."

Wes slowed his pace as they neared the house window. It was open. A slight breeze caught the floral lace curtain.

"They say he was mad as hell," Wes continued. "And went to get his gun to teach that dog a lesson."

At the window, Wes paused to clear his throat.

"Well, he tripped and fell," Wes said. "The gun went off and he killed himself!"

"What?"

"That's right, he was dead before he hit the ground."

Eli felt a sudden chill as she gently pushed the curtain aside while Wes looked on, smirking. Still uncomfortable with the thought of being an intruder, Eli peered through the window.

Suddenly, Eli's head recoiled in disbelief. Her blood curtailing scream could be heard echoing through the heavily ladened kudzu woods.

Chapter 52

The sound of rushing, crystal-clear water cascading over a rock-strewn waterfall was a temptation neither Wendall Tucker nor Milt Delany could resist when it came to fly fishing. It was a great passion they shared. Together, they would often steal away whatever free time they could to traverse a remote stream for trout.

It was bright and early in the morning when Wendall pulled into the Highland Ranch in his usual washed-out AC/DC t-shirt, and walked up the porch steps leading to the house. The shrill crow of a rooster could be heard making its presence known from the chicken coop behind the house.

As Wendall knocked on the door, he was greeted by Sarah. The smell of coffee, bacon and eggs filtered through the air.

"Hey there, good morning, Miss Sarah," Wendall said. "The ol' man out of bed?"

"Old man?" Milt bellowed from the kitchen. "Look who's talking!"

"Yeah, he's raring to go," Sarah laughed as Wendall stepped through the door.

"Grab yourself a plate," Milt said. "We don't have all day."

After a quick breakfast, the two headed to Blackburn Creek for a day of trout fishing. Both had their well-worn rods and reels stocked with an ample supply of midge mosquitoes, caddisflies, mayfly nymph imitation flies, and streamers ready for action.

Upon reaching the creek, they pushed through the mountain laurel to find an easy entry through the overgrown bankside rhododendron vegetation. The pair then slipped on their hip waders and eased into the water.

In an unspoken, systematic order, they followed their usual pattern of fishing in an upstream direction to allow their fly a chance to float into the trout's peaceful feeding area. Their target was a large pool where a sizable group of fish usually gathered hidden in an eddy beneath a large rock or submerged log.

"What have you got on the end of that line?" Milt asked. "You going for the big one's?"

"Thought I'd start with a Wooly Bugger," Wendall said, casting toward the far side of the creek that dropped into the pond. "They'll come running once it gets down to a cut bank."

"Good luck with that," Milt said. "They're deep right now. You'd do better with a Pheasant Tail."

As the day wore on, it became apparent that Wendall's strategy of working the creek was not bringing him any luck. He even tried switching to a Zonker and Sculpzilla streamer, but neither were effective.

Meanwhile, Milt had ventured downstream and slowly doubled back upstream, probing small hidden pockets and creek drop-offs. Working methodically, he had caught several rainbow and brown trout under the seven-inch legal limit requirement, which he dolefully released.

During a late morning break, Wendall made his way downstream to check on Milt, who was absorbed in analyzing the creek's most productive spots. Wendall sat on a log, watching as Milt would skillfully loop his line with the ease of an Olympic ribbon gymnastic and swiftly snap his wrist forward to gently land the fly on the water.

"Still into nymphs?" Wendall asked. "Streamers aren't doing anything."

"Oh, hell yeah!" Milt said, splashing his way to the bank. "They're not on the surface or hitting anything deep. Nymphs are the only way to go."

Milt laid his pole against the log and sat next to Wendall. He lifted his wide-brim fishing hat, adjusted the neck strap, and wiped his brow. "Sometimes, it's a mystery where they're at; you just have to play it out."

Wendall looked at the serene, peacefully flowing creek and nodded his head. For a moment, his thoughts were lost in the lush, green landscape and unspoiled natural beauty.

"It's a mystery, all right," Wendall agreed, stroking his white beard. "Kind of like the one they've got going at that farm right now."

"You talking about those dead guys at Carter's place?"

"Yeah, that's the one," Wendall said. "Both guys shot in the back of the head."

"Damn," Milt murmured.

"Sheriff Porter got his hands full with that one."

"He sure does," Milt agreed. "I hope he can figure out who did it."

Wendall reached over for his rod. He fumbled through his fishing vest and pulled out a WD 40 Black Nymph.

"After Porter gets done with those guys on Carter's farm," Wendall said, trying the Black Nymph to his line, "maybe he can help me figure out the mystery about these fish."

Chapter 53

The two bodies at the Carter farmhouse lay motionless in a pool of blood next to each other. The front door was slightly ajar and the windows open. There was no sign of a struggle or any resistance. Both had been shot through the back of the head and were lying face down. The scene was eerily similar to the brutal Badger Creek slayings.

Upon entering the farmhouse, Sheriff Porter recognized Mark Sanders from the Missing Persons bulletins that had been posted. The other victim was unknown, and not immediately identified.

Outside the house, two distraught teenagers, Wes Harder and Eli Mills, huddled together. They had called Jo Yarborough at the sheriff's office with their alarming, panic-stricken message. Both had ventured to the farmhouse on a lark. What began as a laugh had become the shock of a lifetime.

Deputy Wilson was called to the scene. He methodically began to piece together the occurrence of events through a visual inspection and interviewed the teen witnesses. It was a slow, laborious task. The deputy worked diligently to prepare a chronological report of the crime scene. Every detail was followed in accordance with homicide investigation protocols.

Curious onlookers had begun to filter into the area. Sheriff Porter ordered the area cordoned off. No unauthorized personnel, including the media, were permitted near the farmhouse. He did not want to risk contaminating any evidence.

Photographs were taken, evidence was collected, and the county medical examiner was notified. The bodies would require an autopsy as part of the investigation. Arrangements were made for their transportation to a regional examination facility.

Word of the homicide spread fast. When Mr. Andrews of *The Mountain Holler* heard the news, he called Skip immediately. He could literally taste the news potential of a sensational blockbuster.

Mr. Andrews was acutely aware that once the Carter Farm

headlines hit the newsstands, there would be endless advertising revenue possibilities with unlimited follow-up stories. Unfortunately, while the story was a guaranteed regional goldmine, he was unaware that Skip had other plans.

Skip had called Billie Jo and Edward Barnes about their daughter Mary Beth to follow up on The Gap Runners entry into the national clogging competition. He planned to spend a couple days in Gatlinburg, Tennessee, to report the event.

"Hells bells!" Mr. Andrews bellowed when he learned Skip was on the road, halfway to his destination. "Quit farting around with that lightweight stuff!"

Mr. Andrews told Skip he needed to get to the Carter farmhouse and work on a *real* news story, which was easier said than done.

Jo Yarborough took Skip's initial call to the sheriff's department, which was met with stony silence. The department refused to comment, except to confirm that a homicide had taken place. When pressed for additional information, she referred him to the medical examiner's office.

The medical examiner's office referred the call to the Department of Health and Human Services. Skip was told the call would be handled, in turn, by the Communications Department. Since it would be days before the examination was complete, there was no immediate comment available.

The medical examiner was also faced with the task of identifying an unknown victim. A public appeal was made for any information that might help, while fingerprints and DNA samples had proven inconclusive.

Having reached a dead end, Mr. Andrews urged Skip to contact Mark Sanders widowed wife, Staci. Perhaps she could provide some insight into the story and shed light on the tragedy.

Skip made several attempts to reach Staci Sanders but received no response. It was clear she was not talking, except to the sheriff. He even tried appealing to Katie Mae, who had met Staci Sanders while shopping at Two Sisters. She turned him down out of respect for the widow's privacy.

Sanders and her young daughter had gone into seclusion. The only information Skip had gotten was from a family friend. Even then, he only received a few derogatory words about a friend of Sander's named Andy Dodge and some defiant curse words about Mad Mama, which were not suitable for publication.

Chapter 54

Jack Fuller still had not come to grips with the disappearance of Ricky Ehlers. He could not help, but wonder if his "mule" delivery carrier had inadvertently gone astray, gotten lost, or met with foul play. Either way, his anxiety grew with each passing day.

His apprehension grew when the news broke about Mark Sanders body had been discovered at the Carter farmhouse. It was then he began to fear the worst. To worsen matters, he began to wonder if the entire Mad Mama distillery operation was being targeted.

The decision to temporarily shut down the business would be easy. There had been times in the past where he had to briefly suspend operations due to legal reasons, but never as a direct threat. Dodging the law throughout the years was a common occurrence, and he was always careful not to sell to a questionable customer.

Fuller tried desperately to find a logical explanation, or reason, for someone to target Mad Mama. He wondered if someone, or a vigilante organization had been formed as a temperance movement to stamp out the company.

Another concern was the local religious community. Had the distribution of Mad Mama offended someone? Was there a renegade preacher who surreptitiously had gone on a crusade to eliminate the distillery?

Rumors would surface occasionally that a lethal substitute of ethyl alcohol, or "canned heat," was being sold. The deterring gossip would force Mad Mama to halt production until the hearsay subsided. Who started the rumors was anyone's guess.

It was the loss of two "mules" within a short amount of time that meant everyone associated with Mad Mama was potentially in grave danger. Fuller was aware of other small, private distilleries that had been threatened or destroyed in the past. He did not want to subject his operation to suffer the same fate.

Above all, it was the text messages that alarmed him the most. Who were they from? How had they gotten ahold of Bo Benson and Ricky

Ehler's burner phones? Furthermore, the taunting messages made no sense.

As Fuller considered his options, he wondered if a gang or organized crime syndicate had moved into the area. He also considered the possibility of an unscrupulous competitor who might have sought a ruthless Machiavellian approach to eliminating a rival distiller.

In a lost daze, Fuller wandered to the still's shed. He was not ready to toss away so many years of hard work that he had made to develop his customer base, though he wondered about the future.

"He's gone," Fuller heard Latch say softly from the shed's open door.

"Say, what?"

"Ricky's gone," Latch reaffirmed. "Word's out another body was found with that Sander's guy."

"What makes you so sure?" Fuller asked in a shaken voice.

"Rumor's out the other guy was wearing that damned hat backward, and sunglasses like Ricky always wore."

"Oh lord, that sounds like him," Fuller said, holding his head as he settled in a chair next to the still. "Are you sure?"

Latch walked over to the still to secure the tarp over the kettle. He always kept it covered between distillation runs to keep the copper clean.

"Yeah," Latch said slowly. "Sander's wife has been talking to the sheriff, and Ricky's name got into the mess."

"Damn," Fuller said. "Any idea what happened?"

"Had to be a hit," Latch said, folding his arms. "Clear as day, it was a set up."

"Any idea who's behind it?" Fuller asked nervously. "Did you hear anything else?"

Latch shook his head with a deep sigh. He was emotionally drained, and shared Fuller's grieving sense of concern.

"I suppose it's only a matter of time before they come around here," Fuller sighed ruefully.

Latch nodded his head in agreement at the disheartening thought.

"You know," Fuller said, looking toward the ceiling. "It'd be nice if we could turn the tables."

"How so?" Latch asked. "You don't know who, or what you're dealing with."

"That may be so," Fuller agreed. "Whoever's out there might have won the battle, but not the war. And I've never seen a mule that can't kick a dog's ass."

Chapter 55

Being short on cash was nothing new for Ross. He was a survivor. Aside from his short stint working for the Sweet James Garage Door Company, he had learned to live modestly, while Candi was a born grifter.

Candi had no concept or grasp of budgeting. Money slipped through her hands like fine grains of sand. She relied on Ross to be the breadwinner. What little money she earned on cleaning Airbnb rooms was spent on whatever drugs she could afford.

Ross was greatly alarmed about the couple's finances after the Myrtle Beach trip. He did not share Candi's laissez-faire attitude about spending what cash they did not have, which was reason enough to call Salvador.

The call Ross made to Salvador was, fortunately, made at an opportune time. As luck had it, Salvador was out-of-town nursing a margarita in a noisy hotel lounge.

Ross could hear the giddy chatter of women near the phone and an older man's voice, as well.

"Ross!" Salvador said. "How was Mrytle Beach?"

"Oh, man," Ross began. "Me and Candi had a great time thank you."

"Good, good," Salvador said as a girl could be heard giggling near the phone. "I am kind of busy right now, but glad you called."

Salvador's voice tailed off, as two girls could be heard bantering in a flirtatious, playful conversation. The exchange was fun, lively, and full of laughter.

"I was wondering," Ross began to say, when Salvador cut him off.

"Listen, I can't talk right now," Salvador said, amid the snickering. "I got a half-day job coming up, if you're interested."

"Okay," Ross said. "Let's hear it."

"Remember that box truck we dropped off at Gilbert's?" Salvador asked.

"Yeah, wasn't that the one we picked up in Badger Creek?"

"That's the one!" Salvador said. "We need to pick it up. It'll take half a day."

"Sounds good," Ross said. "How much will it pay?"

"I can probably get you $250."

"Any chance you can do better, like $300?"

"Listen Ross, I can get any putz to drive a truck," Salvador said in a sharp tone. "If you don't want the job, I'll get someone else."

Ross demurred briefly. Negotiating was not his forte. Nor did he have the quick wit to barter. Silence was his only tact, though; he was familiar with Salvador's hardened tactics.

"Okay," Salvador said as Ross heard a feminine ticklish squeal resonate in the background. "I'll see about the three bills, but you'll need to be ready in a couple days."

Ross heard Candi awaken with a slight moan. He quickly stepped outside to take the call where he could not be heard.

"Wait a second," Ross said. "Are you saying we're getting that Badger Creek truck?"

"Yeah, why?" Salvador asked defiantly. "Is there some problem?"

"It's all over the news that a couple folks got shot and killed," Ross said. "They're looking for whoever did it, and the truck too," Ross said. "I don't want be part of any funny business."

"No, listen Ross!" Salvador said. "That's not the same truck. We did not do anything. You understand?"

Salvador could be heard pushing the girls away. "I don't know what happened to those guys in Badger Creek after we left," he added. "We did our job and bought the truck for the boss. You have nothing to worry about."

"Thought you said it was the same truck we're picking up?" Ross asked. "The sheriff's been all over looking for it."

"No," Salvador said, repeating his previous statement in a convincing manner. "The truck we're getting is for a mattress company. It has nothing to do with that Badger Creek truck."

"Besides, we were hired to pick up and deliver that Badger Creek truck, which is what we did," he added. "Do want the money, or not?"

"Hmmm, okay," Ross said. "So, what happens next, and when do I get paid?"

"I'll call in a couple days," Salvador said, as the girls could be heard ticklishly squealing in the background. "Then, we'll run over to Gilbert's for the truck. Easy. You'll get paid in cash after it's delivered."

Satisfied that there was nothing illegal about the truck and the upcoming transaction, Ross agreed to the job. At least, he would have some money coming into the household.

As he ended the call, Ross turned toward the house. Candi stood at the doorway glaring at him with her arms folded.

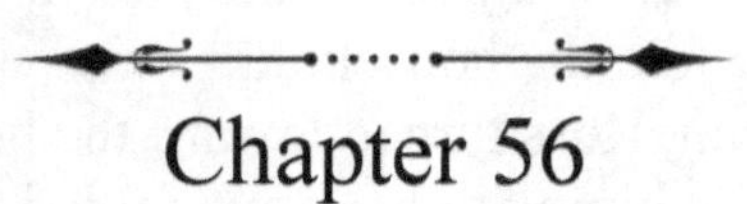

Chapter 56

Deputy Wilson's eyes were riveted to the computer monitor as Detective Halstead downloaded the Bushnell trail cam's SD card. The detective had stumbled across the trail cam on a subsequent trip while investigating the Buckshot Pond murder site.

The first image to appear was an eerie, black-and-white image of a wooded clearing surrounded by weeds and overgrown brush. The occasional glow of a firefly, wayward bat, or moth venturing into the cam's view was the only visible movement. Sweet potatoes appeared to have been laid on the ground to attract deer by an optimistic hunter.

"Nice LCD display," Wilson noted of the cam's clarity. "I've got a Spypoint, but never use it."

"Why not?" Halstead asked. "Those are good cams."

"No time," the deputy sighed. "Besides, I quit hunting some time ago. My butt got sore sitting in tree stands."

The detective and deputy continued to watch the monitor as a fox trotted across the screen on its evening prowl. The nocturnal carnivore paused momentarily to peer at the trail cam before moving on. Its pointed ears, upturned nose, and long, bushy tail could be seen bounding into the darkness of the woods.

"Red fox," Halstead said. "Looking for supper."

A small group of sleek, elegant white-tailed deer moved into the monitor's view. They gingerly entered the clearing with delicate, tender steps. Each sniffed and nibbled at the sweet potatoes strewn across the ground, while the male leader stood with a guarded, regal appearance.

"Whoa, check out the buck," Wilson said in an admiring tone. "That's quite a rack."

"Bet Sarah at Highland Ranch would have a fit if that bunch went through her blackberry patch," he added. "They'd clean her out."

A sudden jolt within the woods suddenly alarmed the deer. Their heads rose in unison. In one quick motion, they turned to leap gracefully into the woods.

"There goes some road kill," Halstead said dryly. "Gentlemen, start your engines."

"Whoever knocks one off better register with the DNR," Wilson said. "Otherwise, it's going to the food bank."

There was a sudden flicker of light that appeared beyond the clearing. The vehicle's headlights appeared to be moving quickly on the road beyond the trees and thick brush that bordered the clearing.

"Hey, look there!" Wilson exclaimed. "What do you make of it?"

"Not sure," Halstead replied. "Looks like a large car; might be a Suburban."

"Wish we could get a better look," Wilson said wistfully. "She's moving like a bat out of hell."

"Hmmm, black sedan," Halstead said as the car sped away. "Either that, or a dark color of some sort."

The screen went dark as the vehicle passed. The two men were left staring at the wooded clearing. Once again, there was the occasional firefly, moth, or stray bat seen buzzing about the camera.

"That it?" Wilson asked. "Anything else?"

"Yeah, but you're going to have to wait," Halstead said. "Gets kind of interesting after a while."

The two lawmen continued to watch the screen intently. There was no wildlife or slightest movement on the screen. Even the insects and bats seemed to have vanished. Soon, boredom set in.

"You know what?" Wilson asked. "Let me see if Jo's made some coffee. I could use a cup about now."

"Ah, hang on," Halstead said. "There's something coming up, you ought to see."

Another set of headlights could be seen through the trees. The headlights were moving painfully slowly, at a snail-like pace.

"Benson?" Wilson asked. "I can't get a clear view."

"It could be," Halstead replied. "Probably a truck. It's got dual headlights like those old Chevy's."

"Anyone else come through?" Wilson asked. "Seems strange anyone would be rolling around Buckshot Pond so late at night. That road's about as dead as they come."

Halstead surmised that the suspect and victim were placed in the vicinity of Buckshot Pond at the approximate time and date of the murder; however, the evidence was sketchy and inconclusive.

Wilson leaned back in his chair, looking perplexed. He wondered if a better view of the vehicles could be seen, as the SD memory card continued to roll.

Suddenly, another vehicle appeared on the screen. It appeared to be the same vehicle seen earlier that Wilson had deemed a "bat out of hell."

The car was racing at a high speed in the opposite direction. Dust from the dirt road enveloped the monitor's picture. The image left a dusty blur on the Bushnell trail cam.

Halstead took the computer mouse, and clicked off the screen. He solemnly looked at Wilson, lowered his eyes, and said, "Welcome to hell."

Chapter 57

The line for game tokens had grown to several kids at Big Ben's Pizzeria, outside Bonner Falls. The restaurant was a popular draw for families with kids who could play an assortment of arcade or video games to win redemption tickets for toys or candy while enjoying appetizers or a meal of various pizzas.

As a youth, Skip had been an avid gamer, but his desire for arcade games had long since faded. Aside from an occasional foosball or dart game at The Red Maple, he rarely ventured into sports bar activities. Instead, he preferred to watch others while nursing a beer.

Behind the counter was a lean, clean shaven young man in his early 30s who enthusiastically greeted the kids. His job was an all-encompassing cashier, food runner, bus boy, gaming and rest room attendant.

After the line had dwindled, the young man took a towel and began to wipe down a group of freshly vacated chairs, booths, and highchairs.

"Busy night," Skip commented as the young man swept past him.

"Yeah, it looks like a full house," he said. "Can I help you?"

"I'd like a beer on draft, when you get a minute," Skip said.

Skip looked at the young man's name tag and asked, "You, Andy Dodge, by chance?"

Andy looked at Skip for a moment with a quizzical, measured look before answering.

"Yeah, that's me," he said as a young child tapped his side for a fresh supply of tokens. "Just a minute, let me help this guy."

Moments later, Andy returned with the beer and placed a frosty mug in front of Skip. The crowd at the pizzeria had begun to thin, which gave him a chance to relax.

"I'm Skip Walker?" Skip asked nonchalantly. "Got a minute?"

Andy took a seat across the table. His eyes narrowed, and lips tightened.

"You that *Mountain Holler* guy?" he asked. "If you are, I don't want to talk about Mark. We were friends, okay? I didn't do nothing.

I'm sick of the things his people are saying about me, especially his kinfolk. None of its true. I didn't do anything, and I'm getting blamed about the Mad Mama."

"I didn't come to talk about Mark," Skip said reassuringly, though it was a lie. He was hoping to gather whatever information he could without overstepping his bounds.

Since Andy was noticeably upset about being blamed for his friend's death, Skip decided to take another approach. He did not want to risk the opportunity to obtain whatever information he could from the meeting.

"Look," he said, taking a sip of beer. "I'm curious who's selling Mad Mama. I'd like to know where I could get some."

Andy looked at the game room's prize counter. Two young kids had stopped to look at the glass case contents and moved on. The inquisitive kids were soon gathered by their mother and led to the restaurant's exit.

It was nearing time to close the pizzeria. Andy and his co-workers would soon be cleaning the counters, floors, tables, and restrooms. Andy checked his watch. He started to rise from the table.

"I don't know," Andy said. "Some guy sells it. He'd come through by and by; order a slice of pizza and beer. Then talk a lot, you know."

"Oh, what'd he'd say?" Skip asked with raised eyebrows, expressing an increased interest.

"Mostly, smack," Andy replied. "He'd brag about his job, and running some dog guy out of business. Good tipper. I never paid him any mind."

"You get his name?" Skip asked, running his finger around the top rim of his beer mug.

"Rick Elbers, or something like that," Andy said hurriedly. "Listen, I have to wrap up for the night."

Skip nodded appreciably, finished his beer, and rose from the table. He left a generous tip, and offered his condolences about his friend's passing.

"Listen, Staci and her friends can say whatever they want, but Mark wanted to try something different, and have a little fun. Okay? That's all. I'm sorry for what happened, but it wasn't my fault."

Andy turned away from the table, then paused. He turned to Skip and said, "Funny, I suppose Elbers was right when he told me that it was a 'dog eat dog world.'"

Chapter 58

The hunt for Rick Elbers brought more questions for Skip, thanks to Andy Dodge's vague tip. He began searching the Internet with a voracious intensity, only to find several individuals with the same name living in places like Allegan, Michigan, Island Park, Idaho, and Tulsa, Oklahoma. None fit the age and location of the individual's profile he was seeking.

After spending hours on the Internet's social media websites, he decided to redefine his research. He focused primarily on company organizations, educational institutions, geographic regions, military service, passports, civil and criminal records - all without success.

Skip's Uncle Em viewed the project as a hapless exercise in futility. With a sardonic smirk, he wryly suggested hiring a private investigator.

"Better get Sherlock Holmes," Uncle Em said mockingly. "And charge fat ass, while you're at it. You can be Watson! A guy like that'll run him down. He'll open the closet and all the hidden skeleton's, including the guy's extramarital affairs will come tumbling out!"

Skip shook his head. He had a story to write and did not need his uncle's unsolicited suggestions nor bawdy humor.

"Hell, I wouldn't be surprised if old Sherlock found out your guy's been shacking up with Irene!" Uncle Em laughed as he patted Fred on the head. "The Wolverine probably was doing him too."

Without saying a word, Skip turned to the porch door. It was clear he was not going to get any work done with his uncle's haranguing distraction. Instead, he would conduct his research elsewhere, and disregard his uncle's facetious suggestion that Fred tag along as the token bloodhound.

Skip decided to take a break, and pay Katie Mae a visit at Two Sisters. She was working a late afternoon shift. He thought he'd surprise her and the owners, Victoria and Veronica, with ice cream sandwiches.

As Skip dipped into his pocket for car keys, he felt the aluminum dog whistle keychain he had been given at Wendall Tucker's birthday party. He had forgotten about his meeting with Bick. Being an advertising sales rep as well as a community news editor, Skip found it interesting that Bick's dog training business had not come up on his radar for a sales call, but that thought had to wait.

After stopping into a nearby convenience store, Skip headed to Two Sisters. Upon entering the store, he gently opened the front door's latch. Upon hearing its cheery doorbell ring, Katie Mae's head turned from the rear counter.

"Skippy!" she exclaimed. "What have you been doing with yourself?"

"Been out and about," Skip smiled as he set a bag of ice cream sandwiches on the counter. "Thought I'd stop by with some treats for you, Miss Victoria and Miss Veronica."

"Why, isn't that sweet!" Katie Mae exclaimed. "Look at what Skippy brought us!"

Victoria and Veronica emerged from the store's rear storage room. Both had a sweet tooth and enjoyed an occasional sugary treat.

"Awww, aren't you the sweetest thing? Why, bless your heart," Veronica drawled. "Isn't he Vicky?"

Victoria nodded enthusiastically, as she unwrapped her ice cream sandwich and thanked Skip repeatedly.

"You out doing your *Mountain Holler* stuff?" Katie Mae asked, tearing the wrapper off her ice cream sandwich. "There's all kinds of stuff going on in the news these days."

"There sure is," Veronica said. "After what happened at Carter's place, we're scared to death to go out anymore. Huh, Vicky?"

"Uh-huh," Victoria agreed, licking her ice cream.

"Well, I'm not worried, none," Katie Mae said. "I was talking to Tammy up on the hill where she lives. She was telling me that Tom heard Gus talking to someone, while they were trimming trees. Sheriff Max has his eye on someone."

"Really?" Skip asked surprised.

"Yes," Katie Mae confirmed. "If anyone's going to get him, it's Sheriff Max."

As Katie Mae concluded her thought, everyone finished their ice cream and tossed the wrappers in the trash. Skip wondered aloud if the victim found with Sanders had been identified. Both Victoria and Veronica lowered their eyes and exchanged knowing looks.

"Words out, it's that young fellow who used to bum around The Red Maple," Veronica said in a hushed voice. "Let me think; off hand, I can't recall the name."

Victoria cleared her throat. All eyes were on her as she said, "Elhers."

Chapter 59

The gate was locked when Salvador and Ross arrived at Gilbert's Body and Paint Shop. There was no sign of any activity, except for the lone bark of a dog somewhere in the rear of the property.

The building had once been the hub of activity and proudly boasted the finest auto mechanical service in the area, but times had changed. Larger automotive competitors had expanded into the region. The paint on the metal corrugated building had long since peeled to reveal a ghastly weathered rust.

Upon their arrival, Ross got out of the SUV to explore the area. Salvador popped open the driver's door and impatiently punched numbers on his phone. He was in no mood to wait for a late appointment, and made no effort to conceal his displeasure.

Unable to reach the garage owner by phone, Salvador got out of the car, cursing. His frustration had reached a boiling point. He angrily slammed the SUV's door shut and lit a cigarette.

Ross walked over to the locked gate. He peered through the chain-link fence while waving off a clutch of mosquitoes that had gathered over his head. He was unable to see the truck they had delivered from Badger Creek. Instead, there was a Carolina blue colored box truck with a Conway Mattress Outlet decal painted on each side.

"What are looking at?" Salvador asked, as he neared Ross.

"Nice truck," Ross said, waving off a mosquito. "It kind of looks like the one we left, but it's not the same with those vents near the roof."

"Don't be so sure," Salvador said, taking a final puff from his cigarette and flicking it over the fence.

As Salvador reached for his phone to make another call, a Jeep Cherokee pulled into the garage's dirt lot. The owner, Chaz Gilbert, got out of the sport utility vehicle with a sheepish, apologetic grin and strode toward the gate.

"About time you got here," Salvador said. "We don't have all day, you know."

"Sorry," Chaz said with a sheepish smile. "Running late this morning."

Chaz unlocked the gate. He called for Diesel, and a Jack Russell terrier came bounding from behind the building. The excited dog jumped on the visitors as they passed through the gate.

"Get that dog off of me!" Salvador growled as he kicked Diesel away. "Got the keys and paperwork?"

"Ah, he's a fun little guy; aren't you?" Ross said as he playfully shook Diesel's ears.

"He's the boss," Chaz said proudly. "Came in the yard one day, looking for something to eat, and never left. Didn't you!"

An elated Diesel jumped into Chaz's arms, and licked his owner.

"Alright already," Salvador said hurriedly. "Where's the keys and paperwork? We've got to go."

Chaz set Diesel on the ground, and moved toward a side door in the building. Diesel obediently followed Chaz, who emerged with a fresh set of keys.

"We had to clean her first," Chaz said, slowly walking the pair toward the blue box truck. "That was quite a job getting her stripped and sanded down."

Diesel still hadn't slowed down and continued to jump wildly. He was noticeably excited about having visitors to investigate, though he avoided Salvador, who found the unwanted attention irritating and repeatedly kicked the dog away.

"Took out the dents, put in the vents, and patched her up here and there," Chaz said, unlocking the cab door. "Took three coats of primer, paint, and a couple coats of lacquer."

Chaz paused to admire his work. "Check it out!" he exclaimed. "Not a run anywhere!"

"That's nice," Salvador said in an even-tempered tone. "Now, let's have the keys and paperwork."

As Chaz handed the keys and an envelope with ownership papers to Salvador, Ross looked around the corner of the garage and noticed several cars. There were several makes and models in varied condition that included dismantled, damaged, and wrecked vehicles.

"Wow! That's quite a collection you got back there!" he exclaimed. "What are you going to do with all of those cars?"

Chaz smiled and leaned over to pick up Diesel. "Those fellows are about to hit the chomping block," he laughed. "We'll pull what parts we can and move them out."

"Chomping block?" Ross asked curiously. "What's that mean?"

Salvador turned with an incredulous, agitated look. His patience had worn thin. "It means quit talking and get in the truck!"

Ross seemed oblivious to Salvador's ominous mood and pressed Chaz for more information as he scanned the small field of aging, immobilized cars.

"We tear off the license plate and unbolt the front end from the frame," Chaz said. "Then cut out the windshield, doors, and seats. We'll pull the dash and airbags if they're still good."

"That's a lot of work," Ross said, shaking his head.

"Parts are another story," he continued. "We get good money for the engine and tranny; the problem's the VIN, but that's okay. I got a guy who can crank out any vehicle ID number you want."

Chaz glanced at Salvador, whose impatience had finally worn out. He quickly added that on rare occasions, the shop had been able to body switch a totaled car's VIN to turn a fast buck.

"Yeah, yeah, yeah," Salvador bellowed. "That's great. Now, tell him what it's like when you're caught, fined, or put in jail!"

The thought of being arrested was not one Ross fancied. He took Salvador's lead, and slid into the driver's seat of the box truck.

"You listen here, and listen good," Salvador warned as he leaned through the truck's window handing Ross the truck's keys. "You forget everything you've seen or heard today, unless you want to join him when the sheriff shuts down this damned chop shop!"

Chapter 60

The dual murders at the vacant Carter farmhouse brought a landslide of media to the Bonner Falls area. Jo Yarborough was inundated with calls from media outlets throughout the country.

As the demand for information rose, Sheriff Porter made the decision to hold a press conference to communicate with the media. His goal was to prevent any insatiable rumors from circulating or causing public alarm. Though the news was sparse, he was determined to keep the media and public updated with the most recent results of the ongoing investigation.

In preparation for the event, press members throughout the region descended on the area. Several individuals represented national affiliates, ranging from print, broadcast, and Internet organizations.

Local merchants and eateries, such as The Red Maple, were humored by the enormous attention their "one-horse town," as one discourteous visitor proclaimed, was receiving while the financial benefits rolled in.

Skip was determined to file his *Mountain Holler* story as quickly as possible. He had been the first, if not the only, reporter to interview Andy Dodge and was anxious to break the news he had gathered.

For Mr. Andrews, the story could not come out fast enough. He had already lined up a battery of advertisers in anticipation of a blockbuster issue and was primed for a big payday. He even had a photographer tramp surreptitiously through the woods to document the restricted, off-limits farmhouse through a telephoto lens to support the article.

At the press conference, Sheriff Porter confirmed that two victims had been shot in the back of the head. He also confirmed that one victim was Mark Sanders, a local resident who lived in the area, and was 27 years old. The other victim's name had not been released.

The sheriff added that the killing was done execution style, and death was instantaneous. The investigation team was still trying to determine what type of gun was used, though preliminary evidence suggested a small-caliber handgun at close range was the cause.

During the presentation, the sheriff noted that there were no visible defense wounds or signs of physical injuries on the victims' bodies. He added that the official death certificates, including the cause of death, had not been released pending the contracted laboratory's toxicology and tissue test results.

Several questions followed the sheriff's comments. He assured those media members present that all inquiries would be answered in due time, including the location of Sanders abandoned truck, which still had the inquisitive media baffled.

The reporters struggled to piece together the reasoning Sanders' truck and body were found at different locations. The sheriff conceded he did not have an answer, nor had his investigation team been able to turn up any video evidence that might shed light on the events that had occurred.

A reporter asked if the murders were related to the Badger Creek slayings, which the sheriff dismissed. While the similarities were undeniable, he was unwilling to connect the two, and was non-committal in his response.

At the conclusion of the press conference, the sheriff made a plea for anyone with information about the case to come forward and help solve the horrific homicide. It was the sheriff's hope that someone, somewhere, might know something that would lead to the murderer.

Skip left the press conference feeling confident that he had enough information for a complete story when Deputy Wilson saw him walking toward his car.

"Hey Skip," the deputy said in a weary, acknowledging tone. Clearly, the hours he had spent working on the investigation were taking their toll.

"Hey there, Mr. Wilson," Skip said, nodding in return. "You got her handled?"

"Yeah," the deputy drawled slowly. "We're getting there."

"Well, that's good to know," Skip said assuredly. "That was quite a turn out to hear the sheriff."

"That's a fact," the deputy agreed. "Seems like they came out of the woodwork."

The deputy took off his hat and wiped his brow. The day's humidity started to bear down reaching an uncomfortable level.

"I'll be glad when it's over," the deputy said glumly.

"Give it more time," Skip said empathetically. "Something will come up."

Skip reached into his pocket and pulled out his car keys. For a moment, he playfully twirled the keyring on his index finger. Then he caught the keys in a graceful, acrobatic motion.

The deputy appeared preoccupied in thought, and was about to turn away. He suddenly froze.

"Say, what's that in your hand?"

"Huh," Skip's head jerked curiously upward. "You mean my car keys?"

"No, what are they on?"

"A keyring," Skip said as the deputy moved closer. "Some guy gave it to me."

The deputy took the keyring, and held it for a moment. He studied every nuance carefully, before turning to Skip.

"I need to know where you got that dog whistle."

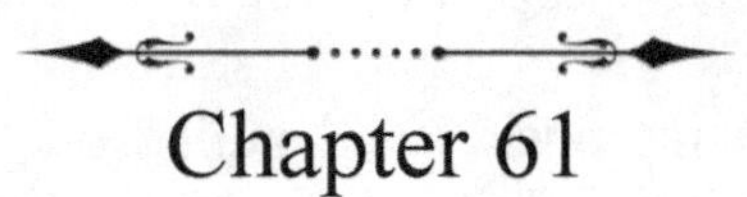

Chapter 61

At first, Skip could not understand Deputy Wilson's fascination with his dog whistle keyring. The non-descript item seemed nothing more than a durable aluminum keepsake that was hardly anything of interest, except to a dog lover.

The deputy's interest seemed to heighten as he poured over the black aluminum's gift souvenir. He seemed to have fallen into a meditative, hypnotic déjà vu-like trance as he starred at the Hellhound logo.

After a moment of fondling the keyring, the deputy turned toward Skip with an apprehensive look in his eyes. A slight tug at the deputy's mouth sent a clear message that the deputy was far more interested in the keychain than Skip could have possibly imagined.

During their conversation, the deputy asked Skip if he would not mind coming to the sheriff station. He wanted to further discuss the keychain's origin and include Detective Halstead in the conversation. The deputy wanted to cull whatever information could be learned about its source and hear whatever thoughts the detective might have to offer.

At the sheriff's office, Skip was led to the conference room. Several questions surrounding his meeting with Bickerson in the sweet tea line at the Highland Ranch pig pickin' birthday party for Wendall Tucker ensued.

At first, the conversation was a casual, lighthearted discussion of the birthday party. The deputy mused about the black balloons that decorated the party's stage, and the detective chuckled about the "over-the-hill" theme.

The group bantered about the party's food, music, and entertainment. Skip laughingly shared Katie Mae's comments about the "hog-eyed boys" at the duck pond, which drew guarded laughs, while the keychain was tossed on the conference table without being given any significance or special attention.

It wasn't until Deputy Wilson mentioned the keychain in a

nonchalant, casual manner that the subject was broached. He picked up the keychain and commented on the cleverness of the savvy marketing plan behind the promotional trinket giveaway while wondering about its source.

It quickly became apparent that the focus was evolving beyond the keychain. The deputy and detective began to rapidly delve into Skip's interaction with Bickerson.

Bickerson had become a person of interest.

Skip provided what information he could about his brief encounter with Bickerson. He described his physical, unshaven appearance, pock marked face, noticeable limp, use of a cane and approximate age.

When asked about Bickerson's demeanor, Skip noted that he was vague, dissatisfied with the party's long, slow-moving beverage line. Aside from being impatient, Skip recalled Bickerson insinuating that there was alcohol being passed around at the Highland Ranch duck pond, which seemed to draw his interest.

Skip recalled most of the conversation he could, until Bickerson slipped away amid the deafening cornhole contestant's celebration, which had diverted his attention. He explained that it was only then that he realized that his new acquaintance had slipped away.

The deputy and detective exchanged a discerning look, as the questioning continued. They were aware of the Highland Ranch duck pond and its corresponding events.

Deputy Wilson asked how the keychain entered the beverage line's conversation. Skip talked about his uncle's dog Fred's curiosity in Bickerson, which led to their discussion about dogs.

Skip told the deputy and detective that Bickerson had a dog training school, which he assumed was named Hellhound, based on the dog whistle's imprinted logo. He added that Bickerson wore a silver dog whistle around his neck. Owners whose dogs graduated from the school were given a certificate and black aluminum dog whistle keychain as a commemorative gift token.

At that point, Jo Yarborough was summoned. The deputy made a note, which he handed to her. She glanced at the paper with a nod and promptly left the room.

When asked about the dog training school, Skip shrugged his shoulders. Aside from the dog whistle Bickerson pulled from a backpack, he did not have any further information.

As the backpack was discussed, Skip admitted the owner's original name was different than Bickerson's, which was how he learned his name. The detective asked if he could recall the name on the backpack, but Skip's memory failed.

Moments later, Jo Yarborough returned to the room. She slid a note to the deputy and thanked her. The deputy solemnly turned to Skip and Detective Halstead.

"Jo ran a quick check in the Better Business Bureau, National and several social media databases," he said. "There is no record of a Hellhound dog training school."

In a pensive mood, the deputy tapped the note on the table with a pen. He studied the note for a moment, cleared his throat, and added, "The records also show there is no one named Bickerson in the area."

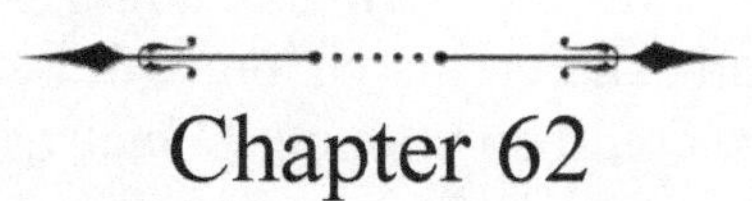

Chapter 62

Jack Fuller was determined to continue selling Mad Mama, despite the loss of Ricky Ehlers. Once Ehlers name hit the headlines, Mad Mama became a target of the local law enforcement agencies.

It was time for a change. Rather than continue struggling with mules and burner phones, Jack sought to find a better, easier way to sell Mad Mama; however, he would need to restructure the organization.

Jack took a hard look at the company's business model. He knew Mad Mama was popular, but selling a couple jars or cases at a time was hardly worth the risk. A better plan was needed.

A new strategy was needed to identify Mad Mama's goals that would enable the company to capitalize on its products and services. Jack also took care to study the company's current strengths and weaknesses, overhead costs, cash flow revenue losses, competitive and legal threats.

It would be easy for Jack to close shop and simply disappear. The other distillers before him had quietly come and gone. He had enough money to relocate. There was no need to keep taking chances, but that was not the issue. It was drive, determination, and motivation that kept him going. For some unknown reason, there was a driving force that made him believe moonshine would increase in popularity and Mad Mama would someday be a household name.

After evaluating the risks and previous horrifying experiences he had encountered, Jack sought a safer solution. In discussing the matter with his master distiller Latch, they began looking at the internet to market Mad Mama.

Taking Mad Mama on the online seemed like a sensible safe option. Jack was confident that Mad Mama had an ideal niche in the marketplace and was perfect for younger adult males. By going online, his mules could avoid physical harm and legal threats, while increasing Mad Mama's market share.

Despite the challenge of developing a website, Jack wanted to rebrand the product. He wanted to create a new and exciting product that would increase consumer demand and generate a whole new group of followers, and shared his vision with Latch.

"Any idea what we could do with her?" Jack asked Latch, who was polishing the still. "We really need a reset, with something new."

"I'd go with a few different flavors," Latch suggested. "Market the hell out of it. Call it authentic hillbilly mountain juice! Folks will eat it up!"

"Not a bad idea," Jack said, rubbing the back of his neck. "What flavors do you have in mind?"

"Peach, apple and cherry," Latch said cheerfully. "Keep it simple. Then, put a spin on it like 'Pa's Southern Peach Elixir, or something catchy like that.'"

"Hmmm, I like that, but what about the internet?" Jack wondered. "Got any thoughts on who can set up a website?"

Latch stopped polishing the copper kettle. He rolled his eyes, looking upward and said thoughtfully, "Yeah, as a matter of fact, I do. I know a gal named Mei Wang. She can do all that stuff."

"She some kind of computer nerd?"

"Ha, I suppose that's what you'd call it," Latch laughed. "But let me tell you, when it comes to computers, she's probably forgotten more than you'll ever know."

"That so?" Jack said. "Where'd you meet her?"

"At the community lodge by The Red Maple," Latch said. "They had a fish fry to repave the parking lot. It was a fundraiser. She was there with a bunch of school friends."

"Boy, those gals were running wide open; whooping and hollering. They were having a ball," he added.

"You say she's in school?"

"Nah, not no more," Latch said. "She got out some time ago and was living in Richmond, or someplace like that. The gals were sightseeing and heading to the train depot to check the schedule."

"Can you get ahold of her?"

"Yeah, I got a friend who knows her," Latch said. "Not sure if she's working. I heard she was offered a job in California, but turned it down."

"Well, in that case, let's get her in here," Jack said. "Mad Mama's about to get a makeover!"

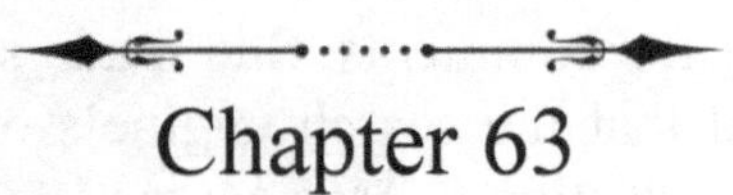

Chapter 63

Mei Wang was a soft-spoken, demure, bespectacled software engineer who had graduated with a Computer Science degree from a major university in Virginia. Throughout her undergraduate years, she worked as an intern for various software companies on a wide range of e-commerce applications and worked on several interactive website designs.

She was an accomplished full-stack software developer with the ability to build a website's front and back end. Mei's expertise in software bundling enabled her to integrate business logic code, API applications, data processing, and data components, while lowering costs to develop the applications.

Her experience also included the creation of e-commerce API integration sites, which would be an invaluable asset in developing Mad Mama's website, provided Latch could locate her.

It took weeks to locate Mei Wang. Jack was ready to give up when Latch learned that Mei and a group of friends were planning a whitewater rafting trip on the Nantahala River.

Jack wasted no time to arrange a meeting with Mei. Upon meeting Mei, he immediately described Mad Mama's software website needs and maintained that it was a confidential consulting opportunity to get on the ground floor of a potentially lucrative company. Mei would be well compensated for her work, as well.

Mei was intrigued by the offer but dubious. She had already turned down several substantial offers, which entailed relocating. It was the enticement of working in the beautiful surroundings of the Smoky Mountains that she found irresistible, though she insisted on setting her own hours and would have carte blanche in the creation of the website.

Jack was overjoyed. Mei first sought to source a website builder to customize the web page appearance that he wanted. Within a short amount of time, she registered a domain name and developed an attractive website.

In almost no time, Mei developed a user-friendly website with stunning graphics for an online store with videos, a picture gallery, and a customer blog for comments. She made sure the menus were easy to navigate and that the search engine's optimalization words were highly visible in relation to Mad Mama.

When the website was finished, Mei searched for the appropriate search engine that required password protection. Consequently, due to the illicit nature of the product, she used a virtual private network (VPN) as a resource to connect Mad Mama's novice, fledgling website and keep the IP address footprint anonymous.

Jack could hardly wait to launch the new website. He had been working with Latch to create new flavors of Mad Mama and was anxious to see Mei's finished work. Nervously, he logged onto the computer and searched for Mad Mama – nothing. His search came up empty.

Again and again, Jack searched the internet but was unable to find the Mad Mama website. Exasperated, he called Mei, who laughed at his naiveté.

"What's so funny?" Jack asked. "I can't find a thing."

"That's a good one," Mei chuckled. "That shows it's working."

"Huh?" Jack stammered. "I thought we were set?"

"You are," Mei said reassuringly. "You need a specific link to access your website and a password for authentication, which means your viewer or buyer will have to register, then log on to get on your site."

"You're kidding!" Jack exclaimed. "How am I going sell Mad Mama if no one can find me?"

"Don't worry," Mei said. "You have an encrypted VPN that will keep your IP address anonymous, because of the nature of what you're selling. Until you get a Federal Distilled Spirits Permit, you cannot sell Mad Mama legally. That's the reason your website is hidden."

Jack tried to make sense of Mei's explanation. He was confused about the veil of secrecy and concerned about his customers being unable to find his site.

"A VPN?"

"Yes, a VPN is a virtual private network that encrypts your data and routes you through another provider's server to hide or disguise your identity."

Jack listened quietly as Mei described how a VPN was essential for

Mad Mama's website. Its purpose was to protect the company from computer hackers and malicious virus threats that had the potential to breach the company's system.

"Do not worry, Mr. Jack," Mei said. "Once word gets out, you'll be swamped with orders."

"A virus?" Jack said. "That doesn't sound good."

Mei further explained that she had set up an antivirus program for the website as a precaution against malicious threats and to monitor any stolen data that might be leaked.

"I highly recommend your customers use cryptocurrency to purchase Mad Mama," Mei added. "Your customers will stay anonymous, and your funds will be protected."

"Crypto what?"

"Cryptocurrency," Mei explained. "It's digital currency that's funneled through a decentralized system that has no tangible form."

"What?" Jack asked. "So, it's not really money?"

"Where have you been, Mr. Jack?" Mei laughed. Cryptocurrencies operate on a blockchain system with an encryption that is designed to make all transactions secure."

"So, then it's really money?" Jack pressed. "It still doesn't make sense."

Mei began to explain the procedure of using a digital wallet, but realized Jack was unable to grasp the virtual concept in the simplest of terms. Jack wanted cash that he could put in his pocket, not an imaginary form of payment. Furthermore, he was concerned about computer hackers stealing from his account.

"No worries. The best way to go is a P2P payment service that is connected to a bank account, credit card, or debit card," Mei suggested. "That keeps the transaction private."

"P2P?"

"Yes, peer to peer."

"Is that when I get my money?"

"Kind of," Mei said. "You have to go through a centralized exchange, use a broker, money transfer app, or get a crypto ATM card, and there will be fees that go with it."

In closing, Mei asked if Jack had any questions. He racked his brain, trying to absorb the avalanche of material he had not been able to comprehend.

"No," he said, mentally drained. "Not at the moment."

Mei assured him the website was secure and would be successful over time. She suggested he take time to adjust to the new search engine.

"Welcome to the dark web."

"You know, this whole thing is bullshit," Jack said wistfully. "There's got to be a better way to get a Benjamin."

"Benjamin?"

"Yeah, that's what they used to call 'money.'"

Chapter 64

Anytime Skip's Uncle Em fired up the gas grill, there was bound to be cause for excitement. It was an unspoken rule that the porch was off limits when the grill was lit, and a forgone conclusion that Uncle Em's infamous beer can chicken would be grilling.

The preparation of the entrée was an exact science, known only to Skip's uncle. He would carefully apply a rub consisting of exact amounts of kosher salt, chili powder, black pepper, oregano, granulated onion, and garlic, covered with a fine layer of paprika and a splash of lemon. The process could easily take an hour.

The final touch was a 12-ounce can of room-temperature beer, which was a joke. It was a well-known fact that any beer left unattended on the porch was open season for Uncle Em, and liable to be swept away in a couple gulps.

Once the chicken was ready, Uncle Em would place a drip pan with oak wood chips under the grill, light the burners, and insert half a can of beer into the chicken. Then, he would stand the chicken upright on the grill and grab a beer for himself.

Skip always watched the action from a safe distance. He would often joke that grilling utensils in his uncle's hands were like an illegal weapon and that his life insurance policy needed updating.

"That your phone going off?" Uncle Em barked at Skip on hearing a beep. "Can't you shut that damn thing off?"

"Hmmm, let me see," Skip said, checking his text messages. "Oh, the Carter farmhouse story is out."

"What?" Uncle Em said, walking toward the grill. "Fat ass got off his butt, and finally got that rag out?"

Skip rolled his eyes, shaking his head. He reached down to pat Fred, sat back on the deep-seated cushion, and swiped his index finger over his phone's messages.

"Oh, my God," Skip shrugged. "I've told you before *The Mountain Holler* is a well-respected publication within the community. It provides up-to-date news on local meetings and events."

"Humph, tell that to fat ass," Uncle Em huffed. "That rag's his cash cow. There's nothing happening around here. It's not like Daytona. Now, that place was always hopping."

"Like chicken burning?" Skip wryly observed. "I suppose you're going to tell me that's not news?"

Uncle Em opened the grill's lid to find the chicken had fallen over, flamed up, and beer draining into the drip pan.

"Damnit," he growled. "Why didn't you say something?"

"I did," Skip said with a rueful smirk. "I'll have to buy you a roasting rack that doesn't fall over for your birthday."

"Oh, hell no," Uncle Em snarled. "Those things are for people who don't know what they're doing. Can't you see, I've done this before?"

Skip raised his eyes, smiled at Fred, and kept quiet. The dog seemed to have an extra sensory perception in regards to the conversation's comical turn of events.

Uncle Em set the chicken upright and slipped an aluminum foil packet on the grill filled with okra and potatoes that he had prepared in advance.

"Now, don't screw it up," Uncle Em warned. "Keep on eye on the burners, and quit playing with your phone."

The Mountain Holler's issue featuring the Carter farmhouse story had begun to spread through the community. The brutal murders had made a sensational headline, as Mr. Andrews predicted. Skip immediately received several text messages and various comments from friends, and readers alike.

The article recounted the events that took place at the Carter farmhouse, and identified the two victims as having met over a moonshine transaction. The murderer and motive were still unknown.

Sheriff Max Porter was quoted as warning people to avoid buying, drinking, or selling illegal alcohol. He also noted the potential for unforeseen danger, such as the savage slayings that had occurred.

In the article, Skip made a sly, contemptuous editorial observation that the murderer most likely had the low mentality of a whiny, cowardly dog, which raised more than one pair of eyebrows.

Skip continued to receive text messages, much to Uncle Em's disgust. The constant, rapid fire cell phone beeping disrupted the peaceful evening, and even Fred's head jolted upward, taking notice.

"I'm about to throw that damn thing in the creek," Uncle Em grumbled. "Even Irene didn't text that much during our divorce!"

Uncle Em lifted the grill's lid and shut off the propane burners. He looked across the yard, and held a pair of barbecue tongs deep in thought.

"Come to think of it," he said thoughtfully, watching over the grill. "I did get quite a few letters from the Wolverine's attorney."

Chapter 65

The familiar face of Corny greeted Salvador and Ross as the black SUV and freshly painted box truck rolled through the gated fence. With the wave of a hand, Corny guided Ross to back the truck toward the spacious storage complex. Somewhere, deep within the structure, a warm, soothing sounds of a Brahms concerto could be heard.

As the electronic door began to rise, a man wearing a well-worn Carolina hat limped forward on a cane with two snarling rottweilers. He tugged slightly on their chain leash and moved to inspect the box truck.

Once parked, Ross jumped out of the truck, inches from the enraged dogs snapping jaws. Clearly, they were ready to pounce on the slightest offending provocation.

Salvador parked the SUV and walked confidently to the garage entrance. A lack of expression belied his true, uncertain feelings, especially when meeting with Copperhead. He was secretly fearful, and nervous the boss might not approve of the box truck's condition. Fortunately, his concerns were soon relieved.

"Nice," Copperhead said in an agreeable tone. "The logo looks good."

He continued to walk around the truck, as though he were on a pleasant stroll with the agitated dogs. "Conway Mattress Outlet," he said to no one in particular, with a smug look. "I like it."

"What do you think, Cornelius?" he asked his elderly property caretaker and master distiller. "Even the air vents were installed; nice."

The dogs' behavior had reached an almost unbearable crescendo with their menacing, uncontrollable, atrocious barking. Both drooled with a foamlike substance from their clinched, barred teeth and lunged forward.

Finally, Copperhead yelled, "Stop!" He jerked violently on their chain leashes, and slapped the most aggressive one on the head. The dogs obediently obeyed, and broke off hostilities.

"That's better," Copperhead said cooly. "Must be time for their meds; now where were we?"

Corny opened the box truck's rear door and pulled out the tuck-under liftgate. The group of men peered inside, inspecting the interior. Corny and his boss seemed most interested in the truck's interior length, width, and height.

"Are you able to work with it, Cornelius?" Copperhead asked. "Looks clean."

"Yeah, I think so," Corny replied slowly as he walked into the truck. "We'll start with the insulation an' subfloor, then go from there. Prob'ly lay some vinyl."

"Good, are you going put the cages in once the walls are framed?"

"That's right," Corny agreed as he glanced around. "We'll also get the plumbing, electrical and drain installed."

Both Salvador and Ross watched quietly as the two men discussed the box truck conversion. They were unsure about the truck's future, use nor interested. Their interest was getting paid, though there was still some paperwork to handle.

"You got the pink slip?" Copperhead asked Salvador as he patted one of the subdued dogs. "We need to make sure we're street legal."

"Yes, everything's here," Salvador said, setting the manila envelope on the liftgate of the truck. "Gilbert handled the documentation."

"Good," Copperhead said turning to Corny. "Cornelius, would you check the VIN?"

Corny opened the envelope, and sorted through the paperwork. He had previously worked with Gilbert's Body and Paint Shop in the past, and felt confident about the company's ability to replicate VIN numbers.

Once Corny confirmed the paperwork, the meeting appeared to be finished. As arrangements were being made for payment, Copperhead gave Corny the leash for the rottweilers. He asked that the dogs be placed in their pen.

"There are a couple things I'd like to discuss," Copperhead said, limping toward Salvador. "If you don't mind, I'd like to speak to you alone."

Salvador motioned for Ross to wait in the SUV.

"It has come to my attention that Mad Mama has a website."

"Oh, I wasn't aware of that," Salvador said, genuinely surprised.

"He's moved onto the dark web, and has a website that was designed by some Asian gal."

Salvador sensed that the conversation had taken a sudden, intense turn. There was a darkened, antagonistic look that came across Copperhead's pockmarked face. The tempo in the Brahms concerto began to build. Still, he kept quiet.

"No one, beats Copperhead. Hellhound is, and always will be, the top number one brand around here."

Copperhead's voice started to rise, as the Brahms concerto could be heard reaching its irrepressible climax. He was angry and visibly shaken.

"Apparently, that Mad Mama smartass did not learn his lesson at the Carter Farm. That *really* pisses me off!"

The look on Copperhead's face intensified.

"It's time that boy gets some religion!"

Salvador did not need any clarification, or further explanation. He clearly understood the task, though Copperhead was not finished.

"You read that article in *The Mountain Holler*?"

"No," Salvador said, shaking his head, with the added admission that he did not subscribe to the newspaper.

"That punk-ass reporter did some snooping, and wrote a story on the Carter Farm."

"What'd he say?"

"I'll tell you what," Copperhead bellowed, as the music concluded with a deafening crescendo, "it's time someone shuts him up!"

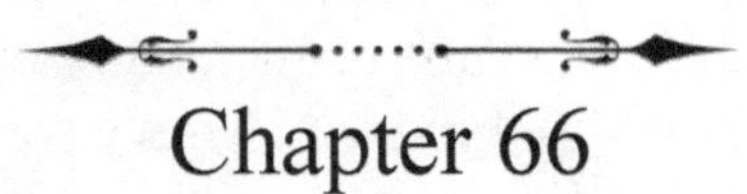

Chapter 66

The steady, fast-paced strumming of the bluegrass guitar, jangly mandolin, and twangy banjo of The Reedy Creek Stringbusters could be heard echoing through the lush, spruce-fir laden Smokey Mountain Forest as Skip and Katie Mae made their way into the Bonner Falls Street Festival. Throngs of people crowded the annual event, as festivalgoers of all ages gathered to celebrate the community's rich Appalachian heritage and enjoy numerous events including food, crafts, and live music.

After the Carter farmhouse news, Mr. Andrews began running advertisements for the annual celebration. He promised the promoters that *The Mountain Holler* would run a follow-up story on the various events, while hoping to attract a surge in vendor advertisements.

Skip did not mind the assignment. He was certain the story would be far more pleasurable than the horrific slayings he had covered at the Carter farmhouse. It was also a chance for Katie Mae to enjoy the colorful pageantry, authentic food offerings, arts and handmade craft displays.

Tom and Tammy tagged along to join in the excitement. Together, they planned an afternoon to stroll the streets, enjoy the food, music, and vendor offerings.

"Boy, isn't this crowd something!" Katie Mae exclaimed as they merged into the crowded cluster of people. "They're packed like sardines!"

"It's a blowout," Skip agreed. "Mr. Andrews is going to be happy."

"Ugh, that poop head," Katie Mae said, wrinkling her nose. "Who cares what Mr. Andrews thinks?"

The music grew louder as the couples strolled leisurely to the end of the street where the Stringbusters were playing. An older man wearing blue jean overalls, a bandana around his neck, and a rustic, floppy formless felt hat was seen giving an exuberant freestyle clogging demonstration, accompanied by the music.

"Boy, look at him go!" Tom said. "Makes me thirsty for a beer."

"Tom! It's Sunday. Where's your manners?" Tammy said, scoldingly. "It's not even noon."

"Well," Tom said sheepishly. "I figured it's noon, somewhere."

Skip laughed as he took a few pictures of the crowed street while the girls were distracted by a cane chair repair demonstration.

"What the hell are they looking at?" Tom asked, as Katie Mae and Tammy joined several ladies watching the demonstration intently. "We don't have any stuff like that around the house."

"Who knows, with those two?" Skip said, shrugging his shoulders. "Better hope they move on, before Tammy takes one home."

The girls continued onto several more booths featuring arts, crafts, and pottery. They were enthralled by the intricate displays of beadwork, quilts, and decorative baskets.

While Katie Mae and Tammy fully immersed themselves shopping for handmade jewelry and scouring each vendor's booth for the perfect souvenirs, Skip and Tom headed to the food court. Among the most popular food stands was a unique, Native American fry bread counter.

"What do have there?" Katie Mae asked as she plopped down on a picnic table's bench, watching Skip and Tom savor their lunch.

"I don't know," Tom said. "But, it's awfully good."

"It's a fry bread taco," Skip offered. "Got all the fixings too. Shredded beef, onions, lettuce, cheddar cheese, sour cream, and jalapenos."

"Jala what?"

"Jalapenos."

"Here," Skip said as he slid her paper plate over to Katie Mae. "Have some."

"Mmmn, that is good!" Katie Mae exclaimed with a mischievous pirate smile. "Skippy? Would you mind?"

Skip saw the request coming. He braced himself for a long, slow-moving line of hungry fry bread enthusiasts.

After lunch, the girls continued to shop. They impulsively bought assorted clothes, jewelry and decorative baskets. Both were particularly enamored with the reasonably priced beaded hand bags they had discovered.

"Whew, me and Tammy sure went to town," Katie Mae said, setting her bags down. "Probably could have bought the place out. Isn't that right, Tam?"

Suddenly, the festival's large mascot came through the crowd in a Bigfoot costume and good-naturedly took pictures with small kids.

The legendary creature had long been rumored to cohabit in the area, but no conclusive evidence had ever been produced.

"That there's what'd you call putting on the dog!" Tom quipped.

Katie Mae smiled weakly, while Skip blew Tom's comment off as his typical unpredictable, capricious humor and reached for his cell phone.

Tammy's jaw dropped with a wide-eyed, exasperated look of amazement.

"Careful, Thomas Thayer," she warned. "You'd better be house trained before you run with that dog!"

Throughout the day, Skip had received messages on his phone. Most were boring, innocuous notifications with an occasional emoji or cliché thought to be clever regarding his recent Carter farmhouse article in *The Mountain Holler*.

The final text came from an anonymous caller. It read, "Stop writing that trash, or it'll bite you in the ass!"

Chapter 67

At Detective Halstead's request, Jo Yarborough conducted an exhaustive search to see if any Suburban's in the area might have been reported stolen. She also checked local traffic violations, misdemeanors, or felonies in hopes of locating the Suburban seen on the trail cam; all without luck.

Jo also contacted local law enforcement agencies in nearby areas and checked with the National Insurance Crime Bureau. Unfortunately, no one was able to provide any assistance.

As a last resort, the detective checked with local garages. He thought the Suburban could have, at some point, been serviced locally, and a mechanic or service manager might be able to recall the vehicle.

As Detective Halstead entered the office at Marsh Auto Center, where Leonard Barlow once worked, he was coolly received by the car lot's manager, Ed Meyers. It was apparent he had worn out his welcome on his previous visit.

"Detective," Meyers said without bothering to rise from his desk. "You buying today, or here to ask questions? If so, I don't have time."

Despite the car lot being totally devoid of any customer activity, the detective smiled dutifully. The manager might have been busy, but car sales were not a factor, including the vacant garage. Still, the detective kept his pose, saying he would only take a "minute."

"Well, good," Meyers said. "Because, a minute's all I've got. Besides, we already talked about Lenny."

Halstead took a moment to gather his thoughts and look around the office. He gathered that the car dealership was not out to win any interior decorating awards.

The furniture appeared to be a collection of second-hand castoffs, while the dealership's faded advertisements on the white-washed walls had long since lost their colorful luster. A dusty bowling trophy lay atop a bookcase, along with some knickknacks and a wall clock that had stopped at 12.37.

"Nice place," the detective politely observed. "Looks like you're ready to sell some cars."

"Yeah, we like it," Meyers said indifferently. "Pays the bills."

There was a loud, almost intrusive squeal that shattered the tense office air as Meyers leaned back in his wooden armed banker's chair. The sound was repeated when Meyers leaned forward, as well.

"Hmmm, that doesn't sound good," Meyers said dismissively. "Chair sounds like she's about to fall apart."

The detective quickly offered that he had a similar situation in his office and suggested using a lubricant like WD-40.

"Good idea," Meyers said. "Now, what can I do for you?"

Detective Halstead nodded in appreciation. He realized Meyers was not going to be an easy interview, and got to the point.

"I'm trying to locate a Suburban," Halstead began. "Is there any chance you might have sold, or serviced one in the recent past?"

"Ha, you've got be kidding," Meyers said with a pointed, sardonic jab. "If you want one of those fancy cars, you'll have to go to Charlotte or Atlanta. There's nothing like that around here."

"What about service?" The detective asked, unmoved. "You ever service one?"

Meyers leaned back with a pensive look on his face. Another squeak screeched from his chair. As he thought, Halstead looked out the dirty louvered windows and saw what appeared to be a mechanic smoking a cigarette outside a garage.

"Let me call Billy Ray," Meyers said. "He might know. Excuse me, while I get the bean counter on the horn."

Amid the muffled conversation, the detective stepped out of the office. He feigned interest in a GMC pickup truck, and wandered near the man smoking a cigarette.

"Nice truck," the detective said, approaching the man. He could see the name Miguel on his grimy, untucked blue shirt, along with the company logo.

"Oh, yes," Miguel agreed. "She's beautiful. She got an 8-speed automatic transmission, a 6.2-liter V-8 engine, and four-wheel drive."

Miguel paused to offer the detective a cigarette and ask, "You like?"

"Absolutely!" the detective said emphatically as he accepted the cigarette.

Although he did not smoke, the detective was not about to miss the opportunity to ask the mechanic some questions.

"Say, you by chance work on Suburban's?"

"Oh, yes," Miguel replied. "I do everything. My uncle, he teach me in Michoacán."

"Mexico, nice," Halstead said thoughtfully. "You ever get any Suburban's in here to work on?"

"Suburban? Hmmm, maybe one time. A guy, he come in mad with a flat tire."

"Oh, really?" The detective said, taking a puff off the cigarette. "What happened to the car?"

"He bent the rim on a rock, an' air was leaking," Miguel said. "I replaced the rim an' air value. Easy."

"How long ago?"

"Oh, I don't know," Miguel said, shrugging his shoulders. "Six, seven months. Maybe more. Long time."

"Did you get the guy's name, or put the VIN number on the bill?"

"Oh, no," Miguel chuckled. "Mr. Ed, he likes cash. No questions."

"Do you, by chance, remember what he looked like?"

"Little guy with dark hair, an' mustache; like this," Miguel put a finger under his nose to simulate a mustache, and laughed.

At that moment, Ed Meyers stepped from the office and called for the detective. Halstead thanked Miguel for his time, tossed his cigarette on the ground, and turned toward Meyers.

"I checked with Billy Ray," Meyers said. "We've never had a Suburban in for service. You need to check somewhere else."

Chapter 68

Candi was enraged when Ross returned home from delivering the box truck; though, he did not care. The freshly earned cash felt good in his pocket. He wasn't about to be brought down by Candi's antagonistic remarks about working with Salvador.

Bills had to be paid. No matter how Candi felt, Ross knew that past-due bills were starting to mount, and her complaints were not paying the rent.

As Ross made his way to the kitchen, he reached for a jar of Hellhound and poured a drink. Moonshine was one of the benefits he got while working with Salvador. Being an avid beer drinker, it was a perk he seldom indulged in, though Candi thoroughly enjoyed.

"So, were you out with that little prick again?" Candi asked as Ross settled into a lounge chair and reached for the TV remote. "I know you weren't playing with yourself in that half-ass deer blind."

"What about it?" he said, flipping through the channels. "Where I've been, isn't your business."

The response was the opening Candi had hoped for. The gauntlet had been thrown. She was in full attack mode, and went after Ross with a ruthless vengeance.

"What? None of my business!" Candi ragged as she seized the TV remote, and threw it across the room. "I'll tell you what, I'm making it my business."

"Go ahead," Ross said, finishing a shot of Hellhound. "See if I care."

"Well, you're going to care when I'm done," Candi raged. "I don't know how many times I've told you to stay away from that little ass."

Ross let out a noticeable sigh, and shook his head. It was the same repetitive argument he had heard before. Without a word, he reached for the jar of Hellhound and poured another drink.

"You know what?" he said. "Get over it."

"Listen, you get over it!" Candi shot back. "How many times have I told you to call Mr. Cunningham at Sweet James to get your job back? Oh no. You've got to piddle around with that batshit friend of yours."

Ross took a sip of Hellhound, and let out a slight, choking gasp. The moonshine felt like hot lava running down his throat. After swallowing, he ran his tongue across his lips while contemplating his response.

"Listen, thanks to that 'batshit friend,' we got a free trip to Myrtle Beach. And you seem to forget that if you hadn't of spent all our money gambling, we wouldn't be in this mess."

Candi's mouth dropped in shock. She theatrically threw her hands in the air to emphasize her point.

"So, now it's my fault? You're telling me it's my fault? You're the lazy ass who doesn't do anything except sit around drinking that cheap ass bootleg shit, who gives out those crappy dog whistles."

A smirk came across Ross' face as he took another sip of Hellhound. He was struck by the irony of the situation. Candi had no problem spending whatever money he brought home on drugs and alcohol, yet, had the audacity to call him a "lazy ass."

"Well, at least that 'cheap ass bootleg shit' helps to pay the bills."

"So, you're telling me, that because you can pay the bills with the shit your friend does to rip people off, it's okay?"

"I didn't say that."

"Well, what did you say?" Candi asked in a challenging, provocative tone. "If you weren't three sheets to the wind, we could have a decent talk."

Ross was exhausted. He was tired of Candi's criticism, which was intentionally demoralizing and degrading. He defiantly poured another drink.

Candi was worn out, as well. She left the room, which gave Ross a brief respite, only to return moments later with another flurry of hostile accusations.

"You know, I ought to tell Sheriff Max about that batshit friend of yours," Candi said brashly. "I'll bet he'd like to get him to the station. That little shit would be sweating like a sinner in church."

"You better not start any games," Ross warned. "Salvador doesn't fool around. He plays for keeps."

Chapter 69

Once the Mad Mama website was ready to launch, Jack was eager to get back into business. He wanted Mad Mama to grow on a scale never seen before. To help move product, he hired another mule named Jeff Hargrave.

Unlike his previous mules, Jeff was born and raised in the Appalachian Mountains. He was a tall, lanky, easygoing individual in his mid-30's who styled his dark, thick hair much like Elvis Presley's famed pompadour.

Although Jeff struggled in high school with grades and attendance, he completed his GED certificate in hopes of enlisting in the Army. Unfortunately, he found the Army's disciplinary requirements too harsh, and restrictive. Instead, he decided against the move, and bounced around in various nondescript warehouse jobs doing remedial work.

As Jack introduced Jeff to the Mad Mama team, he walked him through his daily tasks, which included maintaining the newly implemented database. He would be responsible for managing inventory levels, processing orders, and coordinating shipments.

On occasion, he would make a delivery, though, Jack was hoping to convert most of the Mad Mama's business to online sales, despite some holdouts who did not have access to a computer. Ultimately, Mad Mama would become a covert organization, operating with the utmost secrecy.

Jeff clicked immediately. He was ready to roll up his sleeves and go to work. He was impressed with the Mad Mama team, the company's organization, and the product.

To further distance himself from any unwelcome suspicion, Jack chose several mail station companies miles away from the distillery to ship Mad Mama using a fictious company name minimizing the organization's exposure.

Jeff's first task was to learn how to operate the computer software that Mei Wang had set up, which proved to be a challenge. Jeff had never learned to type, and was reduced to a hunt and peck method;

which, was painfully slow and time-consuming. Nevertheless, Mei made sure he understood the software, how to process orders, operate email and use the company's burner phone.

"So, what do you think?" Jack asked Jeff after walking him through his upcoming assignments.

"It's all good," Jeff said enthusiastically. "It's been sometime, since I worked one of these computer gizmos, but I'll get it."

"Well, if you need help, call Mei," Jack said. "She can walk you through any issues."

Jack walked Jeff to the distillery for a brief tour. He invited him to sit outside under a maple tree with a jar of Mad Mama for a private conversation.

"You know, there's one more thing I need to run by you," Jack said, opening a jar of Mad Mama. "And it's kind of important."

Jeff followed Jack's lead, and opened the jar he had been given. The moonshine was clear with no sediment, or impurities. Jeff could tell by taste, color, and smell that Mad Mama was distilled of the highest quality.

Under the maple tree's lush, canopy shade, Jack tapped Jeff's jar with a healthy "cheers," and took a sip of Mad Mama. As Jeff followed suit, he let out a slight gasp. The liquid was pure, with no harsh aftertaste.

"Whoa," Jeff said, with a slight cough. "That's good."

"We run between 80 to 100 proof," Jack said proudly. "Latch has a hydrometer to measure the liquid's temperature, and samples each batch as he goes along."

Jack took another sip, and looked at the maple tree's majestic leaves. Jeff also admired the tree, as he licked his lips, with an occasional nod of appreciation at the enjoyment of a good, satisfying drink.

"Once she's ready, Latch bottles and stores each batch in a well-ventilated, dark area," Jack said. "That's what sets us apart from other brands. We don't rush the process, like Hellhound."

"Hellhound?"

"Yeah, Hellhound," Jack said. "They're a pain in the ass. You'll want to avoid them as much as possible."

Jack paused to swirl his jar of Mad Mama, as Jeff listened intently.

"See, neither of us have a Federal Distilled Spirits Permit," he said. "I'm working on the paperwork, but there's a lot of red tape in getting a license from the Alcohol and Tobacco, Tax and Trade Bureau."

"So, where's Hellhound come in?"

"Hellhound's run off everyone except us," Jack said, shaking his head. "We've also dodged the law, as well."

"Okay," Jeff said cautiously. "Where do I come in?"

"Everything you do is confidential," Jack warned. "Keep to yourself. Don't tell a soul. If anyone asks where you work, tell them Hines Distribution, or make up someplace like that. Don't breathe a word about Mad Mama."

Jack took a final sip of Mad Mama, coughed, and leaned back with a deep sigh. A gentle breeze rustled through the leaves of the maple tree, as wisps of sunlight playfully filtered to the ground.

"That tree's been growing a long time," Jack noted. "Hope we can grow like her."

Chapter 70

A fine, early morning mist that had settled over Lake Boswell. The eerie scene could have easily been taken from a B-rated horror movie. It would be hours before the fog would lift, but neither Milt nor Wendall cared. They had planned a day of fun and relaxation on the lake in a small aluminum boat that Milt kept stored at Highland Ranch.

As the boat's electric trolling motor puttered along, both men kept a keen eye for any zealous fish that might have broken the placid water's surface for a careless frog or insect. It was like a cruel game of hide and seek, where there were no rules or boundaries. The fish seemingly jumped at will, taunting the fishermen audaciously.

Milt's first move was to take the boat along a shallow grass bank where predatory bass were known to hide in the aquatic vegetation. The bass would ambush baitfish using stealth-like tactics, and proved to be the perfect place for an angler's weedless plastic worm or spinner bait lure.

"What have you got on that line?" Milt asked as the boat inched near the weed bed.

"Hmmm, going with a chartreuse spinner, safety-pin and skirt," Wendall said cheerfully. "Those big boys like chasing the skirts."

"Could work, but you can't go wrong with a worm twister," Milt said thoughtfully. "They're tried and true!"

Wendall flipped his line inches from the weed bed. He let the lure sink a couple feet before playfully jerking back on the line.

"Guess I'd better warm up the net," Wendall said mischievously while moving the lure with an enticing, wobbling motion. "Hope your guys remembered to put one in the boat."

Milt smiled as he tossed his twister several yards from the boat and began reeling slowly.

"I don't know," Milt groaned. "After Leroy's last escapade, I'm ready to throw the net over him."

"That so?"

"We sent him to Tolbert's, but he got lost somewhere. Lord only knows what goes through his head at times. Anyway, we called Jeremy at the feed store, but he hadn't seen him. He flew the coop!"

Milt kept reeling, then stopped to give his line a tug. His line tightened as he pulled hard.

"Got something?"

"Naw, it's a snag. Damn."

Milt moved the boat over the weeded area where his lure was stuck. He gently pulled on the line. He slowly worked the lure loose from the weeds and reeled in.

"Well, I could probably use that net on Harold," Wendall said, tossing his lure several feet from the boat. "He missed a couple days work awhile back. Connie and me went crazy covering his shift."

"Hmmm," Milt nodded, dropping his newly freed lure into the water. "These fish are driving me crazy; let's move."

Both Milt and Wendall reeled in their lines. The sun had burned off the morning fog, and the fish were no longer jumping on the water's surface. It was time to move to a deeper location.

As the boat glided into a quiet cove, the pair rummaged through their tackle boxes to switch lures.

"Alright, let's show them who's the boss," Wendall said with an upbeat cast. "I'm going to throw a deep diving shad at them."

"Crankbait?" Milt questioned. "You might get some action off the bottom. I'm dropping my line midway with a jerk bait."

Although the fish were not biting, neither Milt nor Wendall were bothered. The day had blossomed into a warm, sunny day. The sweet-smelling pines that surrounded the lake, interspersed with hardwood forest maple trees and chirping birds, made the day rewarding enough.

"Say, whatever happened to the Gap Runners?" Milt asked. "How'd they do after you and Darci held that fundraiser?"

"I believe they got an award in the junior traditional line category in Gatlinburg," Wendall said. "I have been meaning to get with Billy Jo and Edward to see how Mary Beth and the gals made out."

"Aw, good kids," Milt said, bringing in his line. "Thought the Stringbusters was running hot that day too."

"Yeah, they were; wide open!" Wendall agreed as he jerked his line. "Opp, thought I had a hit."

Wendall reeled in his line, checked the lure, and tossed it out for another drag across the lake's deep bottom.

"Did you happen to read that *Mountain Holler* story about the Carter farmhouse?" Wendall asked. "Man, those bootleggers are scary."

"Yeah, they are," Milt said. "Fish seem to be running scared too. Sheriff must have showed them the article?"

"Maybe," Wendall said, reeling in for another cast. "In that case, Sheriff Max ought to come out, and set them straight. My butt's getting sore sitting here."

"Well, that's not going to happen," Milt said dryly. "I believe Max has got bigger fish to fry."

Chapter 71

Skip's cell phone began to beep as he and his Uncle Em settled down for the evening news. Their usual routine was to have a light dinner that Uncle Em had made or something Skip brought home, set their TV trays in the living room, and watch the evening news. Fred would usually sit between the two, hoping for a treat or food scape.

At first, his uncle was mildly annoyed. He pretended not to hear the phone and turned up the television's volume. The strategy worked until another call came through, followed by another.

Uncle Em's eyes grew wide, and jaw dropped. He began to grow exasperated. After a text message beep, he turned to Skip with an incredulous look. Skip could feel a profane-laced tsunami about to be unleashed, and reached for his phone.

"Would you shut that damn thing off?" Uncle Em said angrily. "Can't we have a little peace and quiet during the news?"

Skip nodded, though found the comment ironic. His Uncle Em rarely watched the news without making an obscene or politically incorrect comment, but that was his uncle's way of decompressing from the day.

It was during a commercial break that Uncle Em wanted to know why Skip was getting so many calls and text messages.

"Okay, what's the story?" Uncle Em asked. "You're either a pimp, or Katie Mae is pissed off at something you've done. What is it?"

Skip shook his head with a slight smirk. As usual, Uncle Em was direct, blunt, and to the point.

"Remember that *Mountain Holler* story I wrote about the Carter farmhouse?"

"Yeah, what about it? I doubt you'll win a Pulitzer Prize, but go on." "Well," Skip said, overlooking the snide remark, then pausing to carefully consider his words. "I've been getting hassled."

"Hassled?" Uncle Em said, with a surprised look. "Like, what kind of hassle?"

Skip's mouth tightened cheeks rose and eyes narrowed. He grew tense and hesitant for fear of upsetting his uncle, though the truth would come out sooner or later.

"Threats," Skip said quietly. "All kinds of threats."

"How bad?" Uncle Em asked, shutting off the television. "And why didn't you say something before now?"

Skip shrugged his shoulders. He started to explain that he did not want to upset his uncle, but Uncle Em cut him off.

"Listen, no SOB is going threaten my nephew!" Uncle Em bellowed. "Tell you what, I'll kick is ass!"

As Uncle Em cooled down, Skip explained that the harassment was coming from an unknown source who told him not to write anymore articles about the Carter farmhouse murders. There would be serious consequences, if he did not stop.

"Fine," Uncle Em said defiantly. "Tell fat ass to get some other pansy to write their own bullshit. You don't need the aggravation. Besides, what he's paying doesn't amount to a hill of beans!"

"Mr. Andrews told me not to worry, and that stuff like that happens all the time," Skip said. "Besides, he's from Newark. He says reporters up that way go through worse."

Uncle Em was seething with anger. His eyes widened, and mouth fell open in disbelief.

"Jersey? Those boys used to come down to Daytona and get their asses handed to them in the biker bars," Uncle Em said, while pausing to relish the memory. "Even the Wolverine could kick ass on those pantywaist wimps!"

Skip shook his head. He had heard his uncle's imaginative war stories before; but was not about to interrupt. His uncle's ranting would usually stop after he felt justified in making his point.

"So, how'd you leave it with fat ass?" Uncle Em asked. "Did you tell him you're off the story?"

"Not exactly," Skip said. "In fact, I had a phone interview with Sheriff Porter, who gave me an update about the investigation."

Uncle Em reached down to gently pat Fred, who had been lying between the two the entire time.

"Hump. So, tell fat ass to go pound sand and get out of this mess," Uncle Em said belligerently, waving his hand. "I'm about ready to throw that damn phone in the creek."

Skip looked down at his powerless phone and winced. "Well, I wish I could," he stammered. "But story's been filed."

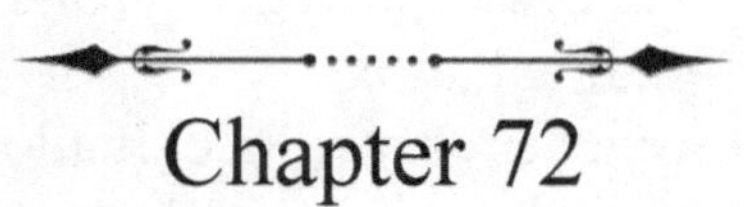

Chapter 72

The usual luncheon crowd had nearly faded at The Red Maple when Candi O'Neil walked into the diner. Her steps were slow and deliberate as she made her way to the diner's counter.

As Connie immediately came over to greet her. She noticed Candi's thin, pale face had broken out with a mass of acne blemishes. Dark circles had formed under her eyes. Her clothes seemed to hang on her emancipated, skeletal frame, while she picked uncontrollably at her arms and disheveled hair.

"Hey there, Candi O!" Connie said, with a warm, amicable smile. "Where ya been hidin' girl?"

"Oh, I been out, and about," Candi said in a slow, rasping voice. "Me and Ross went to Myrtle Beach awhile back, which was nice for change."

"Myrtle Beach!" Connie exclaimed. "That musta been a hoot!"

Upon hearing Myrtle Beach, Harold poked his head through the diner's order window. He was curious to hear what the excitement was about.

"Whattaya think, Harold?" Connie laughed. "Myrtle Beach! Ain't that sump'n?"

"What?" Harold cracked. "That place ain't fit for a hog!"

"Guess he ain't a fan," Connie said, turning to Candi. "Oh, well. Can't win 'em all. 'Sides, that's his favorite sayin' on thangs he don't like."

Connie squirted the counter with her disinfectant spray bottle, and tossed a damp towel down. "Lemme see, the last time I saw you, you were havin' sex on the beach. Still into that?"

"That sounds good," Candi said, "but I'll have a sweet tea."

"You got it!" Connie said enthusiastically, as she finished wiping the counter clean and turned away.

Candi looked around the diner. She did not recognize anyone, which was a great relief. In her troubled mind, she was not in the mood to socialize and wanted time alone.

Money had always been an issue with Ross. There was never enough. They always had to scrape to get by, and his association with Salvador was a never-ending battle.

Drugs and alcohol were her only refuge. It allowed her to get away from the harsh realities that the couple confronted every day. Unfortunately, when those outlets dried up, things got bad.

"Here you go," Connie said, setting the sweet tea on the counter. "Opp, lemme get you some Chex Mix. I'll be right back."

For a moment, Candi turned back the clock and thought of herself as a little girl growing up in Port Arthur, Texas. She loved tagging along with her father, as he would fish on Sabine Lake. She would often help net the fish he caught.

It wasn't until Candi met a young man named Troy O'Neil that she fell in love and married the future Marine, who relocated to Camp Lejeune, North Carolina. The marriage deteriorated after Troy's bad conduct military discharge. Things worsened, as his roving eye could not be contained and he became romantically involved with another woman. Candi was soon abandoned, and left to fend for herself.

When Connie returned, she set a bowl of nachos and two plates with napkins in front of Candi, who had snapped back to reality. As Candi began to refuse the order, Connie plopped down in the seat next to her with a glass of sweet tea.

"I got Harold to whip up sump'n for my break," she said. "Things is slow 'nuff, an' I wanna get off my feet. 'Sides, we're goin' uptown with these nachos! They got jalapenos, guacamole, an' ev'rythin'! An', I gotcha an extra plate, so's you can get you some. Dig in girl!"

Candi scratched the scab on her arm, and nodded with an appreciative smile. Her chipped teeth revealed a history of poor dental hygiene, and severe tooth decay.

"So, you still workin'?" Connie asked, munching on a chip. "Last time we talked, you was doin' sump'n at the school? Whew, jalapenos are hot."

"No, that wasn't me," Candi said. "I work for Airbnb when the tourist season hits."

"Tourist season," Connie grumbled, taking a bite of the warm, melted cheese on a tortilla chip. "The tips are nice when they come through, but don't remind me. Those folks'll make you work yore ass off."

"Opp, I got guacamole on my nose!"

With a giggle and quick swipe of a napkin, Connie dipped her head and wiped her nose. The silliness of the situation brought a laugh from both ladies.

"Listen, I have to go," Candi said. "But there's something I want to give you."

Candi reached in her purse, and handed Connie a sealed envelope addressed to her attention. She took a final sip of sweet tea, scratched her arm and said ominously, "Don't open this, unless something should happen to me."

Chapter 73

Once Mad Mama was up and running on the internet, Mei Wang felt confident she could take on other assignments that did not conflict with her current schedule. Since going online, Mad Mama had been a tremendous success. Orders were pouring in. Both Latch and the newly hired Jeff Hargrave were inundated with production and fulfilling work orders.

Jack Fuller was thrilled. Thanks to Mei's savvy web design, ordering Mad Mama had never been easier. Her simple, user-friendly menu with appeasing graphics and descriptions of Mad Mama's various newly introduced flavors made the moonshine more popular than ever. Money poured in through the P2P cryptocurrency transaction exchange program.

It had taken time for Jack to come around to accepting cryptocurrency, but he soon became a believer. Once he saw the volume of money flowing into the company's bank account, Jack was ready to expand the business to even greater heights.

Since Mad Mama only needed Mei on a sporadic, intermittent basis when there was a need to check the maintenance of the computer network system or install a new program, she began to seek other opportunities to keep her busy. As a result, she began an ambitious search online, while researching potential companies that might need IT assistance. Oddly enough, it was a blind ad in *The Mountain Holler* that came to her attention.

Blind ads were something that Mei tended to avoid, though the ad was simple and straightforward. The headline stated, *Software Engineer Wanted*. Nothing fancy or slick, but simple and straightforward, which appealed to her.

The ideal candidate needed a strong background using an e-commerce platform and the ability to collaborate with the company's marketing and operations departments. Above all, the individual needed to be a team player, capable of handling multiple tasks.

Mei was further intrigued when she learned the job's location was local, offering flexible hours, benefits, and an excellent salary. After careful consideration, she decided it was worth the risk to respond to the ad, despite knowing little about the company.

Several days passed before she got a response to her resume. A recruiter named John McCaskey with Barker Staffing Solutions called. The message on her voicemail said he had a client who was interested in her services. He left his name and number, and asked if she would be able to meet for an interview.

Mei was skeptical. She could not find any record of Barker Staffing Solutions or John McCaskey. A deep search on the internet turned up nothing. There was no company business license, or record of the recruiter's permit. Still, she thought the agency might be working on an undercover freelance basis without revealing the hiring company's identity.

Several scenarios went through Mei's mind as she tried to reason why the recruiting company might be operating under such secrecy. Perhaps the company wanted to keep the position confidential, and not let the employer's competitors know it was searching for a critical position.

Another factor might be that the employer was seeking a candidate who was truly interested in the job, rather than a money grab. Mei was hopeful that if the interview went well, the recruiter would let her know more about the organization for research purposes.

Lastly, the advertisement could be a cloak-and-dagger move on the company's part. An underperforming individual within the organization might be getting replaced without their knowledge. A blind ad would be a way to hide their covert intention.

Whatever the case may be, Mei decided answering the blind ad was worth the risk. She believed she checked all the boxes for the job requirements and was the perfect candidate for the position. Besides, she could always reject the offer, if it was not to her liking.

Without giving the matter any further thought, Mei agreed to meet with the recruiter, and set an appointment.

Chapter 74

Detective Halstead continued to pour over the trail cam video of the black Suburban, while sipping Jo Yarborough's coffee at his desk. He starred at every detail of the video, trying to cull whatever evidence could be found.

After drawing continual blanks, he began scouring local business establishments in the area, hoping someone might have seen the vehicle or had video documentation. He even contacted neighboring law enforcement agencies in neighboring counties, hoping someone, somewhere might have seen, or heard something that could positively identify the individual.

As the detective fidgeted with the black aluminum dog whistle that Skip had left to examine, he thought about his meeting with Miguel at Marsh Auto Center, and the company's reluctance to provide any information. If he could refresh Miguel's memory with a follow-up interview, he might have a lead that could help solve the case.

Upon his return to Marsh Auto Center, Ed Meyers stood, arms folded in the doorway, at the top of his office stairs. As expected, the car lot's sales manager was not pleased to see the detective pull into the parking lot.

"Detective," Meyer's said in an unpleasant, listless, plaintiff voice. "Can I help you, sir?"

"Maybe," Halstead responded with a hopeful smile. "I'd like to talk to that young fellow Miguel, if he's around."

Meyers shook his head, and stepped down the creaky, wooden stairs. On reaching the bottom step, he stopped to lean against the rail.

"That makes two of us."

"Sorry?"

"I said," Meyers said with a disdainful look, "that makes two of us."

The detective looked baffled, but kept his poise. He did not want to jeopardize losing the opportunity to meet with Miguel, and apologized for any misunderstanding.

"Okay, I'm sorry," Halstead said softly. "I don't follow."

"No, I suppose you wouldn't," Meyers spat out.

Meyers walked over to the detective's car, and leaned against the rear door.

"After you left the other day, he took off!" Meyers said. "We haven't seen him since!"

An astonished look of shock and disbelief came across Halstead's face.

"You're kidding," the detective murmured. "Any idea where he got off to?"

Meyers was ready to unleash his pent-up hostility. He was seething with uncontrollable rage, and unchecked fury at losing an employee. The loss had cost the company money, which he blamed on a nosey detective.

"You tell me," Meyers began. "What did you'd do? Threaten to deport the guy? I swear he had a Green Card. The guy was legal. We never had any problems with him, even when Lenny was working here; if you can call it that."

Meyers stepped away from the detective's cruiser, and spit on the ground.

"Mikey was always here, never late or did anything wrong," Meyers paused to catch his breath. "Then, you come along."

Both men stood silently. A light breeze caught the faded polyethene pennants that were strung over the car lot. They fluttered with synchronized precision, as the cars seemed frozen in place, including the older GMC Sierra, which had not moved since the detective's previous visit.

"Miguel told me he once serviced a Suburban," Halstead pressed. "I'd really like to know who owned the vehicle."

Meyers mouth tightened as his eyes bulged.

"I wouldn't be so sure about that," Meyers said. "English wasn't Mikey's first language. He was from Mexico, you know."

"Yes, I know," Halstead acknowledged. "He said his uncle trained him as a mechanic."

An incredulous, dumbfounded look overtook Meyers' face.

"Say, what? He told you that?" Meyers said indignantly. "What the hell's he talking about? We trained him here at Marsh Auto. Everything he learned was right here."

The detective nodded. He decided to try a softer approach.

"Any idea where he lives?" Halstead asked. "Or, what about a phone number?"

"Right," Meyers scoffed. "He never called, so I doubt he knew how to use a phone. Billy Ray pulled his paperwork. You know, the application when he applied."

"Really?" Halstead asked, growing excited. "Can I see it?"

"Bogus, bullshit!" Meyers threw up his hands as he turned to walk back into the office. "The whole thing was a damn lie. We don't know where the hell he lived."

The detective followed him into the tired, unkept office. He knew time was running out, but hoped he might gain even a shred of evidence to help his investigation.

"Out of curiosity, have any other mechanics seen a black Suburban in the garage?" Halstead asked.

"No, sir," Meyers said, sternly shuffling some papers on his desk. "Now, if you don't mind, I'd like to get back to work.

Detective Halstead thanked Ed Meyers for his time, and left his card in case he might be able to offer any additional information. As he turned to the door, he noticed a rack of keys that hung on the wall. Among them, was a black aluminum dog whistle keyring.

Chapter 75

It was not unusual for the Wedgefield Heights estate near the Firestone Reservoir to order several cases of Mad Mama on a single order. In fact, as one of Jack Fuller's longtime preferred customers, it was a common occurrence.

The estate's wealthy owner's parties were legendary for their excessive indulgence and rumored debauchery. No expense was spared. It was the ultimate adult entertainment fun zone for those who had the good fortune to have been invited.

Liberal alcohol consumption, as well as food and music, was among the key ingredients for making the parties a success. It was the estate's on-site bartender Ace's task to ensure that the bar was well stocked for any planned event.

Despite his dislike of Mad Mama, Ace would typically order four to five cases of moonshine to have enough on hand, and quench everyone's thirst. It was a party favorite, though Ace preferred Hellhound.

When the order came through Mad Mama's website, Jeff Hargrave was overjoyed. Sales had gone so well that Jack had started giving the entire Mad Mama sales team a commission. Dollar signs literally lit up Jeff's eyes, as he starred at the computer screen, though, Jack was not as enthused.

The mere mention of the Wedgefield Heights brought back disturbing memories of Ricky Ehlers disappearance, which he still had not resolved. He was unsure if Ricky's raucous braggadocio had gotten him into trouble, or if a more sinister, evil fate had befallen upon him. Either way, he viewed the order with skepticism.

Mei was more direct. She had been in the office to analyze Mad Mama's program needs, and run software tests to upgrade the system. As part of her normal duties, she monitored and maintained the software to ensure there were no glitches, or virus hacks on a regular basis.

During a software update, Mei spotted the Wedgefield Heights order. The order was large enough to require a bill of lading, which meant an additional freight charges. Since going online, Mad Mama had established set shipping rates through the off-site mail stations. Mei warned that the shipping expense would be substantial, should Jack accept the order.

Jack wrestled with the option of sending Jeff Hargrave to hand-deliver the Wedgefield Heights order, as a cost cutting measure. Although Jeff had proven to be reliable, Jack did not want to take any unnecessary risks. Besides, he had grown comfortable with Mad Mama's mail order system. He enjoyed the internet's anonymity, and the safeguards that Mei had built into the system. Still, the lure of having such a large order was hard to resist.

After giving the matter some thought, Jack approached Jeff to get his thoughts on making the delivery to the Wedgefield Heights estate. It would be a quick, routine trip to drop off the product, and return to Mad Mama's headquarters. Since the order would be prepaid, there would be no money exchanged.

Jeff was ecstatic. He was gung-ho on handling the shipment. He assured Jack that he knew the directions to the Firestone Reservoir, and could easily make the run; which, was music to Ace's ears.

Once Ace received confirmation that the moonshine was being delivered, he placed a call to Corny. He knew Copperhead had grown frustrated at being unable to stop the onslaught of Mad Mama's growing popularity. Thanks to the internet, sales had quadrupled, and continued to increase at an unimaginable rate, while orders for Hellhound had fallen substantially.

Corny knew Copperhead would be delighted to know Mad Mama had made a mistake, and finally been exposed. He quickly relayed the message to his ominous, inauspicious boss, before returning Ace's call.

"Hey, Ace thanks for the heads up," Corny said appreciatively. "The news will make alotta people happy around here."

"Good," Ace replied. "Thought it might brighten your day."

"You'll let us know on the time an' date?"

"Yeah, absolutely," Ace said. "We'll get you fixed up."

Corny paused for a moment to clear his throat. There was still one final piece of business he needed to finish.

"I assume you'd like yore usual fee?" he asked nonchalantly.

"Cash," Ace shot back. "Cash'll work."

"Okay, you got it!" Corny said confirming the request. "Get out yore wheelbarra."

Chapter 76

For several days, Salvador tried to reach Ross by phone. In the past, Ross had always been easy to reach. Even text messages, or voice mail were never an issue. For some unknown reason, he was unable to get through on the phone.

When Salvador was finally able to reach Ross, he learned that none of his messages had been received. The phone was on the entire time, and Salvador's number was not blocked, which seemed strange.

Salvador suspected the phone was either disabled due to a technical issue, or Candi might have had access; though, he did not want to cast aspersions. He would deal with that matter later. He had several pending jobs that needed immediate attention.

Ross was nearly broke, as usual. Candi had gone through what little money they had on a drug and alcohol binge. He was desperate for work and scoured the online employment ads through a phone app without success. Aside from a few temporary day labor opportunities, his prospects were bleak.

"Ross, my man!" Salvador began in his charming, rhetorical salesmanship pitch-style voice. "Have I got a deal for you!"

"Okay," Ross slowly replied, somewhat skeptical. He was well aware that Salvador's idea of a "deal," was much different than his, but was willing to listen.

Salvador began by telling Ross he had an opportunity that could potentially be the "easiest" money he ever made. The task was to take a truck to an assigned location for a pickup, then make a delivery.

"What kind of delivery?" Ross asked cautiously. "This isn't something that's going to cause trouble, is it?"

"Oh, no, no, no," Salvador said reassuringly. "This is a simple one-stop pick up and deliver job. Clean as a whistle."

Memories of the Carter farmhouse crept into Ross' mind. Although he had not been implicated in any crime, he was fearful of being accused of any wrongdoing.

"Are you sure?" Ross probed, while lighting a cigarette. "I don't want to get caught doing something I shouldn't be doing."

"No, you're good," Salvador quickly replied. "I guarantee you don't have a thing to worry about."

Ross considered his financial situation. He thought about Candi's drain on their money and the mounting bills that had gone unpaid, took a puff from his cigarette and blew a smoke ring.

"Okay," Ross said wearily. "How much does it pay?"

"Five bills!" Salvador exclaimed. "That's five of the easiest bills you're ever going to make!"

"That's it? Any chance for a little more?"

"Aw, come on Ross," Salvador said in a soothing, sympathetic voice. "You know I always take care of you. Besides, I gave you and Candi that nice trip."

Ross agreed the trip was enjoyable, as he took a final drag from his cigarette and crushed it into an ashtray. He was also aware that memories do not pay the bills, and kept pressing.

"Listen, I'll tell you what," Salvador said. "I have a few things coming where I'll need your help. In fact, I'll double your money, if you'll do this favor to help me out."

There was a pause on the phone until Ross reluctantly agreed. He found it strange that Salvador was asking him for a favor, but accepted the fact as an appreciative form of recognition. The job's time and place would be given to him later.

As he got off the phone, Ross fished his pocket for a cigarette and lighter. Across the room, he noticed Candi was sprawled out on the sofa with her glass pipe, and drug-related paraphilia on the coffee table.

"Sounds like you were on the phone to that batshit friend of yours," Candi said scornfully, slurring her words. "Wish he'd flush himself down the commode."

"You best keep wishing," Ross shot back, while lighting a cigarette. "Because, right now, wishful thinking is about all you got."

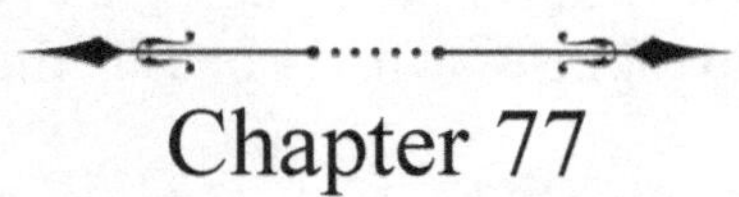

Chapter 77

It had been a long, slow day when Skip picked Katie Mae up at work early before the Two Sisters shop was ready to close. Oddly enough, the owners, Victoria and Veronica, didn't seem to mind. At times, they treated the second-hand consignment store as a hobby, and spent a liberal amount of time socializing as well as gossiping with the customers.

Katie Mae had called Skip, because she felt he needed a break from the long hours he had been spending on the ghastly Carter farmhouse slayings follow-up stories. She thought an evening of fun at The Red Maple with her friends Tom and Tammy would get Skip out of his *Mountain Holler* funk.

"Hey guys!" Connie said cheerfully as Skip and Katie Mae entered The Red Maple. "Nice to see y'all! Grab yerself a seat, an' I'll be right with you!"

Being a Friday night, the ever-popular watering hole was bustling with activity. People were either lined, or seated on a stool at the bar's counter, talking loudly over the music, while some were absorbed playing pool or watching a Charlotte Hornets basketball game. Nearly all the tables, and booths were taken. The ambiance was chaotic, exhilarating and electrifying.

It wasn't long before Tammy came weaving her way through the crowded bar, with Tom trailing close behind. They had planned on arriving sooner, but Tom worked late.

"Hey, there!" Tammy exclaimed. "How we doing tonight? Looks like things are running wide open! Isn't that right, Tom?"

Tom nodded sheepishly, as they took a seat at the table. Moments later, Connie came over with a basket of Chex Mix and took drink orders.

"Say," Katie Mae said turning to Tammy. "I got to run to the little girls' room, before I bust."

"Me too," Tammy said rising from the table. "Let's go."

Both Skip and Tom looked at each other slightly amused. The move seemed to have been a perfectly executed maneuver that would have met the approval of any battle tested gossip monger.

"You know, why is it they always have to go to the bathroom together?" Tom asked. "I never could figure that out."

"Me neither," Skip sighed. "That's one of the great mysteries of life."

There was a sudden cackling hum over the loud speaker as the Stringbusters were preparing to take the stage. Wendall would often bring the local group in on a Friday, or Saturday night as a promotion to boast food and drink sales.

"Speaking about getting lost, what'd you think about that kid at Marsh Auto?" Tom asked, reaching for the Chex Mix.

"What kid?" Skip said, shaking his head. "What are you talking about?"

"Me and Gus were cutting a tree full of carpenter ants at Buzz Wells place," Tom said. "Man, those ants were everywhere. Anyway, Gus got to talking with Buzz, and he told him that some Hispanic kid that works for Eddie Meyers disappeared."

Tom was still chuckling about the ants and pretended to brush them off his arms, as Connie arrived to lay the cocktail napkins and drinks on the table. She checked the Chex Mix basket, and was off to service another table.

"Disappeared?" Skip questioned. "No one disappears."

"No, I reckon not," Tom said, "but the sheriff's looked all over hell's half acre, and come up with nothing. That guy is plumb gone."

"Huh, maybe he quit without telling anyone," Skip said thoughtfully. "I have seen guys walk off a job before. It's not a big deal."

Tom took a sip of his drink. He smacked his lips, and dipped his hand into the Chex Mix.

"I'd agree with you," Tom said, munching a pretzel. "Only, Buzz was saying they don't have any records on him, and the sheriff thinks he might have known about some illegal, funny stuff that was going on."

Upon hearing the comment, Skip's *Mountain Holler* antenna went up. He could smell a potential news story and wanted to hear more, but before he had a chance to fully digest the conversation, the girls came back to the table giggling uncontrollably. It was almost as though they were sworn to secrecy over some clandestine pact.

"About time you guys come back!" Tom boomed. "I thought the parking meter on that commode would never run out!"

Chapter 78

Mei's meeting with John McCaskey for the software engineer opportunity was scheduled for early evening in a nondescript, weathered brick office building on the east side of Bonner Falls. Mei thought it was odd that the meeting was not scheduled earlier, but McCaskey apologized, explaining he had a previous engagement that had taken precedence.

McCaskey assured Mei that his client was impressed with her credentials and anxious for her to meet with him to further assess her professional skills and expertise. He also passed along several complementary accolades, which she found delightfully flattering and further emphasized that the job she was applying for, could be the opportunity of a lifetime!

As Mei arrived at the designated address, she found a building that was cold, dark, and devoid of any personality. There were a few cars in the parking lot, including a box truck, which she assumed was owned by late night workers. Aside from a property management's company sign advertising office space for lease, there was no name or definitive organizational logo identifying the building.

Mei entered the building to find a crude, handwritten sign that directed her to Barker Staffing Solutions at the back of the long, dimly lit hall toward the rear of the building. Mei was seized with an apprehensive twinge, but she determinedly pressed ahead with the confidence that she had the qualifications necessary for the software engineering opportunity.

Upon reaching the Barker Staffing Solutions office door, she found a computer-generated sign that had been taped to the door. She opened the door to find an amiable, heavy-set, balding, unshaven middle-aged man in glasses with a high-pitched, almost girlish-sounding voice.

"Ah, Miss Wang," McCaskey said extending his hand, as Mei entered the office. "Please have a seat."

Mei took a moment to examine the small office's drab appearance. The interior was woefully outdated in dire need of being remodeled.

The desk and chairs were shabby, the indoor/outdoor carpet was threadbare with soiled stains, and the monochrome walls in need of paint.

Aside from a faded Hawaiian vacation poster, which seemed oddly out-of-place, there was no indication that the office had the slightest association with a staffing agency. Still, Mei soldiered on.

McCaskey opened the interview with the usual questions about Mei's background, and how she found out about the job. Standard protocol for any human resources interview. He asked why she wanted the job, and discussed her strengths and weaknesses.

Mei seamlessly answered the questions as the conversation honed in on her online digital store expertise. McCaskey was notably impressed with her vast experience concerning her past collaboration efforts with product development, creative design, and marketing teams for the implementation of new website features, enhancements, and pop-up updates to improve sales.

Once the interview moved into the technical aspects of computer science and electronic engineering, Mei became suspicious. McCaskey seemed unfamiliar with front-end and back-end program technologies. He struggled to comprehend her explanation of computer applications, and how they interact with programable languages, frameworks, and tools for servers and databases.

"Okay," McCaskey said, tentatively shuffling Mei's paperwork. "It looks like you have had experience implementing and managing full-stack integrations. Another thing my client will need is for you to troubleshoot application issues to eliminate any system downtime that might arise."

Mei assured McCaskey that she had extensive expertise in monitoring and analyzing website performance, conducting software maintenance checks, and providing recommendations for the continuous improvement of software systems.

Seeing that Mei had ample technical qualifications as a software engineer, McCaskey shifted gears. He asked about her current job status.

"Software consulting," Mei vaguely replied without specifically identifying Mad Mama. "I have been working with various organizations to build and maintain their software systems."

"What kind of organizations? Do you have samples of your work and references?"

"Absolutely," Mei replied as she handed McCaskey a list of companies where she had interned, while attending school in Virginia. "You can call anyone on the list. They will vouch for my programming experience."

"Great!" McCaskey exclaimed. "I'll make sure this gets to the hiring manager."

McCaskey nervously shuffled Mei's papers and glanced at his watch. Mei sensed the interview was drawing to a close.

"Is there anything else you'd like to know before we wrap up?" McCaskey asked. "I know it's getting late."

"Yes," Mei said. "Could you tell me about the company? I would like to know a little about the organization, and the compensation."

"Oh, the money!" McCaskey exclaimed. "I nearly forget. You're right, that is kind of important."

McCaskey rose from his desk. Mei found the sight of McCaskey's oversized hulking figure repulsive as he adjusted his glasses. His appearance suddenly made the small, dreary office seem frightfully claustrophobic; but she maintained a pleasant smile. Instead, McCaskey turned to the rear door behind his desk.

"I'll tell you what," McCaskey said. "I'll do better than that. I'll let you speak to the client himself."

Mei sat in perplexed silence. She was unsure what to expect. The whole scene seemed surreal as she glanced around the stark, grungy office with the absurd Hawaiian vacation poster. McCaskey opened the door.

Salvador DiMarco stepped into the room.

Chapter 79

When the Mad Mama computer system began to slow down, Jack Fuller was not concerned. There had been minor issues in the past. He was confident a call to Mei Wang would quickly resolve the matter with little, or no interruption to the service.

Jeff Hargrave was the first to take notice of the browser's sluggish connection. The files began taking longer than usual to download, causing a backlog of orders.

As a quick fix, Jeff rebooted the computer and closed the open browser tabs. He checked the computer's task manager and made sure the memory was not overwhelmed by an unseen application. No luck. The system was barely moving at a crawl.

At Jack's suggestion, Jeff freed up the computer's hard drive space, deleted temporary files, and defragmented the system. The computer continued to move at its slow, lethargic pace.

A malware viral infection was suspected to have hit the Mad Mama network. Jack began to panic. A corrupt computer network would have a devasting impact on the Mad Mama operation, especially if the organization's Enterprise Recourse Planning software system were to crash.

Jack called Mei. She would know how to trace any possible bugs that might have infected a switch, router, or workstation. With luck, Mei might even be able to restore the network remotely, which would keep the system up and running.

After placing a call, Jack waited nervously to hear from Mei. It was unlike her not to answer her cellphone, or respond to text messages immediately. As the minutes turned into hours, Jack became acutely aware that Mei was not responding to his messages.

The sight of Jeff's exhausting efforts to work around Mad Mama's computer glitches was more than Jack could bear. He made several repeated efforts to reach Mei by text message, without success. Exasperated, he went to see Latch.

Latch had spent the morning getting ready for another batch of Mad

Mama. He was aware that there had been computer issues in the office, but not concerned. Those were always quickly resolved by Mei. He was preoccupied with checking the still's equipment with a preliminary run of distilled-gallon water to ensure the still had no leaks.

After the water was poured for the still's preliminary run, Latch looked up to see an apprehensive Jack watching the process. Jack's normal placid look had been replaced by one of dreadful consternation.

"Get ahold of Mei?"

Jack shook his head wearily. Being unable to reach Mei was intensely agonizing. He was not only concerned about Mad Mama's computer system, but Mei's well-being as well.

"No, I'll tell you right now, something isn't right," Jack said. "It's not like her to disappear like that."

"She could be out running around," Latched offered. "She might have gotten tied up shopping. You know how ladies like to shop."

"No, that's not like her," Jack said assuredly. "Shopping isn't her thing."

Once Latch verified that there was sufficient heat and cooling to control the still's distillation, he wiped down the stainless-steel apparatus for another batch of Mad Mama.

"What do you want to do about that Wedgefield Heights order?" Latch asked. "Want me to get it ready, or hold off."

"Good question," Jack said. "I'd go ahead and get it ready. Jeff can run it down in his van."

Latch wiped his hands on a towel, and tossed it next to the still. "Think he'll be, okay?"

"Yes, I think so," Jack said thoughtfully. "Besides, we might as well let the mule out of the barn. It's not doing him good to sit around, while the computer's down."

Latch moved around the room with a jar of Mad Mama, and took a seat next to Jack. He unscrewed the lid and took a sip, then handed the jar to Jack.

Jack nodded in appreciation as he took the Mason jar. "Man, it sucks," he said.

"How's that?"

"The whole damn thing just sucks," Jack repeated with an exasperated sigh. He lifted the jar to his lips, took a prodigious gulp. "You take two steps, and get knocked back three."

Chapter 80

After the two murdered victims were discovered at the Carter farmhouse, the boarded-up building become a ghoulish attraction among the locals, including high school kids and young adults alike. Occasionally, an inquisitive visitor would pry one of the boards to peek into the vacated building's living room to view where the bodies of Mark Sanders and Ricky Ehlers had been found.

A visit to the farmhouse had become a game of dare, where people would challenge one another to peek through the window to see where the ghastly murders had taken place. Sadly, unscrupulous adolescent vandals began breaking into the house. Their obscene and satanic graffiti messages, left scattered on the walls, made the gruesome scene even more unsightly.

Upon hearing of the macabre attraction, Ty Fuller coerced Mary Beth Barnes and Charlene Thompson, both members of The Gap Runners, to venture onto the property. An avid soccer player, Fuller had a devilish smile, an unkept mop of hair, and a chipped front tooth with a captivating flair that girls found strangely irresistible.

It took several taunts, but Mary Beth agreed to Ty's goading provocations. Charlene was less than enthused, but agreed to go along. The rumors of Wes Harder and Eli Mills encounter were fast becoming legendary, and many curious onlookers wanted to share their experience.

As the group neared the farmhouse, Ty warned the girls that ghosts and apparitions had been reportedly seen. Mary Beth blew off Ty's nonsense, while Charlene grew notably quiet. The supernatural assertions made her uncomfortable, and she wanted to turn around.

"Okay, is this it?" Mary Beth asked as they stood at the steps of the farmhouse. "Seems like someone's been here, and boarded the place up."

"No problem," Ty said. "There's a loose board on the far window."

"I don't like it," Charlene said timidly. "It looks messed up, like the Devil's Tramping Ground."

"Say, what?"

"Uh-huh, that's right," Charlene said firmly. "My kin took me there once, and that place is creepy as all get out!"

"There's no such place," Ty insisted. "Someone's feeding you hogwash."

Mary Beth listened until she took her cue to confirm Charlene's claim.

"Oh, yes there is!" she said. "It's out near Bear Creek, in Chatham County. It's real, all right. There's a clearing in the woods that's a big circle where nothing grows, and the devil himself walks there at night."

"No, way," Ty said. "I've never heard of it."

"That's right," Charlene added. "You put something in the Tramping Ground's path, or the circle at night, and it'll be gone in the morning! Poof! Gone! He'll throw it out! Just like that!"

"Hmmm," Ty said, shaking his head. "I'll be doggone. Maybe we ought to go there next?"

Mary Beth and Charlene gave each other a knowing look, and shook their heads.

"Naw, come on," Ty laughed. "It can't be that bad."

"I'll tell you what," Mary Beth said. "You can go there, but not us. The Devil's Tramping Ground is his, and you don't mess with it!"

Ty could see the girls were adamant in their claim. Since they were not backing off their tale, he tactfully suggested they move up the stairs leading to the Carter farmhouse front porch.

"You guys ready?" Ty asked. "As I recall, there's a loose board at the far window."

"Not me," Charlene said. "I'm not going near there."

"Okay, I'll look," Mary Beth said. "It can't be any worse than looking at you!"

Ty chuckled as he moved to the covered window. "Ah, now you're getting ugly."

It was a simple matter for Ty to slip his hand under a board. He gently rocked the board back and forth until it was loose enough to be removed.

"There," he said, setting the board against the wall. "You're all set."

Mary Beth boldly walked to the window. She gave Ty a defiant smirk, then peered into the Carter farmhouse living room.

It took a moment for her eyes to adjust to the darkened room. As the images came into focus, a look of horror crept across her face.

Mary Beth turned to Ty and began trembling. "Is this some kind of joke?"

Chapter 81

The call Jo Yarborough received was eerily similar to the one she had gotten when the bodies of Mark Sanders and Ricky Ehlers were found at the Carter farmhouse. Due to the number of prank calls the sheriff station had received since that time, Deputy Wilson was reluctant to rush to the scene. It was only at Jo's urging that the deputy, at the very least, check on a group of possibly emotionally traumatized teens.

When the deputy arrived, he found the young teens gathered near the property's entrance. Despite being badly shaken, Mary Beth agreed to walk the deputy through the chain of events the group had incurred, including the ghastly sight inside the farmhouse.

It was unknown how long Mei Wang's body had been in the farmhouse living room, before it was found in a pool of blood. A bullet in the back of the head easily identified the unknown killer's signature trademark.

As the deputy inspected the body, he noticed a distinct difference from the previous murders. The body had been mutilated by canine bite marks. Bits of splintered bone fragments protruded from the victim's hands, legs, and feet.

Upon closer inspection, the deputy noticed that large chunks of flesh had been brutally torn and ripped from the body's torso. It was the deputy's assumption that parts of the mangled body had been eaten by an animal.

Turning to the teens, the deputy did what he could to calm their nerves. The girls were emotionally distraught. Mary Beth's parents arrived to take her and Charlene home, while Ty Fuller looked on in gloomy silence. Despite his shell-shocked appearance, he remorsefully admitted that it was his idea to explore the farmhouse, but had no idea what lay inside.

Both Sheriff Porter and Detective Halstead were called to the scene. The area was quickly cordoned off. Word of another murder among the nearby residents spread fast. Panic seized the local community, while many coped with the realization that a serial killer might be living in their midst.

"What do we have?" Sheriff Porter asked Deputy Wilson, as he slipped on his protective shoe covers to avoid contaminating the evidence and entered the farmhouse to view the scene.

"Looks like a young, female Asian with a gunshot to the back of the head," the deputy replied. "Am guessing late 20s, no ID."

"Oh, wow," Detective Halstead said, looking at the grisly scene. "Looks like a couple animals got in."

The sheriff approached the body, careful not to step in the blood. He squatted down to take a closer look, nodding his head.

"No," the sheriff said, surveying the scene. "Whoever was here, didn't leave any tracks. And, the lock's intact. That eliminates forced entry."

"Hmmm, a body dump?"

"Could be," the sheriff wondered aloud. "There are no signs of sexual assault, so we can rule that out."

The deputy and detective looked toward the front door of the farmhouse. There was a distinct trail of blood where the body had been dragged to its final resting place.

"Well, let's get some pictures and call the medical examiner," the sheriff said. "Hopefully, the folks at the lab will come up with something."

The sheriff took one last look around the living room before leaving. The room had the Americana appearance of what could have been a setting for a Norman Rockwell painting.

At the doorway, the sheriff turned to ask, "Anything else?"

The deputy shrugged his shoulders and reached into his pocket.

"Yeah, we found this," the deputy said, showing the sheriff a black aluminum dog whistle that was imprinted with the word *Hellhound*.

Without a word, the sheriff nodded and turned to leave. Once again, the dog whistle, which had begun to haunt him, had made its appearance.

Much like the sheriff, Jack Fuller shared a similar emotion, though for different reasons. When Jack heard the news, his stomach was tied in knots. Although the victim's name and identity had not been released, he feared the worst.

A couple days passed, before Jack finally received a response from Mei. It read, "Hi honey, took the dogs for a walk."

Chapter 82

Despite the unknown status of Mei Wang and the failing Mad Mama website, Jack Fuller decided to send Jeff Hargrave to deliver the Wedgefield Heights moonshine order. The customer represented a large account, which he did not want to lose.

The instructions Jeff was given were uncomplicated and straightforward. He was to deliver the order and return to Mad Mama with no personal stops in between. In addition to the Wedgefield Heights delivery, he was to drop off two jars of Mad Mama near the Firestone Reservoir to his longtime customer Roy as a personal favor. He knew Roy would appreciate the "medicinal medication" for his physical ailments.

As a precaution, Jeff was given a burner phone. Jeff was warned to watch for any suspicious people, or vehicles he might encounter and to use the phone should he need help. The burner phone would also eliminate any chance of detection, if anyone tried to track his movements.

Once the van was loaded, a call was made to the Wedgefield Heights estate's property manager, Bubby, who passed the information onto the resident bartender Ace. As preparations were being made to receive the shipment, the bartender quietly sent a prearranged text message to the Hellhound stronghold, where Corny was anxiously waiting.

The drive to Jeff's first stop was nonconsequential. Roy was comfortably seated in his wheelchair, enjoying a pleasant late afternoon breeze. Being given two jars of Mad Mama was enough to bring the elderly welfare recipient to virtual tears. His heartwarming appreciation and sincere gratitude deeply touched Jeff before moving onto his next stop.

Upon arriving at the Wedgefield Heights estate, Jeff was awed by the estate's magnificent security gate. After being buzzed through, he was met by the property's preoccupied caretaker Bubby, who directed Jeff to take the delivery behind the house to the outdoor pool bar.

"You the Mad Mama guy?" Ace asked gruffly as Jeff eased the van to the designated area. "If you're not, you're in the wrong place."

Jeff gave a weak smile and nodded. He began to explain that Bubby had told him to meet the bartender for the delivery, but was waved off.

"Okay," Ace said with his curt, brusque offensive attitude on full display. "Take that shit to the bar near the indoor pool, and hurry up."

Without a word, Jeff began moving the Mad Mama cases to the area, as instructed. He could not help, but notice the bevy of nude girls lounging around the pool. They seemed to be participants in a never-ending party. Some gamboled playfully in the water, while others flashed a coltish, mischievous smile.

Once Jeff finished unloading the cases, he reached in the van for a clipboard. Ace warily eyed Jeff, as he was handed the paperwork with a pen.

"What's this shit?" Ace asked. "We already paid."

"It's a Bill of Lading," Jeff replied. "It's an acknowledgement that you received five cases of Mad Mama."

Ace handed the clipboard and pen back to Jeff. "Keep it," he said. "I'm not signing anything."

Jeff saw no point in arguing. Ace had been blatantly hostile since his arrival. Jack would not be pleased, but he had no alternative. Instead, he took the clipboard and said, "Okay."

Ace watched the van disappear around the estate's vast property perimeter and through the main gate. He checked his text messages with a faint smile, and returned to stocking the bar.

Once outside the main gate, Jeff drew a sigh of relief. He was pleased to have completed the delivery, despite Ace's antagonistic, unfriendly behavior, and anxious to get back to his order desk.

As he drove around the narrow, winding roads within the reservoir's gated community, he slowed to admire the breathtaking beech, oak and hickory trees, interspersed with white pine and American holly bushes. Suddenly, he came upon a disabled truck blocking the road.

Chapter 83

The initial rumors that came into *The Mountain Holler* office concerning the Carter farmhouse began as a trickle. They soon swelled into an undeniable surging tidal wave.

Mr. Andrews was stunned as the reports grew. He had a nose for news, and knew a story when he saw one. More importantly, he knew a sensational story timed right meant increased readership, which translated into advertising sales dollars.

Skip was immediately called to report on the newly discovered Carter farmhouse murder. Mr. Andrews wanted the story covered, before the news broke regionally, or made national headlines.

The word on social media was spreading rapidly. Skip had to move fast, and raced to the farmhouse location.

A small crowd of curious onlookers had already gathered at the farmhouse when Skip arrived. He found the crime scene off-limits to everyone, including the media. Undeterred, he called the sheriff's station, but Jo Yarborough told him that the department had no comment until further information became available.

Skip sought to interview the witnesses who discovered the grisly scene, but found that the families of Mary Beth Barnes and Charlene Thompson forbid their girls to discuss the matter with anyone. Both had been traumatized by the ghastly turn of events.

It wasn't until Skip caught the affable Ty Fuller, while covering a soccer game days later, that he was able to get any information. *The Mountain Holler* was frequently seen reporting youthful athletic events as a public service to the community and Skip was well known among the teams.

Even then, Skip was only able to pry bits and pieces from the flighty adolescent as he toweled off after the match. Ty seemed more interested in getting something to eat with his teammates rather than discussing what he had seen at the Carter farmhouse.

"Great game!" Skip said as Ty changed his shoes and removed his shin guards. "You guys looked terrific!"

"Yeah, I suppose," Ty said, shuffling through the equipment in his athletic bag. "It's nice to tie, but better to win."

"I'm Skip Walker with *The Mountain Holler*," Skip said. "I'd like to ask you a couple questions about the Carter farmhouse, if you don't mind."

Ty looked up, as he hurriedly zipped his bag. His teammates had already started to leave the field. "Come on, Ty," a player called.

"Just a minute," Ty said. "Don't go anywhere."

Ty impatiently turned to Skip. He reluctantly admitted he had been to the Carter farmhouse, and saw Mei Wang's body. Ty slung his athletic bag over his shoulder, as his teammates pressed him to join them.

"Look, I can't talk now," he said. "I've got to go, but I wasn't trying to break into the place. We were just having a little fun, and wanted to peek inside. Okay? That was it. No big deal."

"No big deal?" Skip thought to himself as he watched Ty leave with his friends. Three young people come on the scene of a woman's brutal, grisly murder, and it was "no big deal?" As Skip headed home, he wondered what was a "big deal" to the stripling teen.

When Skip got home, he found Uncle Em on his hands and knees, reaching under the sofa, while Fred looked on. At first, he thought his uncle might have fallen, or suffered a heart attack. A surge of panic overwhelmed him, until he heard his uncle cursing.

"What's going on?" Skip asked as he walked through the door. "Everything okay?"

"Now, what in the hell kind of question is that?" Uncle Em shot back with an annoyed look on his face. "Get your ass down here, and help me find the TV clicker."

Skip took a quick look around the room. Fred sauntered over for a pat on the head as Skip laid his laptop backpack on the kitchen counter.

"Where did you have it before?" Skip asked. "You think to look there?"

"Oh, great," Uncle Em said, reaching farther under the sofa. "Just what we need: a comedian."

Skip's phone began beeping, which was guaranteed to draw Uncle Em's ire. As his uncle turned to view the offending sound, Skip took out his phone and motioned to the coffee table, where the TV remote was in plain sight.

"I suppose," Skip said, pausing to scan his messages, "You might say the joke's on you."

Chapter 84

The report that the body of a Hispanic male had been found in a drainage ditch near the Firestone Reservoir cemetery came to the sheriff's office late in the morning. The body was spotted by a highway maintenance worker, while setting roadwork traffic cones.

Deputy Wilson arrived to find a young man face-down in a mosquito infested creek. The officer assumed death had come quick, as a bullet hole through the back of the head was consistent with the previous execution-style murders he had seen.

The victim's body was covered with a thick, sludge-like layer of green, slimy algae. As in the case of Mei Wang, the body had been badly mauled by a canine animal. Aside from what appeared to be ferocious bite marks, strips of flesh had been savagely torn from the body by an unknown animal, such as a fox, coyote, or even a bear.

Sheriff Porter and Detective Halstead were soon on the scene. Together, they combed the area for clues, while the deputy prepared the crime report. The victim showed no signs of a struggle, which led to their assumption that the body had been dumped.

The detective was certain the body was that of the Marsh Auto Center mechanic Miguel, though the victim's identity remained a mystery. Miguel's name could not be confirmed. He could have been working under an assumed name, but his true identity remained unknown. There had been no missing person report been filed since leaving the used car lot, which added to the mystery.

As the investigators huddled over the body, the ever-present dog whistle appeared. Sheriff Porter literally shuddered, shaking his head as he held the black aluminum dog whistle in his latex gloved hands. By now, he was all too familiar with imprinted Hellhound logo, which he had seen before.

After the body was taken to the county medical examiner's office for an autopsy, Detective Halstead decided to check with the local, nearby residents who might have seen, or heard something related to the murder.

Upon leaving the crime scene, the detective noticed a quaint, white wooden cottage with a handicap ramp on the outskirts of the cemetery. An elderly man, who seemed to be enjoying the day, was seated on the front porch in a wheelchair. As he left the area, the detective nonchalantly strode toward the man's house.

"Hey buddy," the detective said as he neared the house. "How's it going?"

"Fine, jus' fine, an' yerself?"

The detective took a few steps closer, and stuck out his hand.

"Name's Sonny Boy Halstead," the detective began. "I'm with the County Sheriff's Department."

"That so?" the man replied, gently shaking hands. "I'm Roy Weaver, nice to meet you Holiday. Go ahead, have a seat."

The detective knew Roy had gotten his name wrong, but let it go. He was interested in gathering whatever information he could, and unconcerned with such trivial matters as a mistaken name.

"Nice place," Halstead said, leaning back on the creaking porch swing.

"Yeah, I like it, Holiday," Roy said. "Been 'ere 42 years."

"Really?" the detective said noticeably impressed. "Wow, you must have seen a lot of things."

Roy reached for a jar on the table next to his wheelchair, and took a sip. With a coughing gasp, replied, "Yeah, I'd say so."

The detective swayed gently on the swing. For a moment, only the grating creak of the swing's rusted chains could be heard, as he rocked back and forth.

"Say, what's the all the commotion ov'r thar, anyway?" Roy asked motioning to the far side of the cemetery. "The place is crawlin' with people."

"A body was found this morning," Halstead explained. "We're trying to find out if anyone might have seen anything, or heard what might have happened."

Roy took another sip from his jar, smacked his lips and set the jar down. He closed his eyes, and leaned his head back. Halstead thought he might have dozed off.

"That so," Roy said. "The only thang I seen was a big ol' mattress truck that come by."

"Mattress truck?"

"Yeah, a mattress truck," Roy said, nodding his head. "He parked 'er for a wile, 'bout where you boys are pokin' about."

"Did you see anyone?"

"Couple 'a' guys," Roy said, reaching for his jar. "A big guy, and a lil'un."

"Do you recall what they looked like?"

"Not really, Holiday" Roy said. "I was in the kitchen gettin' my medicine. I got rheumatoid arthritis, you know."

The detective could see the Roy's memory was not as sharp, and crisp as he wished. He was intrigued by the information he had received.

"Out of curiosity, what kind of medicine you taking?" Halstead asked.

"Mad Mama."

Chapter 85

Latch was getting the distillery ready for another batch of Mad Mama, when Jack Fuller appeared at the shed's door. He appeared gaunt, weary, and emotionally drained. His eyes were lifeless, with a vacant, expressionless, hollow tearful look.

"That's it," Jack murmured as he took a seat against the shed's wall. "We can't go on."

"How's that?" Latch asked. "You talking about the moonshine?"

Jack nodded meekly. Whatever was bothering him had taken its toll mentally and physically. Jack seemed to be a shell of his former self.

"The computer system is down," Jack said softly. "I can't find Mei, and Jeff hasn't come back from the Wedgefield Heights delivery."

Latch took a seat next to Jack. He sought to put give Jack's spirit a lift, and a positive spin on the situation.

"Mei could still turn up," he said. "Jeff probably got off somewhere. He might have taken the long way home, or wandered off like Ricky."

"No, that's not like him," Jack said firmly. "Jeff's too smart for that tomfoolery crap. He's a straight shooter, and doesn't mess around."

Jack's mood grew tense as he looked around the room. He bit his bottom lip nervously, trying to decipher his next move.

"I think we're licked," he said in a dour, sullen tone. "It'd be best to shut down for a while."

Latch leaned back in his chair, hands behind his head, and pressed his tongue against the inside of his left cheek in deep thought. The idea of shutting down Mad Mama seemed inconceivable, but understandable given the circumstances.

"I was afraid of that," he said. "Got any ideas what you want to do down the line?"

"Maybe." Jack sighed. "I really want to get through where we're at right now, before looking ahead. That seems to make the most sense."

Latch seemed to instinctively follow Jack's train of thought. He shared Jack's frustration at having to take a hiatus, but dread the idea of looking for another job.

"What do we do in the meantime?" Latch asked. "You want me to tear it down?"

"Yeah, let's close shop for the time being," Jack said. "As far as the website goes, I'll see what we can do to take it down. I hate to do it, but we need to lay low."

The website had been a source of pride for Jack. Business was streaming through the internet, and Jeff had become well versed in processing orders and handling daily transactions. The thought of someone hacking into the website was an unbelievable nightmare. Coupled with Mei's disappearance, Jack was stumped and bewildered by the recent turn of events.

"You know," Jack said, looking at his cell phone. "I got the craziest message from Mei."

"See!" Latch said brightly. "I told you you'd hear from her."

"No, now hold on," Jack said. "It's not that simple. In her text, she wrote, "*Hi honey, took the dogs for a walk.*""

"Ah, that doesn't sound like her," Latch said, scratching his head with a mystified, puzzled look. "As a matter of fact…"

"I know what you're going to say," Jack quickly injected. "Mei doesn't have any dogs, and she never called me 'Honey.'"

"You're right, it doesn't add up."

"At any rate, I don't know who, or what is out there," Jack said. "One thing's for sure, they've been coming after Mad Mama hard."

Jack got up, and walked to the door. He took one long, lingering last look at the distillery. He hung his head, and was overcome by a wave of emotions.

"You know, if we lose Mei and Jeff," Jack began, "I'll never forgive myself. We've already lost Bo and Ricky, so I know something isn't right. And, the same goes for whoever's been sending me these messages."

Jack turned to the door, and walked out. Once outside, he turned and said, "As far as I'm concerned, I hope this whole dog thing, whoever it is, bites them in the ass!"

Chapter 86

After a series of unexplained absences Ross had made from home, Candi began to get suspicious. He was suddenly flush with cash, which was a godsend for paying the hard-pressed couple's grocery and utility bills. Still, she wondered if his association with his bothersome friend Salvador was the source behind his sudden wealth.

At home, Candi was complacent. Her alcohol and drug usage had increased. She began to lose focus, and was frequently forgetful. Reoccurring mood swings, became a routine issue. Depression and early signs of dementia had started to creep in.

Candi would occasionally get a call from Airbnb for a cabin cleaning job. The money helped fund her ever-increasing drug habit. She had already passed the stage of having an abhorrent resistance to light, touch, taste, and smell. Life had grown to become a muddled, opaque blur. The euphoric feeling of being high was the ultimate disenfranchised escape from reality, which she craved, until the effect wore off.

Irrational hallucinations began to haunt Candi with intense paranoia. She suffered persistent anxiety attacks at an alarming rate. Disillusion led to panic, and occasional schizophrenia.

Ross was aware of Candi's declining health, and made periodic attempts to steer her from the path of self-destruction. On several occasions, he watched her suffer a severe bout of nausea and violent vomiting, but was always rebuffed when asked if she needed help. Instead, Candi would chastise Ross with a barrage of demonstrative insults aimed at his working relationship with Salvador.

It was on such an occasion that Candi was struggling, when Salvador called on an upcoming job. Candi ordered Ross to hang up. He refused. She became hysterical, belligerent, and abusive. Ross laid down the phone to suppress Candi's unhinged remarks, while Salvador listened to the commotion.

"What's her problem?" Salvador asked when Ross came back on the line. "Sounds like you had to gag her."

"Pretty much," Ross said. "Sometimes, she doesn't know when to quit."

"Man, that woman's got a big mouth."

"Yeah, that's a fact." Ross agreed. "All that bellyaching hurts my ears, at times."

"Well, it's not doing mine much good," Salvador said. "Listen, that's not why I called."

Despite having worked several jobs recently, Ross welcomed the opportunity for another job. The money had been a blessing, though, he had to listen to Candi's constant haranguing speeches complaining about the money's source and her relentless criticism about Salvador.

"How are you fixed for money, right now?" Salvador asked. "With all the jobs we have been doing lately, I have to believe you're set pretty good."

"I'd say so," Ross agreed. "The wallet can always use a little more, you know."

"Good, that's good to know," Salvador said. "I've got a couple things coming that are perfect for you, but first I want take some time off."

Before Salvador could offer any details, Candi could be heard screaming in the background. She was ranting incoherently, while complaining bitterly about Salvador. Once again, Ross had to excuse himself and set the phone down.

"Sorry," Ross said apologetically, returning to the phone. "That was another emergency."

Salvador had heard enough. He did not want to hear Candi's tongue-lashing comments again.

"You know what?" Salvador asked firmly. "Someone needs to shut that woman up. And, I mean shut her up for good."

"Hmmm," Ross murmured. "She's all right, just a little crazy when she's loaded."

"Out of curiosity, is she still working that Airbnb job?"

"Yeah, they call every so often," Ross said. "She mostly works The Oaks Lodge off the Little Tennessee River."

"That so?" Salvador spoke slowly. "The Oaks is a nice place. As I recall, they got some nice cabins that are secluded."

"Alotta tourist hang there," Ross volunteered. "Ha, skeeter country by the river. Not for me."

Salvador's interest in The Oaks seemed to intensify, when he learned Candi typically worked Mondays. Once the guests checked out, it was her job to clean the cottages.

"Too bad they weren't busy enough to keep her there," Salvador joked.

"That'd be nice," Ross chuckled. "Might even get some sleep around here."

"I'll tell you what," Salvador said, "I'm taking a couple weeks off, and will call when I'm back. There's a couple loose ends that need to be taken care of."

Before Salvador hung up the phone, Candi could be heard spewing another blast of vulgar obscenities. He listened to the malicious, rhetorical salvo, and quietly told Ross to let her have her say.

"Just remember," he said. "Every dog has their day."

Chapter 87

The cry of a majestic red-tailed hawk could be heard echoing across the lake as Milt and Wendall slipped their boat from its dock onto the placid lake water. They had planned a day of fishing and relaxation, while enjoying the cool breeze and early morning sun.

Milt took his usual spot at the helm and steered the small boat among the heavily weeded lakeshore banks, before dropping anchor. Specks of sunlight had begun to break through the thick forest canopy, and glisten like dazzling jewels strewn haphazardly across the water.

Silently, Milt and Wendall cast their lures among the dense reeds that lined the lake's shoreline. The sound of their lures could be heard plopping into the water as the red-tailed hawk made one last cry, before making its way across the lake.

"Nice day to be on the water," Wendell said as he slowly cranked his reel. "What do you have on your line?"

"A frog popper," Milt said cheerfully. "Thought I'd start on the top water, walking the dog."

"Careful you don't get snagged," Wendall warned. "Those weeds were the only thing biting, last time we were here."

Milt nodded as he skillfully weaved his lure between some lily pads. With the flick of his wrist, he dragged the lure across the water's surface in a hesitant, taunting motion in hopes of attracting a fish.

"Well, I don't believe I could do any worse than Toby or Leroy," he said with a laugh. "Their idea of fishing is nothing like mine."

"How's that?"

"Magnet fishing."

"Say what?" Wendall asked, looking perplexed as he reeled in his line. "Don't tell me they're doing that crazy thing where they tie a magnet to a rope, and toss it off some bridge."

"That's right!" Milt chuckled as he worked his frog lure among the weeds. "They're going after metal fish. They got themselves a big, heavy duty magnet, rope, gloves, and everything."

Wendall shook his head and methodically reeled in his line. With a light tug, he jerked his reel back to set the hook. Suddenly, the line went taunt. He had snagged a submerged underwater primrose.

"Oh, hell," Wendall bemoaned. "Maybe I should have gone with Toby and Leroy this morning. I am about tapped out losing lures in this place."

"Ha, go right ahead," Milt laughed. "Toby and Leroy have been filling buckets up with all kinds of junk. Bolts, coins, pipes, fishing stuff and even a gun."

"A gun?" Wendall said, looking surprised, as he pulled harder on his line. "You've got to be kidding."

"That's right," Milt said, slowly reeling his frog lure toward the boat. "You'd be surprised at what they come up with."

"I don't know," Wendall said, shrugging his shoulders. "If you're looking for junk, seems like it might be easier to run over to Harley's, and tear off a piece of some old car."

"That might be so, but the guys are even talking about a run over to the Cape Fear River," Milt said, untying his lure. "Ha, treasure hunters! They want be like that Indiana Jones guy."

"Cape Fear!" Wendall exclaimed. "They'd do better at your duck pond. You know, out back where they found that Marsh Auto guy. And now, I hear there's another one missing. Man, there must be something in the water."

"Hmmm, I hear Eddie Meyers at Marsh Auto is about ready to jump out of his skin," Milt said. "He's besides himself."

Wendall had nearly given up on his snag, while Milt changed his lure. He was also anxious to move to another location, and no longer wanted to discuss the duck pond tragedy, or missing the person at Marsh Auto.

"I suppose that beats some of the other stuff Toby was looking at," Milt said. "At one point, he talked about getting an aerial drone with baited hooks."

"Get out!" Wendall said. "That's illegal."

"Well, tell them that," Milt agreed tying a Carolina-rigged worm lure on his line. "Besides, that beats what Leroy wanted to do."

"Oh, lord," Wendall groaned. "What'd he have in mind."

"He wanted to grab his rifle," Milt chuckled. "That boy was never much for sitting with a rod in his hand. No patience. Instead, he got it in his mind to blast the suckers with his 30-06, like that murdering Carter farmhouse creep."

With one final tug, Wendall snapped his line. He was tired of fighting a losing battle.

"Damn, get Toby and Leroy out here," Wendall said. "They need to throw out that magnet, so I can get my lure back!"

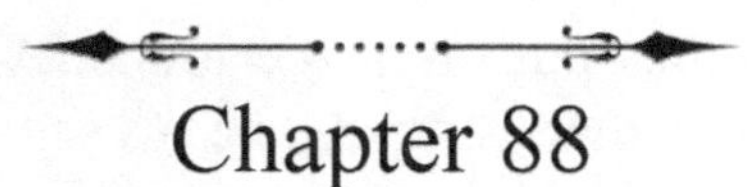

Chapter 88

After the TV remote had been located, Skip stepped into another room to check his text messages. The phone's frequent beeps had always been a sore spot with his uncle, and he did not want to risk antagonizing him further after his frustrating search for the misplaced TV remote.

As Skip scrolled through the messages, he viewed the usual jokes, comments, emojis or inquiries sent by friends and *The Mountain Holler* readers alike. Among the mass accumulation of routine messages, was a stern warning to stop "snooping" around the recent murder crime scenes, or there would be "consequences."

Despite the unnerving threat, Skip said nothing to his uncle, and proceeded to follow Mr. Andrews instructions to follow up on the Mei Wang story. He was asked to write a cover story, complete with Mei's background and whatever information he could uncover concerning her untimely death.

Since Mei had virtually little or no social media presence, Skip went to her former university in Virginia and gathered what few insightful details he could learn from friends, former professors, and work associates. Even then, the pickings were slim.

In addition to the scant information he found on Mei, Skip was able to get a simple quote from Sheriff Porter stating, "We would like to extend our deepest, sincere sympathy to the Wang family, and assure them that we are doing everything within our power to bring the person who committed this heinous crime to justice."

Once the story was filed, Skip made bought a bottle of chardonnay and headed to Katie Mae's house. It had been several days since he had last seen his fiancée, and was planning a romantic evening that included dinner.

"You're late, Skip-A-Roo," Katie Mae said as she opened the door. "Don't tell me Mr. Andrews has you working on another 'special' issue, because those excuses are getting old."

"Guilty as charged," Skip shrugged, setting the wine on the kitchen counter.

"Humph," Katie Mae huffed. "You ought to tell that Mr. Andrews that no one gives a hoot about who won last week's bingo tournament that those fuddy duddies put on at the lodge. About the only news around that place is how many hog-eyed boys show up to stare. News? Even the flies won't touch the molasses on that plate."

The comment caught Skip by surprise, which he chose to ignore. Instead, he gave a weak smile and asked what Katie Mae wanted for dinner.

"Honey, that train left long ago," Katie Mae said, shaking her head. "All you're getting is mac and cheese with cornbread."

Skip slipped his arm around Katie Mae's waist, and gave her an apologetic hug with a kiss on the neck.

"Well, that's not going to work," she purred, craning her neck. "But it's a start."

As Katie Mae turned to take the macaroni and cheese from the oven, she asked, "So, what's this big blockbuster story you've got cooking? You might as well tell me."

There was an awkward moment of silence as Skip looked at his feet.

"Oh, good heavens!" Katie Mae exclaimed. "Don't tell me, Mr. Andrews told you to keep it a secret. I declare, Skip Walker, you tell me that every time some big ol' fat story comes along, and it's always nothing."

"Well, this one's a big deal," Skip stammered. "And, Mr. Andrew..."

"Don't tell me it's about that Asian lady they found," Katie Mae said briskly, setting the macaroni and cheese pan on the counter. "Everyone already knows about it; try something else."

"Really?" Skip said, surprised. "What'd you hear?"

Katie Mae set out plates, napkins, and silverware. She handed Skip two wine glasses as he poured the well-seasoned chardonnay.

"Some gal come in Two Sisters, and told Miss Victoria that a Chinese girl was killed by a jealous ex-boyfriend," she said, pausing to lift her wine. "She said he was a masochist, or whatever they call it, who bit her, and run off."

"Cheers," Katie Mae said, lifting her glass. "Now, who'd do a thing like that?"

Skip clicked her glass silently. He neither confirmed, nor denied the story.

"Hmmm, must be true if you're not talking," she said.

In almost perfect disruptive timing, Skip lifted his fork when his cell phone beeped with a text message.

"Ooh, lordy, lord," Katie Mae said in a jocular manner. "What would we do, if we can't live with that thing turned off for two minutes?"

Skip smiled and reached down to shut the phone off. He could easily have reminded his fiancée about her extensive chat with Tammy during their dinner at Miss Mary's Azalea House, but thought better than to create any issues. Instead, a quick glance at his phone revealed an unknown caller. There was a terse text message.

"We're coming for U."

Chapter 89

Whenever The Oaks called, Candi would pull herself out of her drug-induced stupor to clean Airbnb cabins. The money was good, and work easy; though her deteriorating condition had started to affect her physically.

The Oaks was a small, uniquely secluded resort located in the Smoky Mountains near the Little Tennessee River, managed by Midge and her husband, Larry Bennett. Each cabin had a spacious living room and dining area with a kitchenette, one to two bedrooms, a hot tub, fireplace, and rocking chairs that overlooked the river.

The river featured several popular summertime activities that included fishing, water tubing and kayaking. Guests flocked to the cabins throughout the warm, summer months to enjoy the breathtaking splendor of the Smoky Mountains natural beauty.

As a housekeeper, Candi's cleaning activities ranged from sweeping, mopping, and vacuuming floors to dusting and polishing furniture and emptying trash. Beds had to be properly made with clean linen, bathroom mirrors and sinks free of streaks and smudges, tubs and showers cleaned, and toilets disinfected.

The work could be demanding, but Candi would occasionally slip away on a break, or during lunch to drop an amphetamine. The extra boost gave her the adrenaline energy she needed to make it through her shift.

At home, Ross was supportive of Candi's job. The hours were flexible, and the money was decent. More importantly, the job got her out of the house, which gave Ross a chance to unwind and check in with Salvador about future jobs.

As Candi headed to The Oaks, Ross went through the couple's bills, which had started to mount. He was concerned about several upcoming utility companies that were threatening to cut off their services. The situation was bothersome, and had virtually become a routine, monthly battle.

Ross wanted to call Salvador, but knew he would have to wait. Salvador was on vacation. He would be unavailable for at least a week. His only hope was to tap into Candi's Airbnb money, if she did not squander her earnings on drugs before getting home.

Delinquent bills were the farthest thing from Candi's mind when she arrived at The Oaks. Bills were never an issue with Candi. All of the household bills were handled by Ross. Her focus was getting through another housekeeping shift as quickly as possible and getting enough money to score more drugs.

"Good morning, Miss Candi," Midge said in her usual cheery, upbeat voice. "You must have quite a reputation. The guest in cabin 3-17, said he has heard about you, and requested you clean his room."

"Really?" Candi said, surprised as she slipped on her green housekeeping apron. "That's nice."

Although Candi was pleased that her service was being recognized, she hoped it would translate into a generous tip. She seldom received much in the way of tips, and cleaning fees were never shared by The Oaks.

Cabin 3-17 was hidden deep in the dark woods toward the rear of The Oaks property. It was a stunning two-story, two-bedroom log cabin with a kitchenette, two baths, and a dining area that bordered the river. Downstairs featured a game room with a bar, pool table, ping pong, foosball and large-screen TV. Both the upper and lower decks had oversized rocking chairs with a breathtaking view of the river's rippling water.

As Candi entered the cabin, she thought she heard a noise downstairs, but was unsure. Perhaps it was The Oaks mischievous cat Oscar, who had been known to prowl the grounds.

In record-breaking time, Candi made the bed, cleaned the kitchen and bathroom. She vacuumed the living room, took out the trash, and made a quick swipe with the feather duster over the large-screen TV.

Candi left the room in sparkling, pristine condition as she rolled her maintenance cart away. It was the final cabin on her shift, and she was ready to head home.

Suddenly, there was a call on her cell phone. It was Midge. The guest had requested two additional rolls of toilet paper.

The request seemed strange, because Candi had left both bathrooms upstairs and downstairs fully stocked. Nevertheless, she turned her cart around and headed to the cabin.

Upon entering the cabin, Candi was stunned to see the television had a basketball game on ESPN. She was certain the cabin had been unoccupied when she left, and became alarmed. Cautiously, she glanced around the room. Seeing no one, Candi moved to the downstairs bathroom with the rolls of toilet paper.

The bathroom door was slightly ajar as Candi proceeded to push it open. There was an eerie creaking, squeak at the door. She quickly placed the toilet paper rolls on the bathroom vanity. As she turned to leave, she froze in horror.

Chapter 90

The early morning sun had just broken over the horizon when an anonymous caller notified the sheriff's department of a smoldering, burnt-out van near the Firestone Reservoir. The sheriff and detective responded reacted quickly, racing to the scene, as the local fire crew were already on hand extinguishing the final embers of the blaze.

The van was found hidden behind a utility shed. The small structure was partially melted due to the fire's extreme heat. After the flames had been put out, the firefighters made the gruesome discovery of a body inside a burned-out vehicle.

A medical examiner on the scene suggested the fire had been intentionally set. It was his opinion, that the deceased individual was most likely dead, before the fire started.

Both Sheriff Porter and Detective Halstead were joined by members of the district attorney's and medical examiner's offices, including the county coroner, pathologist, toxicologist, photographer and local EMT's to thoroughly document the scene.

Since there were no witnesses who had seen how the van caught fire, the case would be headed to the office of a forensic anthropologist for an expert opinion. An onsite post-mortem found that the victim was a male, who had suffered a single bullet hole through the back of his head.

A series of bite marks, similar to those found on the body of Mei Wang and the young Hispanic man found recently, puzzled the sheriff and detective. They were at a loss for words on how the body had been mutilated.

A check of the vehicle's VIN number revealed that the van was registered to Jeffrey A. Hargrave, age 36. Aside from a speeding ticket he received years earlier as a teenager on Interstate 95 near South Carolina's South of the Border roadside attraction, his record was clean.

"What do you make of it?" Detective Halstead asked Sheriff Porter. "Seems like we've been here before."

"I don't know," the sheriff replied as the last photos were being taken, and the body removed. "Something doesn't add up."

"How's that?"

"For one thing, what's this guy doing here?" The sheriff said, rubbing his temple. "Also, when did he get here?"

The detective nodded. Neither question had a clear answer.

"Well, he's been here awhile," Halstead said. "It took some time for that fire to burn down, before anyone got here."

The sheriff agreed, shaking his head. "Somehow, I don't get the feeling he was planning an overnight fishing trip to the reservoir."

Both the deputy and detective watched, as the local tow truck driver, Harley rumble into view. He had been summoned after the body had been removed, to take the van to his garage's impound yard. Due to the van's immobile condition, a flatbed tow truck had been ordered.

"It's hard to tell what the motive might have been," the sheriff noted. "I can't tell if this guy was robbed, or what went down."

"This doesn't seem like a good spot to spend the night," Detective Halstead noted. "Based on the awkward way the van was parked; I'd say he was ambushed, or run off the road."

"Hey Mr. Max an' Sonny Boy!" Harley said, hopping out of the cab. "Whew, doggy looks like someone hadda barbecue."

"I wouldn't call it that, but okay," the sheriff said sternly. "You got paperwork?"

"You bet!" Harley said, handing the sheriff a well-worn clipboard. "Yer all set."

The sheriff signed the release forms, and watched Harley toss the clipboard into the cabin. Skillfully, he flipped on the hazard lights, backed the tow truck into position, prepared the winch and tipped the bed.

"You guys might wanna cover yer ears," Harley warned. "Her tires are gone. Them rims is gonna scream comin' up the ramp."

Once the van's frame was hooked, the sound of screeching metal could be heard as the van's metal rims ground their way up the tow truck's bed. Once in position, Harley secured each rim with wheel straps, and the charred frame with additional chains.

The sheriff and detective watched silently, as Harley tipped the truck's bed upward to its transportable flat position. After a brief inspection to double check the bindings, he was off to the impound yard.

The sheriff and detective stood momentarily, studying the new vacant scene. Each deep within their own thoughts.

"You know, I still can't figure out those bite marks," the sheriff said slowly. "I'm starting to feel like a dog chasing its tail."

"You know, you might be onto something," Detective Halstead said thoughtfully. "At least with a tail, you know where to start."

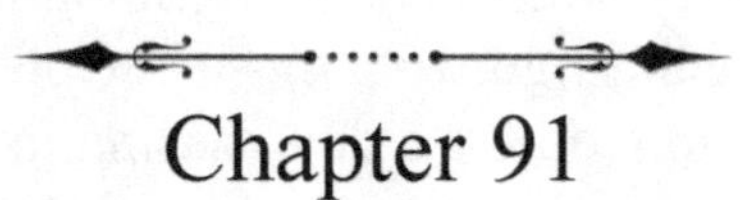

Chapter 91

The familiar aroma of Jo Yarborough's coffee filtered through the sheriff's station, as Detective Halstead made his way into the office. He stopped briefly at the coffee maker for a freshly brewed cup, before moving on.

The detective had spent a sleepless night pondering Sheriff Porter's comment about a dog chasing its tail. His comment kept resonating in his mind that the search for crucial evidence on the seemingly endless murder spree had been frustrating and demoralizing.

Halstead set his coffee on the table, and reached for Bo Benson's notebook. Perhaps there was a scant, trace of evidence he might have overlooked and sought to analyze each line.

As the detective thumbed through the notebook, he turned to the page that had the word "Dog" printed in an old English format. Halstead smirked, as he sipped his coffee. Great care, and emphasis had been taken in printing the letter "D." The letter looked like a poorly reproduced, amateurish replica of the Detroit Tigers logo, a team struggling to make the playoffs within their division.

Even stranger, was the fact that Bo Benson was an avid Atlanta Braves fan. There was no sign, or indication in his belongings that he followed the Tigers. Whether he was dabbling with a logo sketch, or had something else in mind was debatable.

Halstead also thought the emphasis on a dog seemed ironic, as the elder Benson said the family had always been cat lovers. The obsession with dogs made no sense, unless there was an unrelated reason, such as a rock band that Halstead had not heard about.

Lastly, the detective came across the crossed-out "HH." He wondered if the initials were those of a former girlfriend. Perhaps it was a relationship that had soured concerning someone he no longer cared to see.

Halstead starred long, and hard at the notebook. No matter how hard he tried to make sense of the scrawled notes, he could not make any reasonable deductions. Instead, he reached into his file cabinet and removed a small box containing additional bits of evidence related to the Benson murder.

As Halstead opened the cabinet, he noticed the black aluminum dog whistle that Skip Walker had left at the sheriff's office. He was playfully twirling the dog whistle on his finger when Deputy Wilson walked in.

"Haven't given up the ghost, Sonny Boy?" Wilson asked, taking a seat.

"Naw, still chasing it," Halstead said. "And it's starting to haunt me too."

"Better start sleeping with the lights on," Wilson suggested. "Or, better yet, call Ghostbusters."

Halstead stopped twirling the dog whistle keychain, and laid it on his desk. He reached for his coffee, but it had gone cold.

"Damn," the detective murmured. "Another cup wasted, thanks to this Hellhound toy."

Wilson's head suddenly perked upward with a methodical, perplexing look. His mind was working fast, as an overwhelming thought dawned on him.

"You know what?" he volunteered. "What's that dog whistle say?"

"Hellhound, why?"

"HH," Wilson said. "Get it? That could be your HH."

"Hmmm," Halstead said thoughtfully. "I still don't see it."

"Didn't you say Benson was messing with the word 'dog,' an' crossed out HH?" Wilson asked.

"Yeah, but I still don't see the connection."

"When you spoke to his father, didn't he say he was drinking Mad Mama?" Wilson asked. "And he found it under his son's bed?"

Halstead slowly nodded. Still, he was not sure where Wilson was headed.

"Remember, Mad Mama jars or lids that were found at Buckshot Pond, the Highland Ranch pig pickin' and with Mark Sanders?"

"Yeah, what about it?" Halstead asked. "Mad Mama's come and gone. They were online, but that website's been taken down."

"That's my point," Wilson said. "Someone knocked them off. That business got run into the ground."

"Ya, think?"

"Hellhound."

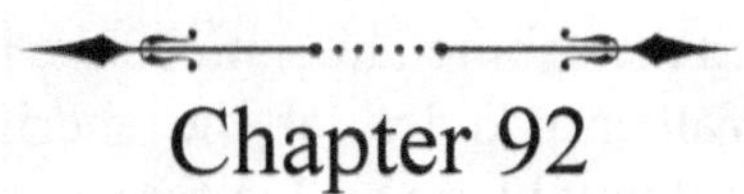

Chapter 92

The fluorescent glow of the evening fireflies flickered through the dense woods, as Skip settled onto a porch chaise lounge with a tall glass of sweet tea to watch his uncle toss a tennis ball across the backyard for Fred to playfully retrieve. Fred seemed oblivious to the cluster of fireflies emitting their luminous, twinkling light above his head, as he was intensely immersed in chasing the ball.

"Those lightning bugs are sure putting on a show tonight!" Uncle Em observed. "They're running around like it's the Daytona 500."

"They're not a bug, but actually a beetle," Skip said. "The one's flying are the males looking for females."

"Ha, imagine flying all over hell for a piece of ass," Uncle Em cackled. "I'll tell you what, one night with Irene, and the Wolverine will have those lightning bugs crying for their mama."

"Beetles."

"Beetles, bugs, whatever," Uncle Em huffed, tossing the ball across the yard. "They're running hot tonight. Guess, it's that time of year."

Fred came bounding onto the porch. He paused at Skip's feet, clutching the ball tightly in his mouth.

"Here," Skip said, reaching for the ball that Fred had clamped down in his mouth. "Let go."

Fred playfully backed up holding onto the ball. He mischievously shook his head like he had found a highly valued, long-lost treasure, and was not going to give it up.

"Now, you've done it," Uncle Em said. "You're going to have to work for it, like your lightning bug friends chasing the gals."

Skip chuckled. He gently clasped the ball, and shook it loose from Fred's mouth. The ball was covered with a thin film of sludgy, slimy salvia, which caused Skip to recoil in exasperation.

"Yuck," Skip said, shaking the ball. "Freddie, we're going to have to get you a towel for this mess."

As he prepared to toss the ball, Fred turned toward the backyard in anxious anticipation. The dog's wet nostrils flared. His alert eyes blazed with excitement.

With a quick flick of the wrist, Skip tossed the ball high in the air. Fred shot off like a rocket. He was determined to get the ball before any unforeseen interloper might interfere.

"Look at him go," Uncle Em laughed. "You'd think he was a pup."

"Yeah, I suppose he thinks he's a kid again," Skip agreed. "Boy, he's getting his exercise tonight."

"Too bad fat ass wasn't here," Uncle Em sneered. "Fred would run his ass ragged, better than any treadmill they got at Dick's Sporting Goods."

"Well, I don't think Mr. Andrews is much for treadmills, or running," Skip said, taking a sip of sweet tea. "Besides, he's got his hands full at the office."

Uncle Em folded his arms, and uttered an unintelligible groan. He adjusted his chaise lounge to an upright position, and turned to face Skip.

"Of course he does," Uncle Em groused. "He's got to milk that *Mountain Holler* cow, and squeeze her for every bootlicking dime he can get to buy more cigarettes."

Fred came racing back to the porch, and dropped the ball at Uncle Em's feet. He was panting hard, his tongue dangling from his mouth.

While Uncle Em was preoccupied talking with Skip, he barely took notice that Fred wanted to continue with the game. Fred grew uneasy. He began to bark, fidget, whimper and wag his tail.

"Ah, come on Fred," Uncle Em said in a coaxing manner. "It's getting dark, and time to go in."

"You might as well toss one more for him," Skip said. "It doesn't look like he's ready to call it a night."

Uncle Em looked down at Fred's sorrowful, woeful face. He was struck by a series of pitiful guilty pangs at having denied Fred his lighthearted amusement.

"Okay," Uncle Em said, reaching for the ball. "One more, for the road."

Uncle Em reached back with the intensity of a veteran pitcher about to hurl the final strike in the seventh game of the World Series. With a mighty heave, he threw the ball to the farthest corner of the yard.

Fred wasted no time. He bolted at reckless breakneck speed to retrieve the ball. His sights were set on a well-planned mission to nab his prize.

Upon reaching the ball, Fred seized the sphere in his mouth. He turned, lifting his head triumphantly to display his hard-earned trophy.

Suddenly, a gunshot shattered the night air. The loud, sharp crack of its explosive sound could be heard reverberating through the thick, wooded trees.

Fred fell to the ground.

Chapter 93

The body of Candi O'Neil lay motionless in a pool of blood hidden in the underbrush near the banks of the Little Tennessee River. Midge Bennett thought it was strange that Candi had not returned her housekeeping cart to the maintenance department after cleaning cabin 3-17, but it was not the first time she had been negligent in her duties.

Midge was aware that Candi tended to wander off on occasion, but was willing to overlook her shortcomings. Candi had good housekeeping skills, and was always willing to work; when she was available. Still, Midge could not help but wonder where Candi had gone on such short notice. Candi would usually confirm when a cabin had been cleaned.

As the hours rolled by, Midge got preoccupied at the resort's front desk and forgot about the cabin. It was late, when she asked her husband, Larry to check on cabin 3-17. She wanted to make sure the property had been cleaned, and ready for the next guest.

Larry took the housekeeping checklist to review each item. A cursory inspection revealed the cabin was spotless. There were no anomalies, such as room damage, leftover baggage, or personal items. The fixtures and carpet were clean, and the towels, pillowcases, and bed linens had been replaced.

The final checklist inspection called for an external property review, which Larry checked to ensure no trash had been left on the balcony or lower porch. As Larry turned to leave the downstairs patio area, he noticed a green housekeeping apron protruding from the brush.

At first, Larry thought the apron had somehow gotten misplaced, or had blown into the bushes during a late afternoon thunderstorm. As he reached down to retrieve the apron, he was sickened by the nauseating realization that the blood-soaked garment was Candi's.

Both Sheriff Porter and Deputy Wilson rushed to the scene, and hurriedly slipped into their shoe covers. The Oaks suddenly became the hub of chaotic activity. Additional investigators began to arrive.

Candi's hands had been zip-tied behind her back, and her mouth was covered with gray duct tape. Her face was badly bruised, and her body showed signs of severe methamphetamine sores from extensive drug use.

Candi appeared to have been beaten, brutally tortured, and dragged to the river, where she was murdered. Severe bite marks from an unknown animal covered the body, and a bullet hole in the back of her head left no doubt as to who the unknown assailant might have been.

Midge was devastated. She was inconsolable. Larry tried to answer the sheriff's questions, but was at a loss for words.

It was determined that a small man with dark hair and a thin mustache named Robert Ryan from Ohio, had rented the cabin for a week. He arrived in a box truck, which was parked nearby, off the resort property's premises.

Aside from a brief encounter with Ryan, which Midge described as "terse," the individual was non-descript in nature. There was nothing noteworthy to create any suspicion, or cause for alarm. She noted he had specifically requested that Candi clean his room.

A thorough search revealed that no one fitting Robert Ryan's description lived in Ohio. Nor did The Oaks have an office video available, or a phone record that would have helped in the investigation.

As the medical examiner's office poured over the body, the sheriff and deputy huddled to compare notes. A pathologist and toxicologist would later confirm what the lawmen suspected regarding Candi's cause of death, but there was one clue they wanted to confirm.

"Did you find it?" Deputy Wilson quietly asked the sheriff.

"Yeah," the sheriff said, nodding his head. "It's here."

The sheriff produced a plastic bag containing evidence that had been found on Candi's body. Both starred silently at the familiar black aluminum dog whistle keyring with its bold Hellhound lettering.

"Are you going to make a statement to the media?" Wilson asked the sheriff. "I'm sure they'll be heating up the griddle."

"Not yet," Sheriff Porter replied. "I'd like to contact Miss O'Neil's kinfolk first, and have Sonny Boy run out to where she was living. Miss Midge tells me she had a boyfriend. I'd like to hear what he has to say."

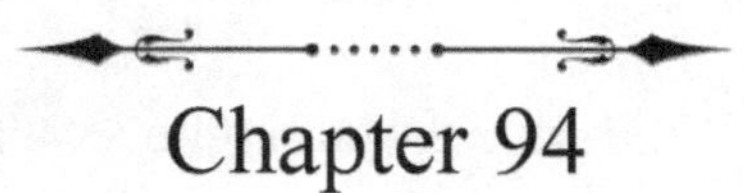

Chapter 94

A faint murmur could be heard near the rear of the Two Sisters consignment shop, where owners Victoria and Veronica were huddled in a deep discussion, as Skip entered the store. There was a sorrowful sadness in their tone, though, Skip could not make out the gist of their conversation.

Katie Mae was helping an elderly woman and her granddaughter sort through a rack of blouses, and did not immediately notice Skip enter the shop. The niece was absorbed in rummaging through every second-hand fashion style, brand, color, pattern, and fabric imaginable. Nothing met her taste. Finally, the exasperated grandmother suggested another store.

"Skippy!" Katie Mae exclaimed, as the couple left. "Where have you been? I thought we were going for a dinner plate?"

"I'm sorry," Skip said apologetically. "I got caught up with Mr. Andrews, and had to call Uncle Em about Fred."

"Ugh, Mr. Andrews," Katie Mae groaned. "That poop head's working you to death."

Upon entering the store, Victoria tapped Veronica on the arm to motion toward Skip at the front door. With a faint smile, she retreated to the backroom, while Veronica moved forward.

"Well, I do declare! If it isn't Mr. Skip himself!" she beamed. "What a pleasant surprise! I heard about your poor dog Ed. Is he doing okay?"

"His name's Fred, and thanks for asking," Skip said. "He's fine. We took him to see Dr. Thomas at the vet's office, and got him patched up."

Both Veronica and Katie Mae gave a sigh of relief, as Skip continued.

"Fortunately, it was buckshot that nicked his shoulder. There was no damage to the nerves or bones. Dr. T says Freddie will be in a splint for a while, but at least he's okay. Funny, he's already got a hankering to go out."

"Well, thank the good lord for that," Veronica said. "I hope they catch whoever did it. They ought to be locked up."

Both Katie Mae and Skip nodded in agreement, as they headed toward the door.

"So, who did it?" Katie Mae asked as they walked toward The Red Maple.

"I don't know, but will say Uncle Em isn't happy," Skip said. "He's madder than hell, and ready to kill someone."

"You can't blame him," Katie Mae said as she stepped through the door at The Red Maple. "My dander would be up too."

"Hmmm," Skip groused. "Right now, he's afraid to go on the porch, and that means no beer can chicken."

The Red Maple was virtually empty when Skip and Katie Mae entered the diner. Both Connie and Harold looked bored. She was folding napkins, and Harold half-heartedly cleaned the grill. Wendell had left for the day.

"Hey guys!" Connie said, in her usual cheerful, upbeat voice. "Nice to see y'all!"

"Where'd everybody go?" Katie Mae said, waving her hand around the room. "Looks like a bomb went off!"

"Ha, no need for reservations today," Connie laughed. "Ain't that right, Harold?"

Harold scowled, and continued scrubbing the grill.

"Ah, he's such a sour puss," Connie said. "'Sides, he's bent outta shape on account 'a' that gal he was sweet on ov'r at The Oaks."

"Who was that?" Katie Mae asked. "Are you talking about that girl who got shot?"

"Yes'um, that's the one," Connie said, wiping the table with a damp towel. "Harold was kinda sweet on 'er."

"Mmmm, that was ugly," Katie Mae proclaimed. "Miss Victoria and Veronica have been talking about it all morning."

Connie laid down menus on the table, but Katie Mae and Skip pushed them aside. Katie Mae was having her usual Cobb salad, while Skip was having a grilled ham and cheese sandwich.

"You know, this might sound crazy, but Candi was in a while back," Connie said, lowering her voice. "She looked sick, an' gimme a letter."

"Oh?" Skip asked surprised. "What did it say?"

"I don't rightly know," Connie said, shaking her head. "It was kinda weird. She said not to read it, unless sump'n happen to 'er."

"Really?" Skip said, bewildered. "Do you mind, if I have a look?"

Chapter 95

A wave of uncertain exhilaration surged through Skip's body, as Connie handed him Candi's handwritten letter. He wondered if the letter was written as a testimonial concerning a personal traumatic event, or a premonition to her possible death.

Once open, he found the letter hastily written, nearly illegible on scrapes of paper. Skip laid the letter in sequential order, and began to read an astonishing account of unlawful, illicit activities that had occurred within the Bonner Falls area.

In the letter, Candi accused Salvador DiMarco of being a violent, murderous thug who lured her domestic partner, Ross Parker, into a sketchy criminal lifestyle. She desperately wanted Salvador brought to justice, above all else.

Candi accused Salvador of being a paid hitman, hired by a mysterious moonshine bootlegger whom she identified as Copperhead. Although Candi was vague, she suggested Copperhead operated the Hellhound distillery from a compound that was fortified by vicious dogs that had once attacked their owner, leaving him with a permanent limp. She added that the dogs were occasionally transported in a box truck for the purpose of savage, sadistic execution-style murders.

The letter claimed that Copperhead was a homicidal psychopath who wore a silver dog whistle around his neck. It was rumored that he killed a man at a birthday party by spiking his drink with a drug overdose over a disagreeable comment. Oddly enough, she noted he was a classical music fanatic who admired fine art and sleek motorcycles.

Despite knowing Ross was deeply involved with Salvador's felonious activities, Candi insisted that he had been blackmailed as an unwilling participant. Throughout the letter, she reiterated Ross' innocence. She repeatedly suggested that he was hoping to return to work for the Sweet James Garage Door Company.

The letter identified several crimes that Salvador may have

committed. She also left a phone number and address for Ross, which Skip hastily took down. He intended to follow up on the lead at the opportune time, though the challenge turned out greater than expected.

It took several attempts for Skip to reach Ross, who was tentative to answer the phone. Detective Halstead had already left a message. The loss of Candi was unbearable. Ross immediately suspected Salvador of having a hand in the foul play, due to his detestable hatred of Candi. Still, he did not want to incriminate himself in any potential legal investigation concerning Candi's demise by meeting with the detective.

"Ross, this is Skip Walker," Skip began trying to coax him into a conversation. "I'd like to talk to you about Candi O'Neil, if you've got a minute."

Without a word, Ross abruptly hung up. He was not taking any calls, especially from an unknown caller he did not recognize.

Skip continued calling several times. He was undeterred, and not going to give up easily.

"Ross, this is Skip Walker and I know where you live," Skip said, leaving a voicemail message. "There's a letter that Candi left that I'd like to talk to you about. If you want, I can come to your place."

After a few more attempts, Ross relented. Candi's letter had piqued his curiosity. He was alarmed that she might have implicated him in some of the crimes Salvador had committed.

"What letter?" Ross asked. "She didn't write no letter."

"Yes, she did," Skip said insistently. "She left it with Connie at The Red Maple, who gave it to me."

"So, what of it?" Ross asked. "What's that got to do with me?"

Skip sensed that Ross was fast becoming inquisitive about the letter. As an item of interest, he wanted to press Ross further for additional information.

"Plenty," Skip said. "She wrote all about Salvador DiMarco, and the things he's done."

"Oh?" Ross said in a nonplussing, disinterested tone. "What else?"

Skip did not want to lose Ross, and risk the chance of having his call blocked. He eased his voice to appeal to Ross in a confidential, friendly manner.

"She said you were blackmailed and forced into working with DiMarco," Skip said. "She also said you guys worked for a moonshine bootlegger named Copperhead."

There was a long pause on the phone. Skip thought Ross had hung up, until he finally came back on the line.

"Look, I know who you are," Ross began. "You're that news guy who writes those articles for *The Mountain Holler*. You don't realize who you're dealing with. You cross those guys, and you're dead. They'll hunt you down, and kill you. And believe you me, no life is worth a jar of crappy moonshine, or a freaking dog whistle."

Before the line went dead, Ross gave an ominous warning. "Mess with those guys, and you can kiss your ass goodbye."

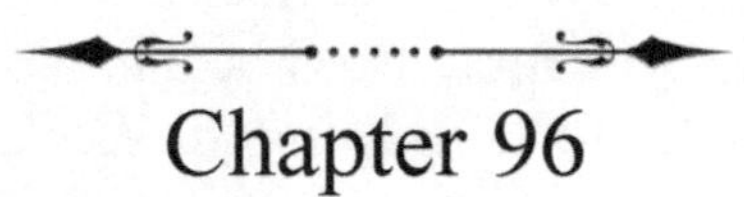

Chapter 96

Once word got out about Candi's murder at The Oaks, Ross went into hiding. He was fearful for his life and well-being, as well as the legal implications that Candi had alluded to in her letter.

Ross' cell phone began to ring incessantly. Calls poured in. The sheriff's department named him a person of interest, and the media was clamoring for an interview.

Salvador was among the callers. He left a message extending his condolences, but Ross knew better. Being sympathetic was not Salvador's style. If anything, he was shrewd, cunning, and calculating. Ross ignored the message.

As rumors about the contents of Candi's letter spread, Salvador became increasingly alarmed. He worried that his trust in Ross had been compromised by Candi, and that the sheriff's department had been alerted to his past transgressions.

Another source of aggravation was *The Mountain Holler*. The biweekly publication continued to run articles on the murderous crime spree that had occurred, with stern warnings about toxic moonshine being sold locally.

The newspaper further accentuated its point by utilizing sensational tabloid-style headlines with embellished stories designed to stimulate and capture the reader's interest through editorialized gossip, criminal news and investigative reporting.

Being a strong believer in eye-catching promotional hooks, the newspaper's publisher, Mr. Andrews knew that an electrifying headline was guaranteed to expand the paper's readership, and increase ad revenue. The gaudy, flamboyant headlines also turned Skip into a small-town local celebrity.

Salvador felt the quickest and easiest way to prevent any further detrimental scrutiny toward himself and Hellhound, was to prevent Ross from providing any harmful information to the legal authorities; but first, he would need to silence *The Mountain Holler*.

Ever since the Benson murder at Buckshot Pond, *The Mountain Holler* had been on the scene of every criminal investigation with breaking news. Salvador was keenly aware of the publication's local prestige through Skip's reporting, which had drawn Copperhead's wrathful ire. To eliminate the bothersome burden, Salvador would need Ross' assistance, which would be a challenge to obtain.

In the past, Ross would welcome any opportunity to work with Salvador. The money was good, and jobs were easy. Going after *The Mountain Holler* would be a simple, straightforward job. Aside from targeting Skip, Salvador planned to hurl a combustible incendiary device into the newspaper's office to drive Mr. Andrews out of town. Unfortunately, Ross was not responding.

Ross lacked the desire and motivation to be a part of Salvador's vindictive retribution plan. He no longer cared about the money, or his clandestine, illicit activities.

The thought of Ross ignoring, or avoiding, his calls incensed Salvador. Ross had always been available whenever Salvador called. Being unable to reach Ross was more than Salvador could bear. The indignant snub sent him into an unprecedented rage.

In a fit of anger, Salvador raced to Ross' house. He was determined to personally confront Ross and settle any issue, or disagreement the two might have.

Upon reaching the house, Salvador was stunned to find Detective Halstead and Deputy Wilson's cruisers parked in Ross' driveway. As a person of interest in Candi's murder, Ross was being sought for questioning, and was nowhere to be found.

Exasperated, Salvador continued to call Ross on his cell phone. He sought to coerce Ross into joining him for another assignment.

"Listen Ross, Copperhead and I are worried about you," Salvador said in a persuasive tone. "I'd appreciate a call to let us know you're okay."

Ross knew better than to think either Salvador, or Copperhead cared for anyone, except themselves. It was a sloppy, transparent attempt to persuade him of their concern.

In another call, Salvador promised a large sum of money to help take down *The Mountain Holler*. Once again, Ross did not fall for the ruse.

The final call was a threat that supposedly came from Copperhead. During the call, Salvador reminded Ross of who he worked for and his past criminal offenses. He strongly suggested he take part in *The Mountain Holler* job, or suffer the consequences.

Chapter 97

It was nearly midnight when Salvador parked his SUV in a cue de sac near Ross' home. Having been unable to reach Ross by phone, he was determined to contact him, even if it meant breaking into his house.

As Salvador neared the house, he could see no cars parked on the gravel driveway. There were no lights, or signs of life to indicate anyone was home. The mailbox was full, and unsightly trash had been strewn across the yard.

Salvador silently crept around to the rear of the house. He knew Ross always kept the bathroom window cracked open, though getting through the window would be difficult.

Although Salvador was not a large man, the bathroom window was small. It would be a tight fit squeezing through the window. With the use of a flathead screwdriver, he pried open the window and removed it from its frame.

An empty five-gallon paint bucket turned upside down served as a makeshift step stool, allowing Salvador to hoist his body upward through the window. Once inside the bathroom, he pulled his Glock 43 from a waistband holster and moved into the hall.

As expected, the house was empty. There were no signs of any recent occupancy. There was a moldy, musty smell that had permeated throughout the house due to being closed. Its repulsive, repugnant smell left an indelible, nauseating impression on anyone who entered.

Salvador began moving from room to room. He found the bedroom in disarray, with men's and women's clothing, shoes, and coats carelessly scattered across the floor. The kitchen sink was cluttered with unwashed dishes and the counter was covered with half-eaten food that had grown a grotesque, greenish fuzzy-gray mold.

In the living room, Salvador found remnants of Candi's drug paraphernalia, old beer cans and overflowing ashtrays. An empty closet revealed Ross had taken his hunting rifle, which meant he was armed. Salvador swiftly holstered his Glock, and slipped out the back door.

Salvador was determined more than ever to find Ross before the sheriff's department, or anyone else. He decided to drive past Ross' house for one final look. In his haste, he absent-mindedly clipped the driveway's mailbox, breaking a headlight. The mishap infuriated Salvador, but he had to keep moving. There was no time to lose.

Unlike Salvador, Skip had better luck reaching Ross. After numerous attempts to learn more about Candi, Skip was able to gain Ross' confidence in taking a call.

"Ross, I'm willing to help you any way I can," Skip said beseechingly. "You need to give me a chance."

"How so?" Ross asked. "What can you do to help?"

"I just want ask a couple questions about Candi," Skip said. "I'm not out to turn you in, or report you."

"Let me think about it," Ross said. "I don't want any trouble, and don't know what happened to Candi."

There was a pause on the phone. For a moment, Skip thought he had lost the call.

"Ross? Are you still there?"

"Yeah, I'm here," Ross said with a heavy, deep sigh. "Listen, I don't want to get blamed for something I didn't do. Candi was a good person. She might not have been perfect, but she did the best she could."

"No one's blaming you for anything," Skip said. "As I said before, if you could answer a couple questions, maybe I can help clear your name."

"I don't know," Ross said. "A detective's been calling me, and don't need all of this. Besides, I can go somewhere where no one'll find me, and not have to deal with this mess."

"Believe me, Ross," Skip pleaded. "I'm here to help."

"I'll tell you what, let me get back to you," Ross said, abruptly ending the call.

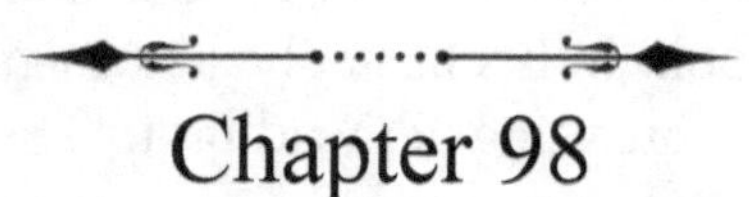

Chapter 98

Ever since he was a small child, Ross had been an avid outdoorsman. His father and grandfather had raised him to enjoy and appreciate the wonderous benefits of nature.

Whenever Ross had the time and money, he would set off to hunt, fish or hike. Being outdoors was a great passion he had held since growing up in the Smoky Mountains.

As a sportsman, Ross was exceedingly adept at surviving in the woods. He would never hesitate to grab his backpack, or fishing pole and head to the woods whenever the opportunity would arise.

Being a passionate hunter, Ross would often take his Browning 30-06 semi-automatic, bolt-action rifle to a deer blind he had built, deep in the woods. The blind was a simple, elevated structure that stood seven feet off the ground. It had corrugated plastic siding, covered with camo netting, and windows that could be raised, or lowered with the pull of a string.

The height of the deer blind gave Ross a spacious panoramic view of the surrounding meadow. At designated areas, he would bait the deer with apples, corn, and sweet potatoes. From the blind, he could watch the deer emerge from the edge of the forest to graze on the food, while the blind kept him well hidden and protected from the wind, rain and snow.

Ross immediately thought about the deer blind after receiving Detective Halstead's message. It was the perfect hideout, a place where he could escape without being seen by anyone. Aside from a stray hiker who might have ventured into the backcountry, Ross was certain no one would find him.

Skip had given up trying to reach Ross. He was not sure if he had shut his phone off, or left the area. Instead, he turned his attention to Midge and Larry Bennett at The Oaks. He sought to gather whatever information they might offer about Candi's demise, and a quote from Sheriff Porter to finish his current *Mountain Holler* story.

Candi's letter had presented an issue. Since Skip was unable to verify its authenticity, he could not publish, or quote any of its contents. He was aware that Candi had given the letter to Connie at The Red Maple, but uncertain if she was the genuine author.

Detective Halstead was still trying to piece together what had happened at The Oaks. He was aware of Candi's drug use. The detective wondered if the murder had been random, or a drug deal gone bad. Even more telling was the gunshot to the back of the head, and the ever-present black aluminum dog whistle.

Salvador had quietly dropped from the scene. No one knew about his whereabouts, except for his boss, Copperhead. Salvador kept him informed through his property and distillery master Corny, as the turn of events unfolded.

In preparing for the deer blind, Ross took a few necessities to survive on a short-term basis. He headed to the blind with some dried meat and fruit, dehydrated meals, water and nutritional non-perishable foods, including dry roasted nuts and granola bars.

Ross wanted time to decide his next move. Since he was unsure about the allegations in Candi's letter, he was hesitant about meeting with the detective and alarmed about Salvador's presence.

The deer blind was a welcome sight as it came into view. The blind appeared to have been left undisturbed. The equipment he shouldered seemed to have grown heavier with each step, and he was anxious to set his backpack, sleeping bag and rifle down.

Upon reaching the deer blind, Ross peeled back the camo netting. He mounted the rope ladder and slid his equipment onto the blind's floor. Before entering the deer blind, he turned to scan the area and make sure no one had followed him.

Ross gently pushed open the deer blind's door. The small room was cool, gloomy, and dimly lit. His eyes squinted, adjusting to the light.

The click of a pistol could be heard, along with Salvador's familiar antagonistic, malevolent voice.

"Hey Ross, Candi's waiting for you."

Chapter 99

After careful consideration, Skip felt that Sheriff Porter should have the letter that Candi left with Connie at The Red Maple. It was his contention that the letter might provide enough leads to apprehend Salvador, or whoever was responsible for the ongoing murders. Skip was also hoping the sheriff might be available to provide a quote for *The Mountain Holler* regarding The Oaks murder.

Upon entering the sheriff's department, Skip found the office immersed in a flurry of activity. The body of Ross Parker had been found. An inquisitive hunter had inadvertently climbed the deer blind's rope ladder, and made the gruesome discovery. The sheriff and deputy had already raced to the scene.

As Skip left the letter with Jo Yarborough, he overhead a radio transmission mentioning Ross' name. He was stricken with the saddened, repulsive thought that Salvador might have struck again. With a heavy sigh, he turned to head home.

The usually gleeful Fred was at the door, when Skip got home. The local town vet Dr. Thomas had done a masterful job dressing Fred's wound, though, it would take time to heal. In the meantime, Fred walked with a noticeable limp that served as a sorrowful reminder of the dark, contemptuous ongoing threats Skip had received for *The Mountain Holler* articles.

"Where have you been?" Uncle Em asked as Skip bent down to hug Fred. "Freddie's been all over the house looking for you."

"Oh, here and there," Skip said nonchalantly. "I had a couple errands to run."

Uncle Em winced and shook his head in disgust. In his opinion, Skip's errands meant the activities were *The Mountain Holler* related.

"Great," Uncle Em growled. "Fat ass got you running again? I hope you're not tied up with that Oaks story. That's about the last thing we need around here, especially after what happened to Fred."

It was apparent Uncle Em was ramping up for a barrage of contentious, pugnacious comments delivered in his unique, irascible style. He had already worked himself into a hostile lather, and was in no mood for casual conversation. Nor did he make any effort to hide his contempt toward whoever had sought revenge against Skip, by targeting Fred.

"Listen, I'd like to get my hands on that goddamned SOB who took a crack at Fred," Uncle Em huffed. "I'd like to tear his ass apart."

"That makes two of us," Skip agreed as he stood up to reach for a box of dog treats on the counter. "Thank heaven it wasn't more serious."

Fred's eyes lit up, as he spotted the box of treats. He pressed his wet nose against Skip's leg, wagging his tail in anxious anticipation of a snack.

"Well, thank your lucky stars that Fred's going to be all right; aren't you Freddie?" Skip said, handing Fred a treat.

A slight scowl came across Uncle Em's face as Fred inhaled his treat. He had repeatedly warned Skip that his association with *The Mountain Holler* was headed down a dangerous path, and felt the local law enforcement had not done enough to follow up on their report when Fred was shot.

"Lucky stars?" Uncle Em replied with an incredulous look. "What planet are you are living on? That sheriff report we filed on Fred wasn't worth a shit. You watch, nothing's going to happen. Those guys are probably laughing their asses off, right now."

Satisfied at having a treat, Fred limped over to Uncle Em and laid down. Uncle Em gave Fred a gentle pat, which seemed to have a decompressing effect on his irritable demeanor.

"I'm sure they'll get the guy who did it," Skip said reassuringly. "It'll probably take some time, but they'll get him."

"I sure hope so," Uncle Em agreed. "It'd be nice if Fred could repay the favor, and take a bite out of his ass!"

Chapter 100

The discovery of Ross Parker's body and letter from Candi O'Neil, sent Sheriff Porter's search effort into overdrive. Armed with fresh information, the sheriff was resolute in pinpointing Copperhead's compound with the goal of bringing him and Salvador to justice.

The hunter who found Ross' body reported seeing a black SUV parked with a damaged headlight along the main highway, boarding the woods. The car appeared to have been hastily parked near a concrete barricade that a construction crew had left at the roadside.

The body of Ross was found face down in a massive puddle of blood. It was the blood that had seeped through the deer blind's side wall and floor that made the hunter suspect something about the tiny structure was amiss.

A crisp bullet hole had been placed through the rear of the Ross' head, with an exit wound at the forehead. It was apparent to anyone viewing the carnage, that death would have been instantaneous.

As Sheriff Porter and Deputy Wilson examined the body, the ever-present black aluminum dog whistle was neatly placed on Ross' back. It was a clear indication that the killer wanted his calling card known.

The deputy cordoned off the area, while the medical examiner gathered what information could be found in the small deer blind. A photographer arrived, but due to the small, confined area, had to wait until the examiner finished reviewing the body.

The sheriff and deputy stood at the bottom of the deer blind, while the body was being prepared for removal.

"Nice area," Sheriff Porter noted. "I used to hunt out here as a kid."

"Really?" the deputy asked. "Have any luck?"

"Not really," the sheriff shrugged. "Those whitetails would be long gone with the racket we'd make tearing through the woods."

A group of wild turkeys, led by a large male, emerged unexpectedly from the tree line across the meadow. Their bare red and blue heads could be seen bobbing nervously as they strode across the grass, foraging for beetles, grasshoppers, nuts and seeds.

"Dinner time!" Deputy Wilson cracked as the turkeys edged their way back into the woods. "That big ol' tom looks like he means business."

"Yeah," Sheriff Porter agreed. "He's got a mean look in his eye."

The medical examiner had nearly finished when the sheriff turned to leave, and allow Deputy Wilson time to complete his report.

"You know, it might be a good idea to get Sonny Boy out here," the sheriff said, rubbing the back of his neck. "There's a good chance some hunter's got a trap camera in these parts."

"Good thought," Deputy Wilson agreed. "There's no telling what might turn up."

The turkeys reappeared at the edge of the meadow. The dominant male leading the flock looked warily across the field with a protective glare. His watchful eye scanned the immediate area, as the flock continued to forage unabated, seemingly without a care, before slipping back into the woods.

"Boy, those guys don't fool around when it's chow time," Deputy Wilson observed. "They get down to business."

"Yeah, you got that right," Sheriff Porter agreed as his phone beeped with a text message.

The sheriff reached in his pocket, and pulled out his phone. He adjusted his glasses, and began thumbing through his messages.

"Oh, looks like a message from Sonny Boy" he said. "He's got something."

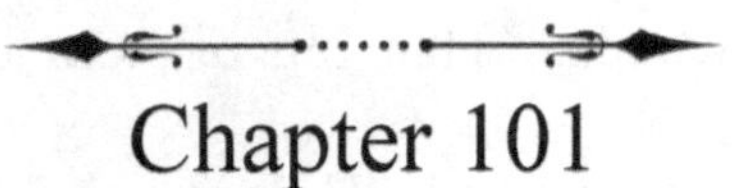

Chapter 101

After his uneasy meeting with Ed Meyers at Marsh Auto Center, Detective Halstead had a surveillance camera set up nearby to monitor the car lot's activity. The detective was suspicious of Meyers laconic, disagreeable, and ill-tempered attitude. He had a hunch that Meyers was withholding information. More importantly, he wanted to learn about the black Suburban that Miguel claimed to have serviced.

It took hours of scoring through camera footage, but Halstead doggedly pressed on. The work was boring, monotonous, and tedious. Still, the detective was focused on the car dealership's suspected clientele.

After viewing hours of tape, Halstead's efforts finally paid off. The grainy image of a black SUV with a damaged headlight rolled into an open garage at the Marsh Auto Center late one afternoon.

Within a short matter of time, the car backed out of the garage. The broken headlight had been replaced, and the driver sped away.

The detective was elated. He quickly noted the date stamp and sought out other CCTV security cameras in the area. Soon, he was able to establish a routine pattern for the driver within the immediate area and enlarged the image pixels for a better view, which he was anxious for Sheriff Porter and Deputy Wilson to review.

In addition to the CCTV footage, the detective scoured Candi O'Neil's letter for clues about Copperhead's residence. The detective made an educated guess that the SUV made periodic trips to the secretive location, and was hopeful the vehicle might lead him there.

By sheer coincidence, the detective hired Clayborne Tree Service to do some yardwork at his house. In talking with the owner, Gus, Halstead learned that there was a fortified residence that fit the compound's description, located north of Bonner Falls.

Gus had worked a job near the suspected compound, and noted that he heard dogs barking periodically throughout the day. He also observed a blue mattress company's box truck multiple times, which seemed unusual for being on a remote, single-lane backwoods road.

To verify the location, Halstead contacted a retired helicopter pilot named Jerry "Gryo" Davis, who had chartered scenic tours over the area. During the tourist season, catching a ride with Gryo was on every Smoky Mountain tourist's bucket list.

Davis claimed to have seen the heavily secured compound on various flights. He described a private, secluded property, well-hidden from view, and provided a crude map drawn from past recollections.

As a final bit of research, Halstead took Gus Clayborne's directions and enlisted the help of Highland Ranch mechanical handyman Toby to fly a night vision drone with a telephoto lens near the compound.

Toby regularly used a drone at the Highland Ranch when checking the rear of the property near the duck pond. In the past, the ranch had issues with feral hogs. The drone was used for hunting purposes to spot them on the property before the hogs became a crop-eating nuisance.

After Halstead and Toby got a view of the residence, the detective took the information to Sheriff Porter. It was time to determine if he had gathered enough evidence to submit a request for a search warrant from the court.

At first, the sheriff was hesitant. He wanted to make certain there was enough criminal evidence to support a property search, owned by an individual named Elliot Culpepper. By linking Candi's letter, and an affidavit from Skip regarding his conversation with Ross Parker that connected Salvador to Copperhead's operation, the sheriff felt that there was probable cause to justify an arrest for the operation of an illegal moonshine distillery and bootlegging activity.

Once the evidence supporting the search warrant was submitted, the sheriff gathered his team to plan their next move. Upon approval, the warrant would give them 48 hours to plan their move.

Chapter 102

The heavy pounding at the door reverberated throughout the house as Sheriff Porter announced in a loud, clear voice, "Sheriff's Department! We have a warrant. Open up!"

A brief commotion could be heard from within the house. Dogs rushed to the doorway. Their abrasive claws could be heard vigorously tearing at the door. The ferocious sound of their unrestrained barking filled the air.

There was a slight movement among the living room's floral lace curtains. Several lawmen led by Deputy Wilson fanned out among the front entrance to the property, as the sheriff resumed his pounding.

"Open up!" Sheriff Porter bellowed. "Your place is surrounded. Come out with your hands up."

The ominous sound of the fearsome dogs began to fade. The group of lawmen began to grow anxious. One member held a battering ram. The hardened steel black tube was poised, ready for the sheriff's command to crush the door.

The sheriff's relentless pounding intensified. Still, there was no answer.

"This is your last chance!" Sheriff Porter roared. "Open up, or we'll break the door down!"

After what seemed like an eternity to the lawmen, a meek voice, along with the soothing sound of classical music, could be heard from behind the door.

"Hold on," the unidentified voice said. "I'm comin'."

The click of a deadbolt could be heard. The door opened slowly to reveal an older, apprehensive man with an alarmed look in his eyes.

"Can I help you, fellas?" the man asked nervously.

Sheriff Porter stepped forward with a pensive, exasperated look on his face. His nerves were already frayed, from having to forcefully dislodge the driveway's main gate. Behind him, the attentive group of lawmen waited eagerly to enter the house.

"I am Sheriff Porter," the sheriff said sternly. "I have a warrant for the arrest of the homeowner Elliott Culpepper, and the authority to search the premises for illegal alcohol that's being manufactured and sold without a permit. Now, that wouldn't be you, by chance?"

The sheriff paused for a moment to glance inside the house. There was nothing unusual, or seemingly out of the ordinary about the house. The living room featured an open floor plan with wood vinyl plank flooring, a gas log fireplace topped by a mantel display of dog trophies, a kitchen with stainless steel appliances and granite counter tops, and a long hallway featuring glossy fine art prints, which he assumed led to the bedrooms.

"Oh, heavens no," the older man said, shaking his head. "My name's Cornelius Webster McDaniel, Corny for short. I check on the place when Mr. Culpepper's outta town."

"Guys," the sheriff turned to wave the lawmen forward into the house. "Is Culpepper here?"

"No, here's been gone for some time."

The group rushed cautiously forward with guns drawn. They began a thorough, systematic approach to clearing the house by checking every door, corner, oversized furnishings and closets.

Dogs could be heard barking uncontrollably toward the rear of the property. Their savage, maniacal intensity left no doubt that they had been trained to aggressively attack anyone perceived as a threat to their territory.

"Where are the dogs?" the sheriff asked. "Are they in the house?"

"No, no," Corny said hastily. "I locked 'em up out back."

"Out back?" the sheriff asked as the men finished clearing the house. "What's out back?"

"A storage garage, kennel cages, an' a dog run," Corny replied. "It's not much."

"Guys," the sheriff said, pointing attentively to the rear of the house. "Garage out back."

The team moved through the house without saying a word. The sound of the dogs grew louder, as the lawmen entered the backyard.

"Where'd you put them?" the sheriff asked about the dogs tumultuous, erratic barking.

"In the truck," McDaniel said, pointing to a light blue box truck with a Conway Mattress Outlet logo, parked near the rear of the yard. "Thought I'd get 'em outta ev'ryone's hair."

In one simultaneous, sudden move, both the grinding of the garage door and rear steel door bordering the backyard wall burst open.

A black Suburban shot out from the garage. It sped recklessly, careening toward the rear gate. The lawmen stood stunned in awkward bewilderment, as the car raced past them.

Chapter 103

Thick billows of smoke from the burning tires of a car's revved engine could be seen pouring from the garage. The black Suburban seemed to have suddenly burst from nowhere, fishtailing from its secluded parking space. The driver gripped the steering wheel, staring hard and fast at the open gate several yards away.

The lawmen investigating the area had to leap from harm's way to avoid being hit. Bodies were strewn across the yard, as the speeding vehicle recklessly accelerated toward the gate. The surprise had been so complete, the men had no time to draw their guns.

A massive cloud of dust engulfed the men, as the black SUV neared the open gate. Through the choking smoke, dust and debris, the men could barely make out the Suburban skidding to a halt.

When the dust settled, the sheriff and his men were caught gagging and coughing to catch their breath. Upon wiping the residue from their eyes, they saw Detective Halstead's cruiser arrive to block the gate.

The driver threw open his door. A small man emerged, pointing a handgun. Shots were fired. The lawmen instinctively backed away. Sheriff Porter shouted for everyone to take cover, but it was too late. Deputy Wilson was down, bleeding from the hip.

The concealed lawmen exchanged fire. The small man dove behind the SUV for cover. He continued to fire rapid, sporadic shots, holding the gun firmly with two hands.

In desperation, the man reloaded his gun. He fired several more rounds and ran to the box truck, trailed by a hail of bullets.

At the truck, the small man crouched in a kneeling military position. Instinctively, he rose to grab the truck's rear door latch handle.

"No Salvador!" Corny yelled from the house, but it was too late.

Salvador climbed the truck's steps and pulled the door open. He turned to empty his gun at the scattered lawmen. Then, with one final blast, he slammed the door shut.

Sheriff Porter yelled for the men to surround the box truck. He warned them to take caution. It was unknown if the truck would be used as a barricade, or sniper's nest.

A series of loud, ghastly, horrific screams were heard from the truck. Desperate cries, pleading for help, filled the air. The sound of snarling dogs mercilessly tearing their victim apart could be heard.

Throughout the gruesome, savage attack, the sheriff rushed to Deputy Wilson's side. The deputy had suffered a heavy loss of blood and needed help. An urgent call for an EMT was made.

Corny quickly made his way from the house and joined Sheriff Porter. The painful cries from the box truck had begun to subside, until they were no longer heard.

"That's it," Corny said. "It's ov'r."

"What do you mean?" Sheriff Porter asked.

"They got 'em," Corny replied, fumbling through his pockets. "Those dogs are rottweilers. Trained killers. Two of 'em. They're released from their cage automatically when someone enters the truck."

Corny took a small wireless remote control from his pocket on a black aluminum Hellhound keychain. With the click of a button, the dogs were no longer heard, and the system was disengaged.

"It's okay," he said. "They're locked up now. Their collars are wired with a program that sends 'em back to their cage. It's all automated."

Corny playfully twirled the remote on his index finger, and watched the lawmen gather around the box truck. The sheriff could not help, but notice the remote control was hooked onto a black aluminum dog whistle keychain.

"What a damn shame," Corny said, looking mournfully toward the box truck. "Anyone who goes in there, doesn't get out alive."

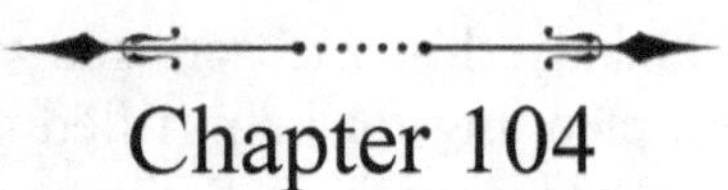

Chapter 104

Mr. Andrews was preparing to leave *The Mountain Holler* office when a call came over the police scanner. Shots fired. An officer down. Backup support, and an EMT was called.

He immediately sent a text message to Skip. Mr. Andrews needed him on the scene, before a major story slipped away. There was no time to lose.

The street was clogged with emergency vehicles, and a temporary Incident Command Post had been established by the time Skip arrived on the scene.

A bright yellow non-adhesive polyethylene tape reading "Sheriff's Line Do Not Cross" had been set as a barricade to seal off the area. Only authorized personnel were allowed onto the property, including first responders, firefighters, and law enforcement officials.

The scene inside the blood-spattered truck was appallingly gruesome. The rabid dogs had savagely severed the artery in Salvador's neck. His body was pulverized, with severe bite marks covering his hands, arms, and upper torso. A portion of his face lay torn on the blood-soaked floor.

The ill-tempered, barbarous dogs growled with barred teeth from their cages at the lawmen entering the truck. Their blood thirsty appetite craved the opportunity to kill another victim, as the first responders viewed the carnage.

Amid the violent commotion, Corny slipped away. He was last seen discreetly, leaning against the garage, intently watching the drama unfold. The pandemonium had created the perfect cover for his escape.

"Where's McDaniel?" Sheriff Porter barked. "Find him. Search the house and garage."

The men moved quickly. As a person of interest, the sheriff wanted to continue questioning Corny about Culpepper. He had planned to ask for more information, when a low-pitched static sound was heard coming from the house.

At first, the sound resonating throughout the house was a slight, annoying distraction. The cacophonic sound caught everyone by surprise, causing the investigation to come to a temporary standstill.

As the volume increased, the crackling hiss of a disrupted radio signal began to reach deafening proportions. The men investigating the truck stepped out to scan the patio around the house. The sheriff, alarmed that the uproar might be a ruse, urged the team to focus on the task at hand.

Over the loud noise, the sheriff heard someone yell, "There he is!"

The sheriff rushed into the garage. Corny had been spotted with a slender, unshaven man wearing a well-worn Carolina hat, hobbling with a cane and a backpack. Together, they ran into a dark, climate-controlled storage room, stashed with an enormous cache of Hellhound moonshine.

The room was poorly lit and crowded with boxes of sealed illicit alcohol ready for shipment. Only the faint silhouette of two men could be seen pushing stacks of neatly palletized Hellhound moonshine onto the floor, blocking the sheriff's path.

The loud, deafening roar of falling boxes and broken glass could be heard as row after row of moonshine crashed violently to the ground. Gallons of moonshine spilled onto the floor. An overpowering smell of ethanol alcohol filled the air.

The slender man flipped a match onto the floor. A wall of clear blue flames engulfed the room igniting boxes and pallets. The entire floor was momentarily ablaze.

Undeterred, the sheriff scrambled over the discarded liquor cases, broken glass and through the remnants of the burned alcohol. He slipped and fell with each step, but hastily recovered to continue his pursuit.

Corny and the slender man moved onto the next room, which was the Hellhound distillery base of operation. The men slid a large metal table against the door and bolted across the room to a rear exit.

The sheriff continued his unrelenting pursuit. He quickly pried the door open. As soon as he entered the room, he caught a glimpse of the men running out the side door.

Outside the garage near the front of the house, the slender man mounted a sleek, aerodynamic X-PRO motorcycle. From his barricade vantage point, Skip could faintly make out the man activating the bike's electronic ignition.

"Boss!" Skip heard Corny call out. "Copperhead, wait for me!"

The slender man turned. He pulled a handgun from his waistband, and raised it slowly. Sharp, explosive pops could be heard. Corny took two slugs to his chest, staggered, and fell to the ground.

Chapter 105

Skip watched the man on the motorcycle toss his Carolina hat to the ground, pull a full-faced Bell helmet over his head, and adjust the backpack over his shoulder. He paused to reach in his pocket for a cell phone. The man's attention was momentarily diverted to watch a pool of blood form under Corny's body.

A faint smirk of amusement came across the slender man's face, while tapping onto his cell phone. He expressed no sense of remorse, sorrow, or sympathy for the Corny's loss. Whatever compassion he might have felt, was non-existent and self-serving.

As Corny lay groaning and gasping for breath, the slender man concentrated on his cell phone. Moving quickly, he tapped a message, or code on the phone. With a quick swipe, he turned the phone off, and started the motorcycle.

Moments later, Beethoven's *Ode to Joy* was heard blaring from the house. Its triumphant, cheerful melody swept through the yard.

The sheriff's men were completely baffled by the music. They froze in dazed bewilderment, and looked toward the house.

Skip heard the music, as well. He immediately recognized the European anthem. Although he knew the music was oddly out of place, as he watched the slender man, throw his head back, laughing hysterically.

With a huge smile the slender man shook his head, and revved his motorcycle. He took one last look at Corny, put on a pair of thick leather gloves, and scanned the driveway's gateway leading to the street.

"Bick!" Skip yelled. "Bick! Hold on!"

As Beethoven's *Ode to Joy* reached its crescendo, there was a tremendous, detonative blast. The box truck was destroyed by a massive explosion. Metal fragments of various shapes and sizes were catapulted into the air. The cluster of unsuspecting men fell wounded from the debris. All that remained of the box truck was a mangled, burning, twisted metal frame.

The slender man released motorcycle's clutch, and the bike began to move. It edged around the house's corner, and gradually picked up speed.

As the driver opened the motorcycle's throttle and sped toward the gate, he was confident his diversionary tactic had worked. Nearly everyone in the house, backyard, and garage had rushed to view the remains of the smoldering truck.

Upon reaching the main gate, a shot rang out. The driver was thrown from the motorcycle. He hit the ground with a thud. Blood could be seen seeping through his jacket.

The driver struggled to his knees, and fell. He rose again, and reached for his gun. It would be his last act of defiance.

Another shot was heard. The driver pitched backward onto the ground. His body jerked with violent, convulsive spasmodic movements, before coming to a rest.

Sheriff Porter called to the motionless man. He approached cautiously with his gun drawn. As the sheriff neared the suspect, he called for the man to drop his weapon.

Upon hearing no response, the sheriff moved forward. He paused briefly to examine the man. There was no movement. The slender man's gun had fallen by his side, along with his backpack.

A painful, agonizing look of bewilderment seemed frozen on the slender man's pockmarked, unshaven face. Aside from a silver dog whistle that hung loosely around the man's neck, there were no other signs of personal trappings.

A backpack tagged "Benson," was the only identity on the unknown man, largely due to the Bell motorcycle helmet's open visor he was wearing. The sheriff suspected he had Elliott Culpepper in his midst.

The sheriff holstered his gun, and stepped back. He unhooked his portable radio, and solemnly announced, "Suspect down."

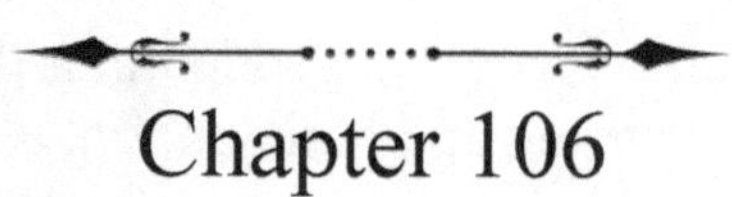

Chapter 106

It was a busy night at The Red Maple. All the booths, tables, and bar stools were filled with people anxious to kick back, relax over a drink, and have a good time.

Wendall vigilantly prowled the length of the bar in his usual ragged AC/DC t-shirt, serving drinks and chatting freely with anyone willing to engage in conversation. Connie moved from table-to-table, taking food and drink orders, while Harold flipped burgers at a blistering pace on the grill.

Skip and Katie Mae sat quietly in a corner booth with Tammy and Tom. The Hellhound story had made sensational news. *The Mountain Holler* had quickly sold out its initial print run. A giddy Mr. Andrews ordered an additional reprint, which he touted as a special collector's souvenir edition.

Milt was seen drinking his usual Turkey Dew, and chatting with off-duty officer Detective Halstead. The detective had brought Deputy Wilson into the diner for a night out.

Since being shot, Deputy Wilson had been temporarily confined to a wheelchair. The bullet had narrowly missed the main femoral artery in his left hip. Despite the leg being saved from amputation, recovery would be a long, slow process.

The talk in The Red Maple was mostly centered on Sheriff Porter's tireless, heroic effort to track down Salvador's murderous killing spree, while shutting down the Hellhound distillery operation.

Hellhound's rival, Jack Fuller, had quietly applied for a liquor license to evade legal issues. He hired a marketing firm to promote a new line of specialized white lightning called Black Eyed Possum Moonshine, with flavors in apple, cherry and peach.

As Jimmie "Jett" Jennings and The Reedy Creek Stringbusters prepared to take the stage, Katie Mae excitedly suggested that she and Skip should take a Caribbean cruise to get away for a week. Both Victoria and Verronica at Two Sisters thought the time off would provide a welcome relief from the recent dramatic events.

"Skippy, why don't we get us some sun, and go on a cruise?" Katie Mae suggested. "Betty Jo told me she and Edward took one, and loved it."

With a devilish smile, Katie Mae added that the Caribbean would be a nice place to get married and honeymoon, as well.

"Boy, I'd jump on that," Tammy interrupted. "Tom never takes me anywhere. I'd take that deal in a heartbeat."

"That so?" Tom asked. "Remember, I took you to Blowing Rock, and we've talk about going to see my cousin in Paducah."

"Hmmm, yes you took me to look at that state park's rock," Tammy agreed, sardonically. "You must have rocks in your head to think that's exciting."

"Ah, come on now," Tom said. "Where else can you see snow fall upside down?"

Tammy rolled her eyes, with a discernable scoff.

"I don't know about taking a cruise," Skip said doubtfully. "Fred's still getting back on his feet, and Uncle Em doesn't move so fast these days."

Katie Mae wrinkled her nose. Skip's response wasn't promising.

"I knew you'd be a poop head," she scolded. "Your uncle needs a good comeuppance. All he does is holler about phone messages."

Skip laughed in agreement, though Katie Mae's admonishments hardly compared to Uncle Em's prodigious epithets.

After a couple drinks, Skip returned home to find Uncle Em and Fred asleep. Fred briefly lifted his head when he walked through the door, then laid back down.

The rare sight of Uncle Em and Fred sleeping blissfully was one Skip savored, until the cell phone beeped with a text message.

"Oh, for chrissakes," Uncle Em roared waking up. "If that's fat ass, I'm going kill him."

Skip pulled the phone from his pocket, and looked at the message.

"Actually, it isn't," he said.

"I don't care who it is," Uncle Em roared. "Even the Wolverine doesn't call at his hour."

"That so?" Skip asked with a broad smile. "Don't be so sure. What if she had an emergency, or something important?"

"She knows better than to call this late, or get she'll get a piece of my mind."

"Hmmm," Skip snickered. "In that case, I'm glad you're in such a benevolent mood."

"Say what?" Uncle Em said, with a perplexed look on his face.

Even Fred's head looked up from his drowsy slumber to see what was happening.

"It's from Irene," Skip said. "She's been trying to reach you. The credit card maxed out, and she wonders when you're getting her another one."

Uncle Em's jaw fell in disbelief. He appeared ready to explode, and unleash a torrid stream of vulgar, obscene comments.

Skip struggled to keep from laughing. Then, with a mischievous grin and quick swipe, he deleted Katie Mae's message.

Uncle Em took a moment to gather his thoughts. "In that case, you'd better call your bank," he scoffed. "Even the Wolverine knows I use your card. Besides, I knew sooner or later that smart ass phone of yours would turn you into a dumbass."

About the Author

R ich Finley is a native of Southern California, born in Los Angeles and raised in the San Bernardino Mountains resort community of Lake Arrowhead, California. He has traveled extensively throughout North America as a marketing communications consultant, and worked in several diverse industries. He is a graduate of Rim of the World High School, Lake Arrowhead, California and earned a Bachelor of Science degree in Communications from Woodbury University, Los Angeles, California in 1976.